I0699765

SHE DREAMS IN BLUE LIGHT

SHE DREAMS IN BLUE LIGHT

A NOVEL

A.R. MALECKI

ANALOGUE HOUSE

Published by Analogue House
www.analoguehousepublishing.com

First edition

ISBN 979-8-9882338-0-0 (ebook)

ISBN 979-8-9882338-2-4 (paperback)

ISBN 979-8-9882338-3-1 (hardback)

Library of Congress Control Number: 2023908643

This is a work of fiction. The names, characters and incidents portrayed in it are the work of the author's imagination. Any resemblance to actual persons, living or dead, events or localities is entirely coincidental.

Cover Design: Roderick Brydon | www.klrcovers.com

For my Cliff under a tree

When you invent the ship, you also invent the shipwreck.

— PAUL VIRILIO

NEW DIALOGUE

Eleanor "Ellie" Crawford
<Software Engineer @Agora>

Tomorrow, connecting the world bits and bytes at a time is going to get easier.

---

114 ❣ 88⚜

1

Eleanor Crawford couldn't really imagine working anywhere other than Agora, even on a normal day. But today, the value of her work would be seen by the world. Today, she would celebrate being *part* of it.

It was her usual 7 a.m. sharp that she approached the curved structure of glass and steel that was Agora headquarters, wonderful and futuristic on the Atlanta skyline. The building featured facade lighting that projected pixel images onto its windows. Today, instead of the usual 1's and 0's, it featured the company's brand new stock ticker: AGX.

Entering the building, she was greeted with couture decorations in the familiar shades of silver and blue in the form of streamers, balloons, banners, and disco balls. Even the front desk receptionist seemed to be exuding more cheerfulness than usual.

Eleanor stood a bit taller and smiled to herself as she walked by the iconic company crest:

Agora
The Gathering Place of the Internet

She filed into the elevator behind three men in suits discussing third-quarter reports, four men in hoodies and jeans looking at their phones, and one woman wearing high heels and a tight black pencil skirt. As she tapped the button for her floor, a familiar voice shouted, "Valley Girl! Hold the elevator!"

She considered quickly jamming the "close door" button but didn't think it would be fast enough. The perfectly gelled auburn hair of one of her teammates, Charley, bobbed towards her, throwing his freckled arm out to stop the doors from closing.

She took a deep breath and held it in. "Morning." When Charley called her Valley Girl, he didn't mean California. For maybe the thousandth time, Eleanor kicked herself mentally for drinking way too much at a recent work party then talking way too much about her small Southern hometown of Aska Valley. In one evening, she'd blown the calculated image she'd spent years building for herself.

"Big day, biiiig dayyyyy," he crooned, sidling in next to her as the elevator doors finally closed.

"Oh yeah, I'm excited."

Ding! Tenth floor. Finance department. All the men in suits got off.

Attempting to block out the overpowering smell of cologne and Charley's presence, she closed her eyes and thought back to when her image was more of a modern day Grace Hopper.

Charley's voice interrupted her reverie. "Did you get invited to the after party?"

"After party?" She shifted a little to lean against the elevator wall now that there was more space. Sure, there were after parties, but did he mean *the* after party?

"Yeah, I got my invite weeks ago." He waved his hand nonchalantly. "But, well, I went to the same Alma Mater as Matthew, and I'm good friends with the CTO, so I guess it makes sense."

Ding! Twelfth floor. Human Resources. The woman in the skirt exited the elevator with the *click, click, click* of her heels.

Eleanor pulled impatiently at her chunky mock-neck sweater,

paired with skinny jeans and high tops. "That's cool. Don't stay out so late you oversleep and miss our launch tomorrow." She added a small laugh to make it seem like she didn't care at all that she'd been left out.

Ding! Fifteenth floor. Software.

There was a momentary dance between Charley, the guys in jeans, and Eleanor as they waited for her to exit the elevator first. *Why must we always do this?*

When she finally got out of the elevator, the familiar metallic smell of hundreds of silicone chips hit her, inducing a kid-in-a-candy-store level of excitement. The buzz of employees clacking on keyboards, shuffling to meetings, and talking to coworkers was dialed up in anticipation of today's event.

Charley was still next to her. "Let's grab some breakfast!"

I'm not going to let him spoil this day before it even starts. She gestured in the direction where their team worked. "I've got to get a few bugs finished before the party."

"Fine, fine. You're such a workaholic." He gave a smug wave and walked toward the gourmet café provided especially for the software floor.

She turned and walked confidently through the maze of modular tables, cubicles, and desks that teams frequently rearranged like children building forts until she reached her own, situated near a large window. Other desks were filled with photos and baubles, but hers only had a small set of technical books in the corner.

She slid into her ergonomic chair with a little spin and put on her noise-canceling headphones. The first thing employees did every day at Agora was spend time on Agora.

Agora Plaza, the center of Internet life, was the place for anyone to converse. Anyone signed up for the platform anyway, but who wasn't?

Eleanor scrolled mindlessly while reading posts from co-workers about the launch today. Her fingers danced across the trackpad until a new Observation from her sister made her stop.

Anne Crawford <*Senior @Aska Valley High*>

It's official, someone other than my mom thinks I'm talented! My drawing got first place in the **SCAD** High School Student Contest: Experimental Medium category!

The image was of a drawing she'd seen Anne working on before. The finished version showed a girl, her face perfectly symmetrical, except where her eyes would be were large glasses made with a reflective material such that the drawing only had eyes when someone was standing in front of it.

Eleanor gave the post Cor and commented:

I think you're talented!

She smiled to herself thinking Anne would get into the art program for sure now, but her smile fell quickly when she noticed her manager, Daryl, had also given the post Cor. Eleanor cringed. *Creepy.*

She closed out the window, ready to get to work. Today her task was to make improvements to Agora's newest feature already making a splash and increasing the company's buzz before the stock launch: Assemblies. *She* had helped build Agora's newest and most exciting feature: groups designed for people to gather, discuss, and share information, ideas, and opinions about any topic that interested them.

She faced a black code editor which displayed a comforting and familiar language to her. Not English, Spanish, or Chinese, but machine code with certain words highlighted in a variety of neon colors. Under her fingers, the keys of the mechanical keyboard crackled rhythmically like a flickering campfire. This was a world she could live in. A world where inputs have known outputs, and rules are made to be followed. Just as the earth creates infinite variety using mountains, trees, and streams, she too could use variables, loops, conditionals, and all the data available to unlock a new world of creation.

Soon the sun was rising over the city behind her and it was nearing 11:00 when her Team Lead Avi popped his head over her monitor and waved. "Okay, Eleanor—no more working today!"

She slipped her headphones off and laughed. "Hey, you know I'm really excited about this event." She looked around for the rest of her team.

"They already went down."

"Oh, you shoulda got me sooner." Not that she was really that upset about it. Avi was the only person on her team she also considered a friend, and she was glad he'd waited for her.

"You were so focused. I didn't want to interrupt." He said.

They joined the swell of people moving in the direction of the elevators, then squished in and rode to the floor everyone called Athens, which housed all the amenities provided to employees.

"Any interesting plans this weekend?" Avi asked her.

"The usual dinner with parents and sister on Sunday, not sure about Saturday yet. You?" She walked past the cafeteria with several restaurants and a coffee shop, then an Entertainment Arena equipped with Ping-Pong tables, arcade machines, and game consoles.

"I think I'm going to the TechTogether Hackathon." Avi waved to someone he recognized in the distance as he said this.

"Oh man, that sounds fun. Do you have a team?" Eleanor thought she might like to join, but the thought of missing a visit with her sister, especially after such a big week, made it a pass.

"Yeah, some friends of mine want to enter the Guardians of the Earth category."

"That's amazing!" She was always inspired by how Avi found time to do things like that on top of all his responsibilities at work.

They reached the Theater of Athena, and the auditorium was buzzing with people in Agora hoodies and t-shirts taking photos and finding seats together. Upbeat, electronic music pulsed throughout the chamber, and the large projector screens lit up with the Agora logo—a colonnade made of 1s and 0s that flipped and animated until it resembled a globe connected by glowing networks.

Eleanor pulled out her phone, centered her face with the screens behind her, and snapped a picture. She opened her Agora app, tapped New Observation, and shared the photo.

"If you hurry, you can get first Cor," she told Avi, who laughed and opened his Agora app too.

They found two seats together and watched as the slideshow changed to a full-screen mural with millions of Agora profile photos for every pixel on the screen, zooming in and panning across to show Agora's global community.

The Gathering Place of the Internet inked onto the screen as a cheer went through the audience. A stiff looking guy in jeans and an Agora t-shirt came onto the stage, and the applause rose higher. Matthew Erickson, creator and CEO of Agora.

The CEO's stony voice boomed from the microphone. "Good afternoon, Agora family!"

Cheers, whistles, and applause filled the room, and he stood basking in it for a few moments. Every time she saw Matthew Erickson, Eleanor felt herself in the presence of a celebrity—and in many ways, that's what he was. The power his role granted him came with constant praise, and constant scrutiny.

"Today is a special day for us. For the first time ever, Agora will issue stock in the company, making us a platform both for the public and owned by the public. But our status as a publicly traded company is about more than just growing our business. It establishes us as a platform that's here to stay. It will take our goal of connecting the world to the next level." He shifted the microphone to his right hand and stuck the left one in his hoodie pocket. "Along with the celebration of our stock, we're celebrating the success of our newest and most powerful feature: Assemblies!"

This is us. The room filled with applause, and Eleanor's spine straightened with pride.

"Assemblies have increased our site traffic by thirty percent since its launch a month ago and has resulted in thousands of new account creations."

When she was in college, the very notion of the mind-numbing chanting that went on at football games made her uncomfortable, but right now, in The Theater of Athena, it felt completely justified.

"A-gor-A, A-gor-A, A-gor-A..." Her high pitch voice stood out among the deep reverberating chorus in the audience.

"And I'd like to take a moment to recognize the team responsible for creating the next generation of Agora features—Avi Kumar and his mobile app development team." Matthew Erickson lifted his hand in a gesture that told them to rise. Eleanor and Avi stood; a few rows ahead, she could see Charley and Reed giving each other fist bumps. She beamed, looking around at everyone cheering for her, and wondered if she was still supposed to be clapping too.

"Thank you guys for your hard work and dedication to launching Agora Assemblies and all those late-night support calls to keep it up and running."

As they sat back down, Matthew's face grew solemn and the entire audience seemed to lean in closer. "We are a social species. Everything Man has achieved is because of our ability to connect with others. To teach, to learn, to share knowledge. We scrawled on rocks, inked on paper, sent pulses through wires, and now we have a light speed web of connections throughout the globe. All of us want to hear and be heard, see and be seen. That's where you come in."

She was helping bring knowledge and information to the world. She and everyone in that room believed any problem could be solved with technology.

"Agora is a free platform, open to everyone and will remain so because that is the only way to connect every single person. Agora already has millions of people in its community, and today represents a crucial milestone in reaching billions. So today, we celebrate, and tomorrow, we get back to doing what we do best! Thank you, Agora Family."

Electronic beats filled the room again, Eleanor's heart rate syncing up with them, and conversation swelled as people stood up and gathered into groups. A fluttery, empty feeling in her stomach was either hunger or excitement—or both. She and Avi shifted through the crowd of other exhilarated, chattering voices to join the food queue.

"Are you excited for your shares in the company to finally pay off?" she asked him.

"Maybe, if the stock does well." He laughed. "I just hope our team gets some more resources now."

"For more developers?"

"Yes, and I think we need a dedicated support team. The late-night support issues are getting ridiculous."

She agreed with that. No matter how much she liked to work, she still wanted to sleep at night.

The disco balls were in full motion, making sparkling lights dance on the walls. As she and Avi reached the front of the line, the delicious aroma of their choices greeted them, everything from sizzling filet mignon to crisp roasted potatoes and organic vegetables. A chef in a stiff white uniform placed food on Eleanor's plate, and she thanked him with a smile.

"Let's go outside. I think I saw the rest of the team go out there," Avi said with a warning look that she understood right away.

"Yeah, alright." She'd much rather talk with him more about his Hackathon than be endlessly subjected to football statistics from Charley. They moved towards large glass doors that opened onto a patio with a view of the city's sidewalks below.

As the rush of fall air hit her, so did a wall of noise that was more than the usual traffic and siren sounds of the city. Avi and Eleanor exchanged puzzled looks and made their way to the edge of the balcony, where Charley, Reed, and a bunch of other employees looked on, taking pictures of something.

"A political demonstration, maybe?" Eleanor looked out to see a large crowd made up mostly of women gathered around the building. Several news crews were set up filming the event.

Avi's face fell to a grimace when he looked at the picket signs. "I don't think so…"

In bold letters, the signs read: *I am a lactivist!* and *Breastfeeding is not obscene!* Others, more simply, featured a giant X over the Agora logo.

She listened to the shouting and picked out a few discerning lines:

"Agora is sexist!"

"Mothers are part of the global village too!"

In the front line of the crowd, a row of women were breastfeeding their babies—right there in the street. Eleanor's first instinct was to look away, and she realized Avi had done the same.

"What the hell? They're protesting Agora?" Her cheeks flushed. *Maybe it's just a PR stunt to interfere with the IPO.*

Charley piped up right away. "They are having a nurse-in," he laughed with an air of condescension, "protesting their Assembly being shut down."

"Shut down for what?" she asked. *We'd never do that. Agora is a free and open public square.*

"Doing *that*." Charley pointed to the row of women nursing.

Far be it for her to agree with Charley, but she didn't wanna see that either. After a minute, she gave voice to her ambiguity. "I mean gross, but we shut down a whole Assembly for that? Couldn't we just take the offending photos down?"

Charley shrugged as if he was losing interest in the conversation. "Who knows. I'm sure the police will clear this up." He waved dismissively at the crowd.

She looked at Avi now, who scratched his head and said, "It was probably up to content moderation. They remove content with nudity, gore, or threats of violence."

Eleanor looked down at the protestors again. Maybe they had been warned and hadn't complied. Maybe it was better for her not to think about it.

More people were crowding the patio to see what was going on, and she was starting to feel claustrophobic.

"Let's go back inside," Avi suggested.

Eleanor nodded, and they retreated to find a table in the cafeteria. As they sat down, her and Avi's phones buzzed with high-priority emails from the CEO.

NEW !!! HIGH PRIORITY EMAIL
SUBJECT: RE: THE PROTESTORS

Agora Family,

By now most of you have seen or heard about the unfortunate
interruption to our festivities occurring outside. Actions are already
underway to quell the disturbance. A quick reminder that it is in all
of our best interests to avoid speaking to journalists or engaging
with the protesters in any way, shape, or form. Thank you for your
cooperation.

Matthew Erickson
Agora CEO

2

———————

Eleanor and Avi read the high-priority email right away. Silence blanketed the room as everyone else read it too. After a moment, the noise level rose again with a hum of speculative conversation.

Before either Eleanor or Avi could utter a word, she spotted Daryl hustling towards them. *Of course.*

"Hey, Avi," he sounded breathless, "you've read the email, correct?"

Before Avi got in a single head nod, Daryl continued. "Okay. Where's everyone else?"

"Probably still out on the patio watching the protest." Avi replied. "We were just th—"

"Ah, I'll go there now. They're going to close off the patio. Don't want to give these disrupters the attention they want." He resumed his rush to assert authority on Charley and the others.

"Quite the day," Avi began eating his vegetarian selection from the party spread.

"Don't you need to go wrangle your team?" Eleanor rolled her eyes.

"I'm already keeping tabs on my most concerning member, so I've got time."

She laughed with him and started on her, now cold, filet mignon. "Man, I was looking forward to this food."

"I was looking forward to Ping-Pong." He started eating a little more quickly and glancing at his phone. "Now, they'll probably call a bunch of meetings."

"For you, not for me." She smiled. "Now *I* can get some more work done."

"Nooo, you're supposed to be having fun today." His smile faded. "You might see if Charley is getting a game going and join in."

She knew he had only her best interests in mind, but this comment still stung. It didn't help when he added kindly, "Then, go home."

She pushed her cold food around the plate for a moment. "So what *is* up with the protest, do you think?"

"They will probably spin it to say that the protesters are trying to manipulate the stock price by wreaking havoc."

"But why would a bunch of breastfeeding women want to manipulate Agora's stock?"

He shrugged. "I doubt they do. There's likely a genuine complaint, but it's not really for us to worry about." He looked at more messages appearing on his phone and quickly shoveled in his last few bites. "As I thought, I have been summoned." He stood up.

"Let me know what you find out!" she said, watching him walk away responding to a message with one hand and carrying his empty plate with another.

"Remember, fun and home early!" he said without looking back.

The last thing Eleanor felt like doing was playing Ping-Pong. She might *just* be a coder, but Agora's mission was also her own, and a threat to that mission was a threat to her and her dreams of bringing everyone Online.

She wasn't going to join Charley even if it did get her in trouble. The day had already been spoiled for her and she didn't think she could bring herself to laugh along with them making fun of the protestors. She returned to her desk to grab her stuff, knowing she would have to walk past the group in order to get home.

Stepping outside, she slipped around the back of the building, and remembering that her backpack had an Agora logo on it, threw her hoodie over her shoulders to cover it up. Eleanor was young enough and dressed casually enough to still look like a university student. She would pass by as if she were nothing more than a vaguely curious undergrad on her way to class.

If I don't talk to them, I can't get in trouble. I'm just walking by on my way home.

By the time she made it around the building and crossed over to the other side of the street, the crowd of protesters had gathered on the corner and was spilling out onto the road, forcing traffic to be rerouted. Eleanor assumed a tired-looking saunter. The gathering seemed relatively peaceful; she also noticed there weren't any men present. A small group of women were chatting, and she listened in.

"Yeah, my account got suspended after they removed, like, three of my photos for 'nudity'." The woman used air quotes, and they all rolled their eyes.

"What about the Assembly group? Is it just suspended, or did they remove it completely?"

"They said there were too many rule infractions for the group as a whole, so it's suspended... but there's no indication of when it will be unsuspended."

"May as well be removed entirely..."

"True, true, I just don't get why they come after mothers—why not like people posing with AK47s or glorifying violence?"

"Uh—because women are an easy target!"

She could hear their sighs of frustration and agreement with one another as she continued to walk past the crowd. She tuned in to some of the voices in the crowd shouting:

"Put our Assembly back!"

"We're feeding your future employees and customers!" *That's a weird one.*

"Hey!" A voice came from behind her. She continued to walk,

hoping to avoid any engagement, but a girl about her age ran up to her. "You want to join our cause?"

Eleanor's eyes darted around, checking if anyone she knew might see her. "Sorry, I'm late for class... plus, I'm not sure this really affects me." Her eyes looked towards the breastfeeding women.

"It affects anyone who cares about free speech but especially women!"

"Sorry!" Eleanor huffed and pushed herself to walk even faster.

A little out of breath, she was now mostly past the crowd and could only hear the faint remnants of the protest. As she approached her apartment building, she was determined to head upstairs and investigate a little further on her computer. She scanned her building's access card and was pleased to find the elevator waiting for her.

On the fourteenth floor, she marched down the long hallway, past loud music and the faint smell of weed seeping through the walls. She had been living in this same building since college, and being within walking distance of work, there had never been any reason for her to move. Midtown rent was too high to live alone, and here, at least, she had her most reliable friend, Emily.

When she reached her unit at the end of the hall, she twisted her key into the lock and kicked her shoes off by the door. The apartment was dark, but that was all right. *Too early for Emily to be home.*

She took a glass bottle of green tea from the fridge and went out onto the balcony. The roar of the city hit her as she opened the door—like when you go to the beach, and the sound of the waves crashing over and over again numbs your ears. A city can do that too. Cars doing eighty down seven-lane highways, and the hum of thousands of mechanical units heating, cooling, and powering the lights that wash out the sky. The occasional siren disrupts the city's murmur. She tipped back the bottle of tea and let the grassy flavor envelop her mouth in an attempt to neutralize the dense smell of combustion.

This place wasn't beautiful to Eleanor. It was the people, the opportunity, and the potential that she was here for. In the distance, she could see the dissipating crowd outside Agora. She emptied her drink and went to her closet, took off her work clothes, and dropped them on top of a pile of other clothes. It was a finely honed system she had—a last in first out queue—the most time-efficient method for clothes she intended to wear several times before dragging them to the dry cleaners. She picked up an oversized t-shirt from the pile and slipped it on.

She sat down at her desk with its two monitors and a glowing, blue mechanical keyboard. Photos decorated her walls—one of a younger Eleanor with her sister, and another of her family at her graduation. A third showed her and Avi on her first day at Agora, and others featured her with a broad assortment of friends. A shelf above the desk was squished full of books like *The Dream Machine*, *Essential Turing*, *Neuromancer*, and an Einstein biography, among others.

She opened a few news websites and the Agora site. Once there, she navigated first to the private Assembly for Agora employees, called *Agora Family*, and began to scroll. Stickied to the top of the group was the same message that was sent to their emails. There were already several Dialogues and Observations posted about the protest. One Observation was a photo of the demonstration that showed the line of women who were "nursing-in," but a blurred smear had been inserted over the actual... nursing part. The caption read: "Fixed."

It already had over a hundred comments on it, and as she skimmed through them, most seemed to agree that Agora was right in taking the groups down.

The next Dialogue read: "Stock price closed less than a dollar above starting price :-(Disappointed."

She didn't add any comments and instead clicked over to the news tabs and read the headlines:

"Agora Faces Disappointing IPO as Protests Loom"

"The Gathering Place of the Internet Doesn't Want Nursing Women in its Public Square."

With a big sigh, she shut down her computer and collapsed on her bed. *Enough of this for today.*

She pulled out her phone and began swiping through notifications—emails, text messages, Twitter, Tinder… She tapped that one—swiping through some of her matches.

Maybe I'll go out this weekend. She came across a guy named Robert. His profile said he worked in IT. She swiped right.

She answered a text from her mom, deleted some junk emails, scrolled through Reddit, then opened the Agora app again. As she scrolled through her Plaza, she saw a photo of Anne with her AP art class and tapped the Cor button. Emily had posted a picture with some friends at a bar. Cor. Eleanor's eyes moved rapidly across the screen, and before she knew it, nearly an hour had gone by.

She wrapped herself in the puffy down blanket, switched on Netflix, and drifted off to sleep, hoping that the events of today would die away quickly without interruption to her work.

ASKA VALLEY COMMUNITY ASSEMBLY

Dialogue by Eudora P.

"I think it's time to move our group somewhere else before we get censored."

Comments:

Mike
Oh please! Unless you post PORN on here, there's nothing to worry about.

Jessica
Women feeding their babies isn't PORN!

Eudora
@Mike Typical man silencing women's problems...

Mike
Not everyone on the internet wants to see your titties.

Eudora reported this message.

Jessica
Then don't look at it?

Mike
How can I not when it's right there in my Plaza?

Eudora
Let's try and keep it civil.

Jessica
Starting an Aska Valley Women's Community, private only. Discourse me for link.

3

―――――――

E leanor woke to the sound of her phone vibrating on the nightstand, chiming a digital melody intended to be peaceful, which, of course, had the opposite effect. She turned off her alarm and rolled out of bed.

She padded down the hallway and peeked into Emily's room.

"Em!" She whispered loudly. "Let's go run."

Emily raised up her arm and swung it around as if to wave her away. Eleanor flipped on the light.

"Ehh stop! I was out late last night." Her voice was muffled under the blankets."

"When are you not? Come on, we have to stay in ship shape so we can find husbands." She flopped on the bed next to her.

"I found one last night actually, so I can sleep now."

"Oh really, what's he like?"

"He likes rum and dances real good."

"Mmm sounds like the recipe for a lifelong marriage." Eleanor teased.

"It will be, once I remember his name." Emily sat up. "I'll run now, but really slowly and only if you go out with me this weekend."

"Maybe. Depends on how much work I get done. I matched with this guy on Tinder last night. Maybe I'll ask him."

"Good, I was beginning to think rejecting all the men on there was a hobby for you."

"I just don't want to waste my time going out with guys I won't like."

"Such a harsh opinion with so little information," Emily said, rolling out of bed.

"What! It seems so obvious to me the guys on there that are just looking for sex."

"Sex can be good too." Emily pulled on some bright orange jogging shorts.

"Not with people I don't even know!"

"Sweetie, you're such a bumpkin."

"Won't you be cold in those?" Eleanor said, changing the subject.

"You're going to make me change my mind. Let's just go and get this over with."

With that, they set out on their usual path up Tenth Street to Piedmont Park, where they were met with other early morning joggers and a group of morning yoga-in-the-park people.

"Ick, isn't the grass wet at this time?" Emily said a little breathlessly.

"I think that's part of the appeal," Eleanor laughed.

They ran along the path around the lake at a pretty slow pace, stopping occasionally for Emily to catch her breath. It was a cool morning, and she did whine about being cold as Eleanor suspected she would. But Emily had those long, tan legs that scream out to be seen. The humidity made their hair whisp around their faces and their cheeks red.

"Let's eat before I barf," Emily wheezed.

They stopped at a cafe they liked on the way back and ordered avocado toast and coffee.

"So aren't you going to tell me about your grand, amazing party yesterday." She waved her hands around in fake excitement.

Eleanor bit into her toast and chewed slowly before responding.

"Yeah it didn't really turn out to be that great." She filled Emily in on the events of the day before.

Emily listened intently, twirling a finger through her curly brunette hair. "Sheeesh, that's crazy. Sucks to have your work literally protested. But really, this is just a small thing right? Doesn't affect you that much in the long run."

"Maybe." Eleanor couldn't shake the feeling that it wasn't a small thing. She began to ruminate on different outcomes that might come from the event when Emily pulled her back.

"So tell me about this guy you might go out with." Emily huffed.

"I don't know. He's attractive, and his profile said he works in IT. I don't really know anything else."

"Well, let's hope he's not a square like some of the people you work with." Emily signed the check with a flourish.

"Hey, I work with some really smart people." She thought of Avi.

"Yeah, yeah, I know. You also work with some real jerks."

"True," Eleanor said, thinking of Charley and Daryl.

When Eleanor got to work, the office was a bit more empty than usual, but she saw Avi at his cube and waved, then sat down and began to go through her usual routine.

Avi popped his headphones off. "Are we still going to pair on that extra story later?"

"Oh yeah." She had almost forgotten about it in all the chaos. "Let me schedule some time now."

"And how was Ping-Pong yesterday?" He smiled knowingly.

"It was great!" Eleanor opened her calendar—he wasn't free till five. She sent the invite for five o'clock until six, and Avi accepted right away. She checked her Agora Plaza and the Agora Family Assembly again this morning, but little else was being said about the events that took place yesterday. To Eleanor, it felt like everyone had already moved on, but she still wanted to find a way to do more.

Today, Eleanor was working on a feature she'd advocated for that would give users more control over the content they see in their

Plaza with the creation of an Inner Circle. They would choose who they wanted in their Inner Circle and content from them would show up first.

Eleanor felt herself slide into the time warp that was her code editor, and before she knew it, her calendar chimed an alarm for a three o'clock meeting labeled: "SmartData Partnership." Realizing she hadn't even eaten lunch, she went to the cafe to grab a ready-made Super-Greens Salad from the fridge and ate it quickly at the counter, laptop in hand.

With a couple minutes to spare, she walked over to the Apollo Conference Room. Daryl was already sitting at the head of the table, looking pleased with his own punctuality.

She stopped short, momentarily thinking she might go back for a drink to avoid sitting alone with him, but then Avi went in and sat at the opposite end of the table. Daryl greeted Avi and began to discuss something from a previous meeting. As she took a seat next to Avi, she wondered what exactly it was that Daryl spent his time doing. A few of the other devs and the database administrator walked in and took their seats.

"I guess we can go ahead and start," Daryl said with a voice that was too loud for the room. "Agora has decided to partner with SmartData in our efforts to improve the efficacy of our ads. A click isn't the only indication an ad was successful; a user may see an ad on our platform then buy that item in a physical store."

Eleanor looked around the room, *No one looks interested in this.* She figured going public would result in some work related to profitability, but she'd gone on assuming she could keep worrying about real features for users. But the Agora mobile app had been their best source of revenue so far, and lots of companies were eager to buy ads on the platform.

"If we can show our ads are effective offline as well as online, we can charge more for them," Daryl continued. "If you don't know, SmartData has offline purchasing data for millions of people from loyalty programs across several major retailers, so it's a huge data set. We're rolling this out on mobile first, and it's top priority. Avi, you want to explain the technical details?"

"Sure, so basically, we're going to create anonymous IDs for some advertisers and send that to their API along with hashed information like the email address they used to create their account. They will then cross-reference that with their purchase records and match a customer purchase in store with the relevant ad campaign."

Avi and the database admin talked back and forth about which tables to add to the database, but Eleanor tuned it out, receding into her own thoughts. *Their dataset is large enough that you could probably identify the people... It doesn't seem so anonymous.*

"Eleanor, can you start on this today?" Daryl shook her from her thoughts.

"Oh... yeah, as soon as I finish the Inner Circle feature."

"Oh, I forgot to tell you, that feature is going in the icebox for now; it's not high priority."

"Oh... but I'm close to done—"

"We'll re-evaluate it at the next planning meeting." He leaned back in his chair.

She was annoyed now. "Okay... So, do the customers who joined the loyalty programs know their information will be connected with their Agora Persona?"

"They should—that's what a loyalty program is. The company gives you perks or discounts in exchange for your purchasing behavior." Daryl didn't even break eye contact with her.

"Yeah, but they probably don't expect that to be linked with their Agora Persona. Shouldn't we offer an opt-out feature?" The whole room was looking at her now, and she suddenly felt like she might have misspoken.

"Well," Avi began in that mild-mannered tone he was so good at, "I think we could add that feature later."

"There is no opt-out feature here. Users agree to this when they create their account and agree to our terms," Daryl said addressing the room.

"But no one reads that," Eleanor said, surprised by her own desire to push the subject. She stared directly at him across the table, and there was a momentary air of a standoff that no one dared interrupt. Daryl turned up the corner of his mouth in a smirk that reminded everyone of the power he held, and, with that, he ended the meeting.

Eleanor smacked her laptop closed and marched back to her cubicle. Instead of finishing the feature she'd already been working on for days, she spent two hours reading documentation on *SmartData* until Avi meandered over to her cube for their five o'clock.

"Ready to pair?" he asked.

"Yeah, definitely," Eleanor said, eager to do something else.

She changed the setting on her computer to mirror the same image on each of the two monitors mounted in her cubicle. Avi paired his bluetooth keyboard and mouse, and they were ready to go.

She grabbed the sticky note she had written this morning, and they went over it. They worked efficiently for about an hour, writing test cases, passing keyboard and mouse control off, writing code, testing it, repeat. Before they knew it, the four-point story that should have taken several hours was completed in one.

"You're a machine." Avi looked a little tired.

"Thanks." She glowed. The office was quiet and dark since most everyone had gone.

Avi hesitated, then said, "I'm sorry about the meeting with Daryl. I only just found out he was ice-boxing your feature at the meeting before."

Eleanor took a moment to think before she responded. "It's okay. Just one of those things I've had to make peace with to work in this industry—and for one of the top companies. My job is to write code, not make decisions."

Avi shook his head, "But that shouldn't be normal. You should at least feel like your voice is heard."

"Millions of people use Agora every single day. Where else could I work that would impact so many people?"

"Even if that's true, you should be heard more." Avi frowned.

"My work can speak for itself. I don't care to be the loudest voice in the room."

"You might someday though."

There was a momentary silence while Eleanor thought about

what he'd just said. "I do think we should have an opt-out feature though," she whispered.

It was Avi's turn to think for a moment, and when he spoke, it was in the same hushed tone Eleanor had used. "Do you have any plans for dinner? We shouldn't talk about it here."

Eleanor nodded, and they packed up their stuff and left the Agora building together.

NEW EMAIL

SUBJECT: FUN OUTING!

Agora Family,

Considering the stressful events of this week, each team will have a mandatory Fun Outing this Friday (tomorrow). See your manager for details.

Matthew Erickson

4

———

With the Agora building towering over them, Avi and Eleanor stood on the corner of Peachtree Street. It was starting to get dark, and the glass building reflected coral hues from the sunset. An autumn chill stood the hairs on her arm up as they waited at a crosswalk. Eleanor looked up the street at the precise repetitions of identical elm trees that lined the sidewalk. Each was almost bare but hung on to the last of their leaves as if they could delay winter by doing so.

Some people say that cities sparkle at night. At least Eleanor had dreamed they did when she was growing up in Aska Valley. Maybe they do from far away or when you're passing over in an airplane, but when she found herself standing on the concrete surrounded by artificial lights and frequent car horns, the magic dissipated.

Avi's phone rang.

"It's my mom. I always talk with her about this time." He sounded apologetic.

"I don't mind," she reassured him.

"You pick the place. I'll follow." Avi answered the phone and began speaking in rapid, clipped words and long drawn-out expressions. Eleanor listened as she began to lead the way to one of her favorite restaurants.

When Eleanor was selected two years ago to join Agora, she underwent a two-week-long orientation that culminated in choosing the team she wanted to join. She picked the mobile application team for two reasons: because her work would reach people directly, and secondly, because Avi was there. Although many other new hires had requested the same team, she had particularly distinguished herself in Android and iOS programming in college.

For her capstone project, she built a study group app whose members averaged twenty percent higher grades. When she presented her project at the Expo among e-commerce sites, mobile games, and inventory management systems, not only did she win the "Community Builder" award, but she also met Avi. Eleanor knew right away that he was someone who could help her be successful.

As she listened to the lyrical sound of him talking with his mother, it occurred to her that she'd never really spent much time with him alone outside of work. This made her feel a little awkward, and when she looked over at him, he smiled and rolled his eyes at his phone.

She stopped in front of a small ramen bar and waited for him to finish his call. "Sorry about that," he said.

"It's no big deal. I'm close with my family too."

"Yes, but Indian mothers are very… involved." He laughed a little. "She's always asking if I'm ready to get married."

She laughed with him. "That's universal. My mom is always bothering me about my love life."

Avi pulled open the door and waited for Eleanor to go in first. "True, but is she always trying to set you up with good matches?" he asked, walking in behind her.

"No, you got me there… Not so many eligible matches in Aska Valley." She slid into a booth, and Avi did the same across from her.

She liked this place because it was small and not too noisy. She liked being able to hear the *clink* of sake glasses and *slurp* of noodles. All the wood textures and soft lighting made her feel instantly warmer.

Avi started to laugh again. "I just don't think it's so important though—marriage."

"I feel the same, although I'm probably one of the first generations of women to not really *need* marriage to survive."

He studied her face as the waitress came over and filled their glasses with water. "Hey Eleanor, good to see you."

"Good to see you too." She smiled at the middle-age waitress whose name she knew was Naomi. "This is my co-worker, Avi."

Naomi nodded at Avi and then turned back to Eleanor. "Would you like your usual?"

"Sounds good." Eleanor said, sliding her menu to the edge of the table without having opened it.

"I'll have a vegetarian ramen." Avi smiled at the waitress and handed her the menus.

Eleanor sipped from her water glass, wondering how to restart the conversation they had whispered about back in the office.

"The meeting with Daryl today." He seemed to read her mind. "You're more than just a programmer, and he should treat you that way."

"I think I would have to deal with that anywhere though. Agora is becoming larger than anyone ever expected, but I feel lucky to be a part of it."

"Yeah, but building software is supposed to be collaborative… agile… An engineer shouldn't just be a component of an assembly line," Avi continued. "Look, I've been here five years. Agora used to be about connecting people, but it's not that simple anymore."

"We need to make money?"

"Yes, that's one part of it, but the protests yesterday too. Agora is dealing with things none of its founders ever experienced or could even think to expect."

"Yeah, it seems like everyone just ignored the protests…"

Naomi returned, placing two steaming bowls of ramen in front of them. Eleanor picked up her chopsticks and snapped them apart. "And now this SmartData thing is so lame."

"It might seem that way, but there are conversations happening."

She perked up, noodles dangling in mid-air. "Meaning?"

"I won't pretend to know everything—" he waved his hand dismissively, "—but Agora certainly doesn't want more bad press, and while they're not going to address it publicly, they're going to take steps to try and keep this from happening again."

"Like what?" She chewed her food slowly, focusing on what Avi was saying.

"Well, for one thing, they're going to start taking moderation more seriously, with more clearly defined rules and more moderators."

"Okay, but what can I do?"

"I'm glad you asked!" He slurped some noodles from his bowl. "I actually have something that will distract you from SmartData work."

She set her chopsticks down.

"There's this little committee forming."

"A committee for what?"

"It's a small group of people that are concerned about free speech and moderation. They meet to discuss these issues and vote on policies."

Now she was interested. "Are you on it?"

"Ha! They asked me to join, but I don't think Daryl will let me have anything else on my plate right now. They're looking to get some more people after yesterday. I do think *you* should join. Represent our team on this issue."

Too many thoughts were pummeling her brain: Avi cared about this, wanted to help her do something, *and* knew what it was she should do. That she could have a say in these matters. "So, how do I join?"

He leaned back, nodded, and smiled. "I'll loop you into the email chain, and there's a private Assembly for it. I'll add you."

I'm so glad I worked late and came to dinner with Avi. Eleanor was finished with her ramen, even though there was still a little left in the bowl.

"But are a bunch of Agora employees really going to be allowed to write these rules?"

"Well," he began, "there are other people involved for sure, but I think a democratic approach is going to be really good."

"Feels kinda weird that I'd be the one making those choices." She was fidgeting her fingers.

"I think you're just the right kind of person to be participating in these conversations." He smiled encouragingly at her.

The moment was broken when the waitress placed their checks on the table. "How was everything?"

"Great, as always." Eleanor beamed, and Avi nodded in agreement.

"I'm glad we talked about this," Eleanor said as they got up to leave.

"I'll help in any way I can," Avi replied. They stepped back into the cool night and began walking in the direction of their apartments.

Maybe it was her small town roots, but she didn't always feel safe walking alone in the city at night. When she found herself alone, she would walk briskly or talk to someone on the phone until she reached her destination. She was glad she wasn't walking alone tonight.

"What will you do when you get home?" Avi asked, interrupting her thoughts.

"Oh, I've been reading this book about a guy who leaves his job and hikes the Appalachian Trail."

"Getting any ideas from him?" Avi chuckled.

"Nooo, I mean it's something I'd like to do, but going hiking on the weekend mostly satisfies my craving."

"Oh, where do you go hiking?" Avi sounded genuinely curious.

"Well, I go visit my family on the weekends sometimes, and there's lots of trails there. It's actually not too far from where the Appalachian Trail starts."

"I always try to get in some kind of outdoor activity on the weekend; I sometimes play cricket. Have you ever played?"

She shook her head.

"The professional games sometimes last for several days." Avi laughed. "Oh, by the way, did you see the email about the outing tomorrow?"

She sighed, "Yes, unfortunately."

Avi chuckled in agreement as they approached her apartment building. She reached to get her wallet so she could scan in.

"Well, I'll see ya tomorrow." She gave him a half-smile.

"For the social event, no skipping." He winked.

"Yes, of course." She rolled her eyes. "Night, Avi."

"Yeah, have a good night, Eleanor."

With a beep, the door opened, and she went inside. She got in the elevator and pulled out her phone, opening the Agora app. A notification flashed for an invite to join the Assembly: Agora Content Policy Committee. She clicked *accept*.

AGORA ASSEMBLY
CONTENT POLICY COMMITTEE (PRIVATE)

Welcome to the group, everyone! This is a place for any and all Agora employees who are interested in free speech and keeping Agora a fair and safe place for everyone.

Next Event: Kickoff meeting Monday, 10 a.m., Hypatia Conference Room

---

Comments:

Rebecca
Glad to be here, everyone! First topic of discussion... the protests. Is it possible for us to speak to any of those with complaints?

5

———

The next morning, Eleanor got ready with a little less spring in her step. She put on jeans and Converse, deliberating for a moment before pulling on a t-shirt that read "I cheated on the Turing Test."

As she walked to work, she thought more about her conversation with Avi last night. *If he thinks I need to speak up more, then it must be important.* He was successful in the way she wanted to be. He did good work, and everyone knew it from experience. He might not command a room like Daryl, but he was someone people could go to.

This wasn't the first time Eleanor had struggled with being heard. In her computer science classes, she often sat in large lecture halls comprised of mostly men, feeling herself stand out. She had to work twice as hard in any group project to be taken seriously or to be *allowed* to do work. Over time, it became clearer: She was nothing but an anomaly an entire system was shifting around. The more she got talked down to, not taken seriously, excluded, or hit on, the more she understood why she was a minority.

Like a chameleon, she learned to blend in. She dressed down, laughed at derogatory jokes, played video games, drank beer, and even began to dislike her own sex. She convinced herself it was their fault for not adapting or working hard enough. *She* was able to survive here; why couldn't they?

But most importantly, she strived to always be the smartest person in the room. She read books, code documentation, took extra training courses online, started homework the day it was released, did side projects, hackathons, coding challenges. Everything. Eleanor learned to breathe and dream code. She would never allow herself to become the stereotype.

She'd run across girls who tried to use their femininity to slide by —smudge their grades, cheat on tests, get extensions, wheedle homework help, and so on. For thousands of years, women have been the dependents of men, and they somehow have a hard time resisting that behavior even when they do have autonomy in the world.

Over the years, she had grown bitter towards women who acted that way. She was constantly trying to fight that stereotype. She didn't care about First Wave or Second Wave Feminism; she cared about building something.

Avi is right, Daryl should take me seriously.

Agora headquarters was now in her vision, the sun rising behind it. She might not care for skyscrapers and urban sprawl, but this building was art and architecture. A colonnade of glass and steel whose facade lighting she had participated in, on several occasions, manipulating the colors of. Right now, they showed their usual 1s and 0s. The building sparkled, and coming here every day made her sparkle too.

When she got up to her desk, she opened up her Agora Plaza and went to the new group, Content Policy Committee. She posted an introduction to herself and added the first meeting to her calendar. Then she opened Agora and navigated to a page only employees had access to—the Acropolis, which was a live feed of all the content currently being shared on the platform. This was one of her favorite 'unproductive' activities.

Endless new things revealed themselves when she scrolled—a man posing with a reluctant smile in front of a graveyard, a young woman with glasses and a messy bun reads to a wistful crowd in autumn, a new baby swaddled and squinting from the bright lights of a new world—these snippets of human life fascinated her.

She could click on the photos, read about what's really happening to those people, and sometimes she did. But she didn't know them, nor would she, and she sometimes assumed the mysteries of their photos were far more fascinating than reality. After about twenty minutes had evaporated, she closed the browser tab and decided to do some real work for a bit.

All programmers at Agora were given five hours per week to spend on Hacking, which basically meant trying anything that sounded interesting or creating new features to something that already existed. She figured she could devote a few of those hours to her Inner Circle feature. It might be in the icebox for now, but she figured it would get implemented eventually.

She worked on this until around half past eleven when Avi popped his head up from his cube on the other side. "You ready for the team outing, Eleanor?"

"Sure." The truth was, she'd rather stay and work.

Daryl strode down the row of cubicles, looking way too eager. "Is everyone ready to synergize?"

The room was mostly unresponsive.

"Yeah, let's go," Avi humored him.

The group started moving towards the elevators with a general murmur of conversation, Eleanor lagging at the back.

"Ellie, I like the shirt!" Daryl called out to her.

She rolled her eyes internally, *like he actually gets the joke.* "I go by Eleanor."

"Your Agora Persona says Ellie," Daryl insisted.

"That's for friends and family." *Is Daryl stalking my Persona?*

"What's the transportation arrangement?" Reed asked.

Daryl faced the group. "We're going to the pub next to the Escape Room. Whoever is driving, keep the parking tickets to get reimbursed later. I can take four people with me!"

"Avi, you walked, right? You two can ride with me," Daryl

pointed to Eleanor forcefully as they stepped into the elevator. She saw no way out of this unfortunate arrangement.

As they entered the parking garage, the large group broke into several smaller ones and dispersed to different vehicles. Daryl led them towards his car, a black Range Rover. One of the managers who was friendly with Daryl hopped into the front seat, and the two of them began chatting about something.

Eleanor looked at Avi as if to say, "What are we doing here?" when another of her teammates, Aditya, opened the Range Rover's backdoor and slid in next to her. She found herself squished in the middle with Avi on one side and Aditya on the other.

As they fumbled with the seatbelt buckles, Avi offered a quiet apology. Aditya paid her little mind, which was typical, since he also would rather be back in the office working. For the most part, he always kept to himself.

Eleanor caught Daryl's eyes in the rear view mirror as he backed out. He was chuckling, but she couldn't tell if he was laughing at her or at something the other manager said. These forced bonding arrangements were supposed to make teams more cohesive or something, but Eleanor really felt they wasted time and money and were inordinately annoying.

She chatted with Avi some as they bumped along the city roads littered with potholes—some patched, others wide open—all of which made the car's passengers bounce and sway awkwardly. Eleanor wasn't surprised to find that Daryl was the kind of aggressive driver who liked to inch his way into lane switches and accelerate like a Nascar driver as soon as a traffic light turned green. As such, they were the first to arrive at the spot chosen for the day's festivities: a tacky bar and grill that looked like it had been designed to cater to more unique sporting game interests.

The place was loud with layers of noise from TVs, country music, and kitchen staff clatter. They were escorted to a long table in the back that was already set up for their party, and Daryl immediately went to flag down a waiter, demanding more chairs and an appetizer platter.

"That poor waiter is going to wish he'd called in sick today," Eleanor whispered to Avi.

He stifled a laugh. "Where should we sit?"

"At one of the ends."

"Let's go down there." He pointed to the corner farthest away from Daryl. "There's a cricket match playing on that TV."

As they found seats at the far end of the table, the same waiter was hurriedly filling about twenty glasses of ice water. Daryl was playing host to the Agora entourage as they started to trickle in. Eleanor stared at an Esports match playing on one of the TVs.

"Oh cool, a pro DOTA match!" Charley, sat down next to her, somehow already holding a beer. "So, how's it going? Feel like I don't see much of you even though we're on the same team."

"Oh, good. You?"

"Just working hard, you know." He jutted out his chin with a swig of Blue Moon.

"Yeah, I've been working on a side project, and I took some of Frank's stories this week." Eleanor fully realized this would sound like a challenge to Charley.

"So, what are you aiming for, Eleanor?" He locked eyes with her.

"Aiming for?" She gave him a puzzled look.

"You're not working that hard for no reason. What are you trying to get promoted to?"

"Well… I don't know."

He looked astonished that she didn't have an answer for this.

"Well, I'll give you a tip." He took another swig of his beer and hushed his voice. "Did you ever notice we're in the minority here?" His eyes flicked to Avi and Aditya, who were deep in conversation about the cricket match, and then back to her.

Eleanor was used to being a kind of minority. She raised her eyebrow, which she knew gave her a quizzical expression.

If Charley noticed, he didn't show it. "We're positioned in a way to go straight up the ladder, if we want." He looked satisfied with himself.

She looked at the cluster of people chatting with Daryl—all of them managers—and Charley's message started to sink in.

"I hadn't noticed." She forced a smile. *Who even says something like that out loud?*

He shrugged then took another swig of his beer. "Advantages are to be had if you look for them."

She shifted in her chair, wondering if it was too late to move, or if Avi had heard any of the conversation, but people were beginning to sit down to eat, and Avi was still chattering away about Cricket.

What if someone overheard the conversation and thought she agreed with Charley? He seemed completely unaware that the conversation he'd just had with her was anything other than normal.

She was about to join in on Avi's conversation when she noticed a tall, brunette woman she'd never seen before enter the restaurant and walk straight up to Daryl, who smiled brightly and waved her over.

Maybe someone Daryl knows from marketing.

The woman followed Daryl over as he came to the now mostly full table. To Eleanor's surprise, the woman didn't take a seat with everyone else, but rather continued to stand next to Daryl as he clapped his hands together and folded them in front of his chest. "Welcome, Everyone! This somewhat last minute event was designed for us to all unwind from this chaotic week and reset our team synergy. I also wanted to take this opportunity to introduce someone new to our little umbrella of Agora. This is Bethany Dawson." He gestured to the woman, who upon closer inspection, Eleanor could see was wearing riding boots, Levi's, and a silky pale-pink blouse. "She's going to be filling the brand new role of Engagement Engineer!"

He began to clap loudly, and everyone, Eleanor included, mimicked this action. *An engagement… what? That's not engineering.*

Bethany stepped forward now, her lips slightly parted, eager to give her own introduction. "Hey, everyone," she said with a honeyed southern drip, "I'm *so* excited to be part of this team. I know how critical you guys are to the Agora we all know and love. Agora has succeeded more than anyone else at connecting the world, but to really build a global community, we have to do more." She smiled with perfect white teeth, and her green cat-like eyes attempted to make contact with everyone in the room. "We've brought people online, and now, we have to keep them there. My main task is going to be helping in the redesign of some of Agora's core features to be more fun and engaging. I look forward to working with y'all!"

Redesign? Eleanor snuck a look at Avi, who shrugged lightly.

Bethany and Daryl took seats right in the middle of the table, and as food began to arrive and more alcohol was poured, Eleanor strained to listen to the deluge of questions everyone was asking the pair.

"Did you know that we're doing a redesign?" she asked Avi.

"A redesign is always in the pipeline, but I didn't know it was happening this soon. Or maybe they've prioritized it."

She picked at various fried food items with little enthusiasm and put together that Bethany had studied digital marketing (so she was spot on there) and psychology, was brand new to Agora, but had worked at another tech company before.

Daryl clapped his hands to get the attention of everyone in the room. "Okay, everyone! Before we have too many drinks, let's get to the main event." The Agora staff began to make their way to the door and over to the Escape Room. When they reached the venue, they were greeted by an overly cheerful employee who was giving instructions and dividing them into groups.

Eleanor hoped she wouldn't be put into a group with Charley. Being literally trapped in a room with him sounded like a good working definition of hell right now. Slips of paper were being passed around to designate groups, and clusters were forming in the numbered areas. Eleanor had been given the number five.

She really wasn't all that surprised when Charley sauntered over and gave her a knuckle bump. Oh, God, she mutely cursed her luck. Worse yet, Daryl followed behind and exchanged high fives with him. She was officially doomed to spend the next hour locked in a room with an all-boys club of arrogant power seekers. From across the room, Avi shot her a sympathetic smile.

For the final cherry on top, the famous Bethany started walking their way. "Team 5! Yeah!" She threw her arms up in a cheer, and rose gold bracelets jingled on her wrists. Eleanor was forced to participate in more high-fives.

"Hey! You're Eleanor, right? I hear you're a really great developer." Bethany smiled and swung her arm to give Eleanor a side hug. "I'm so excited to work with you!"

Eleanor complied with a smile as false as Bethany's eyebrows. "Yeah, I'm all about making Agora the best it can be."

"Then we'll be allies." She winked.

Their group was led into a room decorated to look like a casino. There was a giant timer over the door that indicated how long until they'd be released from their confinement, unless they escaped sooner, but Eleanor had her doubts. On another TV screen, another overly cheerful Escape Room employee—this one dressed as a blackjack dealer—was giving instructions.

The general idea was to search the room for clues to discover where a missing agent went. Team Five moved through some of the more obvious clues, like those hidden in doors in the wall or underneath stuff, relatively quickly. But then they hit a snag. The current clue said they needed to "gamble the expected value of a spin of the wheel." They agreed that meant they needed to gamble a specific amount on the slot machine but were tripped up on expected value.

In the bag with the clue was a five-dollar chip and the number seventeen. Eleanor had slogged through tons of casino-themed problems in her Probability and Statistics class to know what needed to be done. "It's asking for the expected value if you bet the five-dollar chip on seventeen."

Why were they looking at her like that? Hadn't any of them taken statistics?

Charley snapped his fingers. "Yes, and if you won, it would be a hundred seventy-five dollars! So that's what we need to gamble in the slot machine." He sounded so damn confident as he bent over, ready to try his own suggestion.

Eleanor corrected him swiftly, "No, expected value is the average of all the outcomes."

"Let's just try it real quick." Charley strutted over to the slot machine, put in the chips equalling one hundred and seventy-five dollars, and pulled the handle.

Of course nothing happened.

"Let's try Eleanor's suggestion!" Bethany's face glowed with a message: *girl power!*

Eleanor did a quick summation in her head. The expected value was that the player would lose twenty-six cents. She reached into the tip jar on the table, pulled out a conveniently placed penny and quarter, and slipped them into the slot machine.

It chimed loudly, clicking on 7-7-7 and opened to reveal the final clue.

"We've almost escaped! Let's do this!" Bethany gave her a swift high-five, but Charley and Daryl just moved on to the last puzzle.

Everyone crowded around Eleanor to see the final hint; the aroma of several unique but equally overpowering colognes, and just a hint of something fruity, made her head pound.

As Eleanor began piecing things one by one in a cogent order, hands reached from behind her, helping at times but just as often making things worse. Finally, they guessed that the agent had gone to Ireland. The game-master announced their victory, and the door clicked open.

As the final high-fives went around, everyone filed out of the room. Team Five seemed to be the first group to escape their room, but the three other groups trickled out soon after.

Eleanor eagerly escaped the small room. She couldn't wait to get away from the tacky casino decorations, poker table, and that obnoxious slot machine. What was supposed to be a team building activity really just seemed to expose the inadequacies of the team in question.

Daryl and Charley were trying to galvanize a group of people to go out for beers, as if they needed to drink anymore. Eleanor readily declined and rode back to the office with someone else to grab her backpack and go home.

NEW DIALOGUE

Avi Kumar
<Lead Software Engineer @Agora>

Bonding with my team today. Hope we can find a way to get out of this room!

Comments:

> **Eleanor**
> You are a great team lead

> **Daryl**
> Your team is lucky to have you

> **Charley**
> We're going to get out before you

6

After spending a quiet Friday night at home to recoup from the social event, Eleanor was ready to keep her promise to Emily to go out on Saturday. She lay sprawled out on the couch while Emily poured wine in the kitchen, the room warm with the afternoon sun.

Eleanor's Tinder match, Robert, had messaged her the night before, and they exchanged a few words before deciding to make plans for the weekend. They seemed to have enough in common, and Eleanor wasn't sure how much more could really be learned without meeting him first.

"So what's on the agenda for tonight?" Eleanor didn't look up from her phone.

Emily laughed. "I'm not your Outlook calendar, Ellie."

"You know what I meant." Eleanor rolled over so she wasn't facing her and looked at her phone again.

"Sure, sure. Well, I want to go try that new taqueria, then I figured we could hit a bar."

"Drunken Goat?"

"Hell yeah!" Emily popped the cork off of a brand new bottle of Rosé.

"Okay, I'll tell Robert." She clicked the virtual keyboard with the details and pressed send. "He said he's trying to bring a friend for you."

"Eh, whatevs, I can find my own friend. Time to pregame." Emily plopped on the couch and swished a wine glass at Eleanor. "So how much do you know about this Robert guy?"

"Eh, not much. We talked back and forth some last night. I definitely need you to stick around for a bit to make sure he's not weird." Eleanor sipped her wine.

"Fine, what are you going to wear?"

Eleanor tilted her head back on the couch and smiled. "Whatever you tell me to."

"Good choice, we'd better go to my closet since you have nothing but boss bitch outfits."

"Well, that *is* my day job, you know." They both laughed.

Tipping back their glasses and emptying them, they went to Emily's room where she pulled open a closet stuffed to the brim and began to dig through it. She pulled out a black strapless stretch dress and held it up.

Eleanor shook her head. "It's too cold for that, plus I'll look slutty!"

"It's not that bad." Emily rolled her eyes.

"I'm taller than you!"

"Fiiine." Emily squished it back in the closet and began sifting through other dresses. "You have a great body, Eleanor. It's no crime to show it." She pulled out a powder blue cocktail dress with long sleeves. "There. Now you can be toasty warm."

"Sure, I'll try it." Eleanor stepped into the bathroom and slipped into the dress. She sighed. It looked okay, and maybe the world would even consider it good. It had a deep V that she filled out exactly the way the designer would have liked, and it hugged her waist just so. She did find comfort in the long sleeves that the wrapping layers of the dress tied into perfectly.

"It doesn't fit!" she yelled to Emily from the bathroom.

"Bullshit!" Emily peeked in. "It looks better on you than it does me."

"Can I wear tights at least? It's so short."

"Sure, tights and what shoes?"

Eleanor put a finger to her cheek in contemplation. "Boots?"

"Wrong." Emily laughed. "You're hopeless."

"Not heels; there's too much walking."

"But flats would be an insult to how good you look right now."

"Fine, but you're rubbing my feet tomorrow." Eleanor went to her room to curl her hair and put on makeup. When she was through, she slipped on a pair of black suede pumps over her tights. Emily came out wearing the black dress she'd tried to put on Eleanor coupled with a pair of shoes that jacked her up enough inches to match Eleanor's height.

They grabbed their purses and set out into the night. When they reached the taqueria, there was one guy standing outside. Had to be Robert; looked like his picture.

"He's cute," Emily whispered.

He had on a flannel shirt and slacks, and his short hair curled on top. "Not bad," Eleanor agreed.

"Eleanor and Emily?" His southern drawl took Eleanor by surprise.

"Yes, I'm Eleanor and this is my friend, Emily."

Emily gave a big wave. "Nice to meet you."

"I apologize, my friend wasn't able to make it."

"That's okay." Emily shook her head. "I'm here to make sure my Ellie is safe."

He nodded with a smile. "You girls look lovely! Let's get some food."

Eleanor felt a subtle gag reflex in her throat at the way he said this. She tried to temper her judgment as they went inside. The trio sat down at a high-top table, and Eleanor was trying to figure out why she already disliked this person when he started talking.

"Have you been to this place before? My parents own a couple franchised Mexican restaurants, and I managed one of them while I was in college, so I ate food there all the time."

"Nah, this place just opened recently." Emily smiled at Eleanor. "We have this thing we do, don't we, Ellie?"

Eleanor smiled now. "We've been looking for the city's most unique taco."

He raised his eyebrows, "Oh, and what've you found?"

"Hmm, so far I'm voting for this one that had fried pickles in it." Eleanor said.

"Korean BBQ taco for me all the way." Emily added.

"Well let's see if this place has something to beat it." Robert took up his menu with a grin.

A waitress came to the table to get their drink orders. Eleanor ordered a margarita and noticed Robert ordered a beer without even making eye contact with the waitress.

"So, Eleanor, you said you're a software engineer, right? Where do you work?" He asked.

"Agora." She picked up her menu.

"Wow, really? That's impressive!" His country roots seemed to drag out the word impressive in the most patronizing way.

"Eleanor is *so* smart," Emily joined in. "We were roommates freshman year of college and have been besties ever since."

The waitress returned with their drinks and took their orders. Eleanor downed the rest of her margarita and ordered another as well as some tacos. Feeling a bit warmer, her inner critic quieted some. "What's your place of business, Robert?"

"Oh, I work for a local software company doing IT."

She lifted her second drink and let her lips taste the salt around the rim. "Like, technical support?"

"Uh, yeah, preparing and deploying hardware, maintaining servers, and we're spinning up cloud services now. You know, all the stuff that keeps your code running every day." He didn't seem to lose any confidence.

She was perfectly aware of the value of the work he did; it just wasn't impressing her for some reason.

"That's cool." She sipped more of her drink.

He was double-dipping in the salsa. "You two into any sports? I played some football in college, and I really love following that."

"I like tailgating!" Emily laughed.

"Who doesn't! I'm a total grill master. I usually host a few big tailgating parties a year."

"Sounds fun!" Emily smiled and stole a glance at Eleanor, who was reaching the bottom of her second margarita, hoping it would help her have more fun soon.

The food came, and the topics of conversation grew no more scintillating while they ate.

When their plates were clean, Eleanor excused herself to go to the restroom before they left for Drunken Goat. On the way, her eyes met a familiar face sitting at the bar, holding a beer.

"Is that Eleanor Crawford?" Daryl's eyes bugged.

Her cheeks grew even warmer than they already were from the alcohol, but she intended to just smile and keep moving.

"What's my little subordinate doing in a place like this?" He slurred his words a bit, not even trying to be professional.

"I have a social life." She didn't try to hide her impatience.

The guy sitting with him looked at her apologetically and then reached out his hand to introduce himself. "Hey, I'm Kitt."

"Um, hi, I'm Eleanor. Nice to meet you. How do you know Daryl?"

"We were in the same MBA program together, and I work at Agora too." He seemed to be studying her somewhat.

"Ah, are you a manager as well?" She felt her back stiffening.

Kitt smiled. "No, I'm a data scientist. Managers are assholes." His dark eyes had a teasing glimmer as he looked toward Daryl.

Eleanor smiled. She was about to ask him why on earth a data scientist had bothered earning an MBA in the first place, but she stopped when Emily and Robert walked up.

"There you are. Thought we lost ya," Robert said.

"Sorry, got sidetracked." Eleanor smoothed down her dress and gave Kitt what she knew was an awkward smile. "Nice to meet you." She turned away but should have known that Emily, who was always happy to have a few more men around, wouldn't leave it at that.

Looking at Daryl and Kitt, Emily piped up, "Unless you two want to come with us?"

"Where to?" Kitt looked at Eleanor for permission.

"Drunken Goat." Eleanor smiled, tipping her head down slightly.

Daryl slammed his empty beer glass on the counter. "I love that place! Let's go." He threw some cash on the counter and hopped up from his barstool.

Robert rocked back and forth on his feet. "Let's get goin' then."

Some people get talkative after a few drinks. For Eleanor, it was the opposite. As they walked up the road, she started to feel the effects of the two margaritas: Her vision was a little blurry, and she would have liked to be holding onto Emily's arm for balance. Drunken Goat was popular in the city and as packed as ever on a Saturday night. Wooden barstools, each with a carving of a goat stumbling on two legs, lined the bar.

"Let's do some shots!" Robert shouted.

"Hell, yeah!" Emily egged him on.

As they moved towards the bar, Eleanor pulled her arm, and they lagged behind the men a moment. "That's my manager, Emily." Looking towards Daryl.

"Oh *shiiiit*—" she laughed, "the jerk you told me about? Well, fine, I'll keep him out of the way so you can flirt with his friend."

"I'm out with Robert."

Emily's eyes showed she clearly understood just how Ellie felt. "Please, I knew the moment he opened his mouth, you weren't into him. Relax, just have some fun." Emily exuded an aura of confidence that made Eleanor feel just slightly envious.

As they caught up to the group, Robert had already ordered everyone a round of shots. Eleanor looked at her shoes. What the hell. Maybe the thing to do tonight *was* just to have fun. She wondered about Daryl, though. There was something different, almost pitiable, about him tonight, not shrouded in his cloak of power.

They all tipped back their shots as the DJ made electronic beats reverberate from the bass through their bodies.

"I want to dance!" Emily shouted in Daryl's direction.

Daryl followed after Emily while Robert grabbed Eleanor by the waist and pulled her onto the dance floor. She went with Robert, but she couldn't help making eye contact with Kitt, glimpsing his muscular frame as he slid onto one of the barstools to watch.

She was attracted to him without a doubt. He was a bit taller than her but not lanky. But above all, it was his eyes that drew Eleanor in. Bright, curious, constantly observing and thinking, they were the kind of eyes that told her a lot was going on behind them. She liked to think she had the same kind of eyes.

By the end of the second song, Robert was so pumped up, he was singing along, his body close enough to hers that she could smell the alcohol and tacos on his breath. Eleanor excused herself to finally go to the restroom. When she returned, she was relieved to see that Emily was now dancing with Robert, and Daryl had found himself back at the bar. She teetered on her heels a little before catching Kitt's eyes again and resolving to go over to him. She slowly climbed onto the tall barstool and ordered a rum and coke.

"You having a good time out there?" He swiveled around so he was facing her.

"Mhm." The corner of her mouth turned up as she took a sip of her drink. "Robert is the result of the brilliant data-driven dating platform we've all come to know and love."

Kitt leaned in closer to her, his crisp, collared shirt tightening on his shoulders, "I can make that data work better for you."

She held his gaze. "I'd like to see you try."

He gestured towards the mob of people dancing, and she nodded back at him, draining what was left in her glass. As she hopped off the stool and stumbled into him a little bit, he caught her and pulled her out on the floor.

Any awkwardness she might have normally felt in this situation had been melted away by the alcohol. She felt the electricity of their connection as their bodies moved against one another. They danced several songs, and she all but forgot about Robert until she caught sight of Emily dancing with Daryl.

"Yuck." She shuddered.

"What?" Kitt shouted above the music.

She gestured at Daryl and Emily. He was all over her, and not in a good way; Eleanor felt the corners of her mouth turn down.

Emily needed her. She and Kitt walked over to them as the song was ending and the decibels of noise lowered.

"Hey, you two," Kitt said.

"Cnya b-lieve I didn get invite t'the after party an that lil' shit did." Daryl slurred.

Eleanor couldn't help but laugh to herself when she realized what was upsetting an intoxicated Daryl.

"He's a bit drunk… Quite drunk, really," Emily said without losing her cheerfulness.

Kitt put up his hand to ward off an oncoming waitress ready to bring Daryl another drink and put his arm on Daryl's shoulder. "Come on, boss. Let's get you some air." When Daryl stiffened slightly, Kitt threw his arms around him in a bear hug, moving him to the door. "I'll get him an Uber," he called to Eleanor. "See you in a few minutes."

While Kitt was sending Daryl home Eleanor asked Emily what happened to Robert.

"Well, I danced with him some, but he noticed you and Kitt hitting it off and decided to leave. He didn't seem mad or anything really."

"I feel bad." Eleanor clicked her heel on the floor.

"Eh, I wouldn't. That's how these things go sometimes. You seem to have a good connection with Kitt though, and he seems cool, so don't waste that. I'm going to have some fun so don't wait for me!" Emily winked and set off to find some new beau to entertain her.

Eleanor sat down again, now in that zone where alcohol takes over the decision-making part of the brain. Kitt came back into the bar and sat down next to her. "All right, I sent him home."

"Will he be okay?"

"Yeah, this is pretty normal for him." Kitt slid a credit card to the bartender to cover the tab.

"Why?" Eleanor was genuinely curious. "Also, here." She pulled some cash from her bag and tried to hand it to him, but he waved it away casually.

"No way, most of it is Daryl's. I'll get him later." He laughed.

"But, you know, I'm not sure Daryl has ever even asked himself that question. Why do any of us drink really?"

"So we can do the crazy things we wouldn't do when we're sober. Or that we'd overthink." She met his eyes, and he scrunched his forehead in agreement.

His eyes lingered on her. "You wanna get out of here?"

It was against her better judgment, but it was just what she wanted to do. The rest was a bit of a blur. Making out in the Uber, being led into his apartment, him shuffling some of the clutter and clothes off the bed before they fell into it together.

Sex with Kitt was just as calculated and thoughtful as she'd been imagining—him exploring her like an anomaly in a data set, determined to learn exactly how she had appeared there. Their eyes exchanging signals on every move and touch. Afterwards, they lay with their bodies merged on top of each other staring up at the ceiling, and Eleanor noticed for the first time that it was covered with glow-in-the-dark stars. She squinted to get a closer look and realized it wasn't just stars; it was the whole freaking galaxy: planets, moons, and the Big Dipper. "I feel like I'm in a kid's room."

She could feel the laughter bubble up in Kitt's chest. "Oh, come on, why does everyone say that?"

"Probably because everyone our age had these in our bedrooms as kids." She heard her own voice sound so matter of fact as she searched for a blanket with her hand.

"Maybe that's why they're comforting." He rolled onto his side to face her, pulling the navy blue linen duvet over both of them. "Well, I've never had sex with a hacker girl before."

"What makes you think I'm a hacker?"

"Oh, I can just tell. Agora better watch out, or you'll take the whole thing down." He smiled a kind of dorky smile.

The alcohol was starting to wear off now, and Eleanor wasn't sure what she was supposed to do. "Should I go?"

"What? No... unless you want to?" The pout on his face made Eleanor's heart short circuit.

"I don't—yet." She settled in, feeling relieved.

"Okay. Good." He tapped his finger to his cheek, "So... tell me… what's the meanest thing you've ever done?"

"Sheesh, that's the first thing you're gonna ask me?"

"Yes, it's good to get these things out of the way. I'll go first even." He waited a moment, probably to see if she would volunteer to answer first, but she just smiled in that "okay, go on then" way.

"Right, so in high school, there was this kid that would always cheat off of me in math class."

"Cliche."

"Yes, but I got really tired of it, so at the end of senior year, we were taking the final, and I did the whole exam on the paper, but I didn't color in the right answers on the answer sheet."

"So he failed?" Eleanor squinted.

Kitt started to laugh uncontrollably. "Worse. I bubbled in the shape of a dick on the answer sheet, and the guy copied it and got expelled."

"He did not!" Her eyes widened.

He tried to bury his cackles in the pillow. "No, I swear, he had to go get a GED and everything."

"How did he not notice that?" She found his laughter contagious and was cracking up too.

"Gestalt perception not fully developed? I don't know."

"Okay, but, he kinda had that coming," she said.

"True, but it still felt mean." He cleared his throat in a "your turn" kind of way.

"Yes, yes, okay… so, in college, I dated this guy, and I found out he was cheating on me."

"The bastard!" He shook his head.

"I only found out because a friend of his tipped me off, but I wanted evidence, so I logged into his Agora account, found the proof, and then posted it on his Plaza for everyone to see."

"See, I knew you were a hacker." Now they were both laughing.

"No, he was just a moron who used the most obvious passwords."

"That's savage. But also, he deserved it. And you just reminded me: I need to go change all my passwords."

She smiled at the glow-in-the-dark ceiling sky. "Hot or iced coffee?"

"Hot." He thought for a moment. "Are there any people you'd give up your kidney for?"

"My sister. Also, don't you mean *one* of my kidneys?"

"Does it change the answer?" He shrugged.

She bit her lip. "No, I suppose not… Okay… What's your favorite YouTube channel?"

"Data Science Dojo." He nodded matter-of-factly.

"Nerd."

"True, and even still, what's one thing you know that I definitely don't?" he said.

"How very humble of you… Let's see." She snapped her fingers. "I bet you don't know how to shuck corn."

He poked her cheeks as if to give her freckles. "You're right. I don't. So you're a country girl *and* a hacker. Weird combo."

She frowned and rolled to her side to face him. "What's more important than work?"

He blinked hard. "Living life."

Eleanor wasn't sure how long their conversation went on before they drifted off to sleep, but when she woke up the next morning, she was only a little hungover. She looked around the room and realized how nice Kitt's apartment was. He had large windows looking out on the city, and from them, she could see even further to the forest that lay beyond the tall buildings and congested streets. For once, she didn't hate looking out at this city.

She reached for her purse to pull out her phone and swipe through notifications. A text from Emily with a winking emoticon; Eleanor rolled her eyes. Tinder, asking her how her date went. She opened that. A survey with a few questions like, "How did this date go?" and "Will you go out with this person again?" She laughed to herself as she tapped 'no' and gave the date two stars.

She clicked the submit button and found herself wondering what difference that data would really make. Next to her, Kitt began to wake up.

"You want some breakfast?" he murmured.

"Sure." She smiled back and tossed her phone aside.

TELL US HOW YOUR DATE WENT

Review your date with:
Eleanor Crawford

2/5 stars

A little bit full of herself. Also she bailed on me at some point.
At least her friend was sweet.

7

<hr>

When Eleanor arrived home later that morning, she was in a bit of a daze, but Emily was eagerly waiting for all the details. "Well, well, this is quite the role reversal." Emily let her feet dangle over the side of the couch arm.

"Aren't you supposed to be at church?" Eleanor teased.

"*Puhhhlease…* Tell me about Kitt!"

Eleanor plopped down on the couch with a smile. "The sex was good."

"Mhmm."

"And, I don't know. He's interesting, definitely attractive, and his place is nice, but we work for the same company."

"So? There's no law against that. It's not like it's someone on your team."

"Yeah true. Someone on my team would be trickier."

"Sooo," Emily raised her eyebrows. "Are you going to see him again?"

"I'm not sure. He made breakfast this morning, but we didn't have 'the talk' or anything." Eleanor shrugged.

"You have a radiant glow this morning." Emily took out her phone and began scrolling through her Agora Plaza.

"I'm hungover." Eleanor placed a hand on her stomach and stuck her tongue out.

"Well, you bear it angelically." Emily laughed.

"Ok, I gotta go get ready for family lunch."

"Have fun!" Emily shouted without looking up from the message she was typing.

Eleanor went to her room to take a shower and throw on some casual clothes. She always looked forward to her regular Sunday lunches with her family and sister. She hopped in her car and drove up the highway about 45 minutes to meet them at a country buffet halfway between Atlanta and Aska Valley.

While waiting for them to arrive, she noticed a Link request from Kitt on Agora. She tapped 'confirm' to add him to her Circle but didn't have a chance to look at his Persona before her parents' familiar F-150 pulled into the parking lot next to her.

A younger and more carefree version of Eleanor hopped out of the backseat and threw her arms open for a hug. "Ellie!"

"Anne." She hugged her sister tight in return. "How's it going?"

"Hey, sweetie!" Her small-framed mother slid down from the high truck and gave her a gentle hug.

"Hey, Dad!" Eleanor waved to the other side where her father, in his classic Levi's jeans and a flannel shirt, was already talking to someone he recognized.

The parking lot was filled primarily with trucks and SUVs and people in church clothes engaged in friendly conversation. She wasn't in Atlanta anymore.

They made their way inside and through the line where they paid to be given plastic trays outfitted with green plastic cups, chipped ceramic plates, and flimsy silverware.

Anne and Eleanor exchanged knowing glances. "To think this place hasn't changed since we were kids."

Eleanor smiled. "I bet I've used this exact plate before." She held it up and pointed to a smiley face etched into the back.

They both laughed even though it wasn't quite true. The cash-only register now took credit cards, the dining area had flat screen TV's on the wall, and the brand new touch-screen soda machine let you mix and match flavors and varieties. Eleanor knew it had been the talk of the town when it first made its appearance.

She filled her plate with all her favorites she couldn't get in the city—country fried steak, gravy, mashed potatoes, mac and cheese, green beans, and those fluffy buttery rolls. The family instinctively trickled to their usual table and sat down to eat.

"So, I hear you had quite the public release at your company this week, Eleanor," her father said before biting into a roll.

"Oh, yes, there's been no end to the news articles."

"What a thing to do, breastfeeding in the middle of the city like that, though." Her mother gave a sigh and dabbed her mouth with a napkin.

A thought flitted into Eleanor's mind. "Hey, Mom—"

"Yeah, sweetie?"

"Did you breastfeed me?" Eleanor had never thought to ask about this before now.

"Did I wh—" Her face reddened, and her eyes blinked rapidly. This was obviously the last thing she expected to discuss with her daughter. "Well, of course I did, just imagine your grandmother if I hadn't. Why?"

"Well, the protests have had me thinking, and I wondered if it was something you did in private—or, er, is it something you do, like, in front of people?"

The corners of her mother's mouth turned up with amusement. "Well, when you were hungry, I fed you. I would've never left the house for two years if I needed privacy every time, but it was usually just in front of friends and family. I probably used a blanket or cover if there was anyone who was uncomfortable."

"But are there... photos?"

She thought a moment. "I imagine so. We didn't have Smartphones back then, so we weren't snapping photos of everything, but your dad took pictures with the Kodak when you were a baby." She smiled nostalgically, "I should go dig some out."

"Did you share them with people?"

"The photos? Well, of course, you were an adorable baby!"

"No, I mean the breastfeeding ones specifically?"

Her brows knit together with confusion as though she hadn't the foggiest idea what her daughter was talking about. "Well, yeah, if they were in the stack, I suppose. I didn't pick them out or anything."

Eleanor set her fork down. "You didn't feel weird about people seeing them?"

"I mean whoever developed the photos would have seen them, which, at the time, was probably your cousin, Marty. He worked at the photo center in town."

Eleanor turned this information around in her head.

"I mean, it's a natural thing to do, breastfeeding," her mom added.

"And you didn't feel like you were 'on display' or weird?"

Her mom pondered this question. "I think you kids are way more on display with how much of your lives are on the internet than I ever was breastfeeding, but you certainly wouldn't see me out there protesting and nursing at the same time."

This wasn't the response Eleanor wanted. "Ok, well, what if when you got your photos developed, they put your breastfeeding photos in a separate envelope marked 'nudity' and said you couldn't share them."

Anne let out a giggle. "Leave it to Ellie to turn Sunday dinner into philosophy hour."

"How would that stop me?" her mother said.

"Just pretend it could. What would you do?"

"I guess if that place said I couldn't share them... I'd get them developed somewhere else? Why would I give my business to a place that tells me what to do with my own pictures?"

"And if there was nowhere else to get them developed?" Eleanor pressed.

"Well this is just silly. Why do they get to decide what I do with my pictures?" Her mother was clearly puzzled by the direction this conversation had taken.

"Well it's like, they decided 'hey, this is nudity,' and some people are uncomfortable with it or don't want children to see it. So they take out photos with nudity so they're not in the stack of photos being passed around at holidays or family dinners." Eleanor felt she had finally made her point.

Her mother obviously disagreed. "But those same children could be breastfed or see their mother breastfeed?"

"Okay, yeah, but the general idea of keeping photos with nudity separate makes sense, right?"

"Well, yes, but who decided that breastfeeding counts as nudity?"

"Isn't it? We don't generally expose our breasts in public?"

"The breast's purpose is to feed our babies though. I've seen more of a woman exposed in skimpy outfits than when she's breastfeeding."

Eleanor put her hand to her temple. *Dear Lord, what have I started?*

Her dad, who had been eating very quietly, now joined the conversation. "I do agree with your mother. There are far more photos on your platform I would consider examples of nudity than breastfeeding could be."

Anne rolled her eyes. "Now imagine the protests if they took down every photo where a woman exposed her body even a little."

A light seemed to click on in her mother's eyes. "Well, if you're talking about sharing pictures of me breastfeeding online, I would have never done that!"

"What? Why is that different, then?" Eleanor swirled her straw around in her sweet tea with a little too much force.

"You never know who might see them there!" Her mother raised her eyebrows. "Ellie, is this still about work or maybe you personally?"

"Mom, no. This is about Agora—the place where I spend all my time!"

"Oh, so you don't have a boyfriend then?" Her mother frowned now, likely disappointed. "God knows there's plenty of men in that office."

Eleanor's and Anne's eyes locked. Ellie understood her sister's silent message—*you're not getting anywhere with this*—and decided she was right. Their table grew silent as the family ate, the only noise the rumble of the full restaurant. Eleanor decided to introduce a new topic. "How's AP Drawing going?" she asked Anne.

Their parents exchanged quick glances, but Anne didn't look up from her plate. "Oh—ridiculous—you won't believe what happened."

Eleanor smiled, and Anne swallowed a mouth full of peas before continuing. "So we get this assignment: 'Draw something beautiful that you see today.'" She mimed a snobby art professor giving a commission. "And everyone brings in the usual drawings of flowers and mountains and waterfalls."

"Well, sweetie, those things *are* beautiful," her mother said gently.

"So what did you draw?" A bemused smile crept across Eleanor's face.

"I drew Cooper," Anne said matter-of-factly, naming their old, three-legged hound-mix dog. The girls had been in high school when they rescued him after he was hit by a car.

"Oh, Anne!" Eleanor stifled a laugh.

"What? Cooper is beautiful."

She imitated her teacher's deep pompous voice again, "This was meant to be an exercise in skill, not interpretation. You didn't follow instructions."

She stuffed country fried steak into her mouth. "He gave me a C!" she said, her forehead wrinkling. "All art is an exercise in interpretation, what a moron."

Eleanor couldn't help laughing now. "That's amazing. Do you have a picture of the drawing?"

"Yes, I do." Anne reached into her purse to find her phone. "I don't see why it wouldn't make a good portfolio piece, and now I'm determined to put it in."

"What do you think, Dad?" Eleanor asked while Anne scrolled through her photos.

"I think your sister's right; Cooper *is* beautiful." He gave a thumbs up to show his unity.

Anne handed her phone to Eleanor, who took her time examining the detailed pencil drawing of the familiar old dog. The shading and proportions expertly depicted Cooper sitting on three legs, his ears perked up in devotion. Eleanor could almost reach out to pet him.

She knew very well what was beautiful about the drawing, but to an outsider that didn't know this dog was loved, they might just see a sad-looking, probably flea-bitten, dog sitting by itself, maybe waiting for the ASPCA to put it to sleep. "It's an amazing drawing, no doubt," she told her sister.

Anne's face twitched. "But you don't think it's beautiful either?"

"*I* do think it's beautiful." She handed the phone back to her sister.

"Besides, who is he to tell me what I find beautiful?" Anne crossed her arms.

"Very true!" Eleanor's plate was mostly empty now. "I think I'm going to get ice cream."

"Me too." Her father got up to join her.

"So how are things at the inn?" she asked as they joined the line for the soft serve machine.

Grayson House had been a part of Eleanor's life as long as she could remember, her town being nestled in the mountains with plenty of quaint charms that brought a regular host of tourists throughout the year. Most of Aska Valley's economy was centered around it. Her grandparents converted Grayson House into a bed and breakfast in the fifties, then her father had taken it over, somewhat reluctantly at first, after a few years of working post-college. Her parents have been running it together ever since.

"Oh, the usual, already fully booked up for Thanksgiving."

Grayson House was more than just a place to stay—it was a historical destination, located on about fifty acres of land along the Toccoa River featuring hiking trails, kayaking, and an amazing restaurant. They also ran a shuttle that would take people to the charming little downtown that had quaint shops and frequently held holiday events and festivals.

"That's great!" She pulled a cone out of the cardboard box on the side and began to pile vanilla-chocolate swirl into it.

"And you'll be proud, we finally hired some help." He followed her lead and grabbed a cone.

"Oh great! Anyone I know?"

"Hmm, I don't think so. His name is Emmett. Had a real rough time of it, but he's a hard worker." He filled up his own ice cream cone, and then they walked back to the table.

The restaurant was continuing to fill up, so the Crawfords relinquished their table and loitered in the parking lot, chatting a bit longer before ending their visit. Eleanor hugged her sister tight, then her mom and dad as they said their goodbyes. In her car on the way back, she wondered how a city could look so beautiful from a distance but so grimy when you were in it. Her sister was right about what people find beautiful, and Eleanor knew that Anne was far better at finding beauty in things than she was.

SMS CONVERSATION

Kitt
I had a really good time. Want to get dinner after work tomorrow?

Eleanor
I had a great time too! Dinner sounds good :)

Kitt
Ok, what time do you finish working?

Eleanor
Now that is a hard question... but I think I can wrap up at 6.

Kitt
How gracious of you!

Eleanor
Have something in mind?

Kitt
Oh yes, you just wait and be surprised.

8

———————

The next morning, Eleanor took a bit more care getting ready by putting on a little more makeup, and leaving her hair half down. She wouldn't have time to come home first before her date, and she wanted to look nice.

At work, she started her usual routine until she checked her calendar and saw that the first meeting of the Content Policy Committee was this morning. *Oh, yeah!*

Eleanor peeked over the cubicles; she didn't see Daryl yet. *Hope he made it home okay.* Avi was in already, of course, and caught her eye. "Good morning! Need something?"

"Morning, Avi." She stood up with her laptop. The meeting was starting soon. "I'm headed to the first meeting for content policy. Thanks for introducing me to it."

"Awesome! I'm glad you're joining. Do you want to fill me in on it later today?"

"Well…" She hesitated. "I actually have some dinner plans. I was going to leave early today."

"Oh, no problem." Eleanor saw a flicker of disappointment in his eyes before he reassured her. "You shouldn't call it leaving early. It's just on time."

"Yeah… I know." She walked around the cubicles. "Well, I'm off."

"See ya." He waved and turned back to his computer.

Eleanor stopped in the break room and made some coffee. While the single-serve coffee machine sputtered away, she looked out the window. Fall was almost over, and the city was descending into that gray cast caused by winter. Winter was by far this city's ugliest season. With the rare exception of those moments that snow actually fell.

Last year, she had watched from this very window as one of the biggest snowstorms ever to hit Atlanta ground life in the city to a halt. The sight of I-75 morphing into a parking lot was mind-blowing. After a while, she couldn't see anything but gray clouds and fat tumbling snowflakes. Everyone got sent home early, and there were snowball fights in the streets. The whole city had shut down for several days, and Eleanor had spent all of them cuddled up with a blanket in her apartment.

Eleanor mixed cream and sugar into her coffee and headed for the conference room on the floor below hers, the one on which she knew Kitt worked. She took the long way around to try and find out where he sat. Walking a little slower than usual, she allowed her eyes to scan the room until eventually, they landed on his. She smiled when she noticed him sitting in his cubicle with big headphones on.

He grinned back and started to take his headphones off, but someone started talking to him. Eleanor looked away and continued to the Atlas conference room, where she sat towards the back.

A few minutes later, her phone buzzed in her pocket, and she couldn't resist pulling it out. As she had hoped, it was a text from Kitt: "Good Morning :)"

She couldn't help smiling as she replied: "Morning! Already hard at work I see."

As other people were filing into the room, she took a survey—there was no one she knew or even recognized. *Am I the only engineer here?* She calculated the average age of those in the room to be under thirty.

For some reason, she'd expected this room to be packed with

people who were all interested in improving Agora, but only a dozen people sat in the room when a guy in a short sleeve button-down shirt stood up and cleared his throat to start the meeting.

"Hi, I'm Jeff. I run the content moderation department here at Agora. We're still a very small team, but as Agora grows, so do we, and last week's events prompted more interest than ever in what we do. I'm excited to form this committee to get input from all the different voices here at Agora and to start refining our policies and practices moving forward." He clicked a remote that started a slide presentation on the screen behind him.

"Today we're going to do a brief overview of how content moderation currently works. Then we'll discuss the current issues facing Agora."

He flipped the slide again, and a screenshot of the Agora web page popped up with the *report* button highlighted on Dialogue and Observation posts. "When someone reports a Dialogue or Observation, it comes to us for review. We have a set of rules, albeit small, we try to follow for how to handle the content. As you all know, our goal is to provide an open gathering space for conversation, so free speech is important to us. But we also want that space to be safe. Just as there are rules for behavior in a public space, we believe there should be rules online, but it turns out those rules aren't as easily enforced."

He let out a dry chuckle and switched the slide again, this time to a screen that showed a message that read: *Your Observation has been removed.* Underneath the message an image of a woman breastfeeding appeared.

"There are currently about fifty people regularly monitoring content, but we will be scaling that up quite rapidly. So far, our main goal has been to keep the worst-of-the-worst content off Agora— porn, violence, and so on. The main questions we are asking are: 'Will this harm our users?', 'What is the intent of this content?', 'Is the intent to cause harm?'"

He clicked for a new slide. "Here are some examples of what a moderator would do." The screen showed an image with two buttons underneath: 'approve' or 'remove'. "Right now, it's really basic. The moderator sees the content that's been reported—in this case, a text post that threatens a specific person—and makes a decision. This time, the content would be removed."

Ok, sure, but how do they know if it should be removed? Eleanor thought to herself.

"This brings us to the biggest challenge we face in dealing with this issue: We need a framework to make these judgments." He clicked to the next slide, a screenshot of a Word document. "These are the guidelines we're currently using." He pointed to a title on the screen: "Agora Content Rules." Below it were four commands:

1. No nudity
2. No blood or gore
3. No violence
4. Use your judgment

"One of the main goals going forward is that we make this document more detailed, but we want to do it democratically. Our first problem is this: We've been flooded with breastfeeding photos over the past couple days; it's like they're continuing the protest in some way." He opened the web browser to the Agora Acropolis page and began to scroll through live content, which, as he said, was overflowing with nursing photos.

"Pictures like these are the only things my moderators have been clicking through since Friday. Thousands of them. It's become a PR issue, and we need to make some kind of rule and justify it."

Eleanor's problem-solving gears started to churn. She was sure there could be an algorithm that would filter most of those pictures out before a human monitor ever needed to see them.

Jeff was still talking. "Really, what we're looking for is a more specific definition for what we think counts as nudity. Until now, we've gone with: 'If you cover it in public, you cover it on Agora.' But, now, this is obviously a gray area. So, let's go ahead and open it up for discussion."

The only other woman in the room spoke first. The aura oozing from her words made clear she felt she *had* to be there; otherwise, there would be no one to make her point. "I'd love to start by providing a *relevant* perspective. I am a mother who nursed both my children. Feeding babies this way is a completely natural and essential part of life, and most laws dealing with indecent exposure make exceptions for breastfeeding."

A man in a suit responded. "Yes, but most women wear some kind of blanket or nursing cover when they're in public."

"That's an option, yes, but no law requires it," she replied.

Another man scratched his chin thoughtfully. "Okay, but you're not differentiating between a short-lived act and a photographic record of said act permanently on display and available at any time."

That's a fair point. Eleanor thought.

"Why does that matter?" the woman asked. "Nursing an infant is something that would exist in the public square, and we are supposed to be a kind of public square, are we not?" The woman shot Eleanor the faintest of glances. Eleanor felt she was being asked for her support.

"Okay, but why do they *need* their breastfeeding photos to be seen by everyone?" The suit guy obviously felt the need to speak again.

Another man spoke up. "As I see it, it's a matter of self-expression, right? That's not something we're supposed to be restricting, right?"

Eleanor joined the conversation. "Isn't there some kind of middle ground? What exactly about these photos would truly count as nudity if feeding an infant weren't involved?"

"The breast?" Suit guy raised his eyebrows, letting Eleanor know what he thought of her question.

The eyes of the other woman in the room narrowed to a squint. "Ever see a woman in a bikini? Wouldn't you agree a large portion of her breast is visible there?"

Eleanor smiled. "So maybe just the nipple then?" she suggested.

There were some nods of agreement.

The woman's eyes blinked rapidly as though she was contemplating all the alternatives. Eleanor hoped she'd accept this compromise as a victory. "So, we can leave the photos up if the nipple is not visible?"

"Which means the child would probably be actively breastfeeding…" Jeff, too, seemed to be considering Eleanor's solution.

The woman sighed. "I think this is a decent approach." She may not have won, but Eleanor hoped she could see that the two of them had successfully nudged the line.

Jeff clapped his hands. "Okay, should we vote on this then? Breastfeeding photos are allowed, so long as the nipple isn't visible in the picture?" Everyone in the room, except for suit guy, raised a hand in agreement.

"Okay, I'll add the relevant clause. This will be a living document, and I look forward to working on it more with you all! Any questions before we wrap up?"

Eleanor decided to ask the question that had been nagging at her since the discussion began. "Do you all have any kind of algorithm in place to automate some of this?"

"Not yet, but we'd love to have someone from Engineering work on that."

"Yes, that's why I'm asking."

"Oh—awesome! If you can get manager buy-in on it or use Hacking hours, I'd love to see what you come up with."

"Okay. Cool." Eleanor was disappointed—she'd hoped they might already have something going she could contribute to—but not deterred. She would build something.

"All right, thanks for your time, everyone." Jeff dismissed them.

Eleanor took her laptop and headed back to her floor. She worked on the DataLogic implementation for most of the day then used her last hour to start researching a moderation algorithm.

When five o'clock finally came, she hopped up to meet Kitt in the lobby as they had planned.

"Hey! You ready?" His shoulders were relaxed, and his face glowed all the way from his spreading grin to his warm.

"Yeah, what should we eat?"

"I have a plan." He smiled then gestured to the large glass

entryway doors.

Eleanor followed him with a twinge of excitement that grew as they approached his car. He opened the door of a Tesla Model S for her.

"Thanks!" Eleanor gave a glossy smile before sliding into the pristine white-leather interior.

She wasn't necessarily one for cars, but electric vehicles as a technology of the future fascinated her. And sure, there were other electric models on the market, but this was *the* one to have. She took in the vegan leather seats, large sunroof, and a digital display, all smelling like a new invention. Kitt got into the driver's seat, and it began automatically adjusting itself.

"Wow, I'm jealous. I've been considering getting an electric car." She tapped on the screen to adjust the air conditioner.

"This is the best one on the market. It's got the longest range of any electric car, and it's fast as hell." He spoke like he was giving a sales pitch.

"And, it'll drive itself one day," she added.

"Yeah, exactly! It can already handle highway driving pretty well. Takes some of the monotony out of stop-and-go traffic."

"I've read some about autonomous driving. I think it's an interesting topic."

"I did a project on it in school!" He looked at her before letting the car go into reverse. "I'm really into it."

As he pulled out of the parking lot, she could feel the car's power. He floored it onto the open road, and her stomach fluttered with a thrill as if she was on a roller coaster.

When he pulled up to a fancy looking restaurant and handed his car off to the valet, she was relieved she had dressed a bit nicer today than she usually did for work. She twirled her loosely curled hair hoping she wouldn't trip on the way in. The place was definitely high class but in a more modern sense. They served Southern farm-to-table style food that had become popular lately. Although people were waiting for a table, the hostess whisked them to theirs right away.

"I know the owner. He was in my MBA program." He pulled

back her chair and waited until she was seated before joining her across the table.

"Oh, cool. I was meaning to ask you about that. Why did you decide to get an MBA as a data scientist?" She spread her napkin on her lap as the waiter filled their water glasses and placed a set of petite cornbread on the table.

"Well, mostly I wanted to have more options. I don't necessarily have any big business plan at the moment. Since Agora offers reimbursement for advanced degrees, I figured I should work on something. And if I ever really want to strike out and do something on my own, I need some business sense. So, that's pretty much it."

"That's cool!" This was one more thing they shared in common —an obsession with learning. "Growing up, I helped my parents out a lot with the inn they run in my hometown."

"Ah, so you've already got the business skills then." he said.

"That's probably not comparable," she laughed.

The waiter came back with a bottle of champagne and filled up their glasses with silky bubbles.

"So how did you wind up at the Big A?" he asked, taking a sip.

"You know," she sighed, letting the bubbles tickle her tongue. "It's a pretty unlikely story, I think."

"Well, statistically speaking, it's pretty unlikely for most people to work at Agora." He tilted his head back with an easy smile.

"You would say that."

"True," he leaned back in his chair, "but I love a good success story. Do tell."

Her face became more animated. "I was born in a really small town. My parents didn't understand computers. I guess no one from their generation did. I knew the first time—when we got one at the inn to handle bookings—it was fate. I was no one, nothing, a blip in the world, but then that screen lit up in front of me, and it all changed. I was no longer confined to the narrow beliefs of my small town. I could find other people out there that thought like me."

He nodded, encouraging her to continue.

"I mean, we were the first generation to grow up in this hyperconnected, globalized world. Suddenly, there's this group of people that have access to all the knowledge and history—more than any group before us—with a million times as much information as the libraries of Alexandria at our fingertips. And it's not just *there*, but we can touch it. We can change it, affect it, manipulate it. We are the movers of the Information Age."

"Okay, so you're really into access to knowledge… Why Agora, then? Why not work for a search engine?" He took one of the mini cornbreads and popped it in his mouth.

"Because knowledge is in the hands of the people—that's social. For most of human history, knowledge moved through social networks. Think letters, scrolls, writings on the wall, gossip…"

"But you don't seem like the type to care about amplifying gossip."

"Yes, but sometimes gossip is true or useful. At my family's inn, I was constantly around families and friends from all over coming together to celebrate holidays, weddings, reunions. I had a supportive community there. It made me think relationships with others are the greatest source of joy in life. The people we meet, the stories they tell, they form our social networks. And the internet was allowing us to communicate faster than ever before, and with people farther away. I believed in the power it had to support our social interactions. Agora seemed like the answer to that. I thought, 'I could help build that. I could help connect billions of people with loved ones who've moved far away or to new people that share their same interests.'"

"But?" he started to say. He was interrupted by the waiter who placed two small Murano glass salad bowls in front of them filled with kale, beefsteak tomatoes, red onion, and gobs of homemade mayonnaise topped with sliced hardboiled eggs between them. "Y'all enjoy," he told them. Kitt locked eyes with him. "Thank you."

Eleanor poked the curly green kale with her fork. "But what?"

"You said *believed*. You don't anymore?"

His question took her off guard. *Did I say that?* "I still do, but it's not so simple in my mind anymore."

"In what way?" He sounded genuinely curious.

"Well, everything that happened last week with these women's groups has had me thinking. I actually joined a committee related to it. That's where I was going this morning on your floor."

"Oh, okay! Continue."

"And all these people in this room, smart and thoughtful people, don't see eye-to-eye on how to handle these images of human babies being fed."

"I agree, there's much more nuance to human nature than people like to believe."

"Exactly!" She threw her hands up. "But it's not an unsolvable problem. I feel like we made a balanced and fair decision."

"Which was?"

"The photos can stay if the nipple isn't visible."

He nodded, and they both took a few bites of their salads before she felt she had to tell him more. "Did you know they don't have any kind of automation systems in place for this?"

"That's not surprising since it hasn't caused any kind of real issue until now."

"But still, I couldn't believe it."

"Speaking of surprises… my friend, the chef, will probably be deciding what we eat tonight." He laughed. "That cool?"

"That's cool." She smiled.

"So, then, Hacker E.C., you're going to make something for them?"

She giggled at the nickname he'd given her. "I think I will use some of my Hacking time to work on it, yeah."

"I can help you get some training data if you're interested."

"That would be awesome, actually."

When the main course arrived, Eleanor was beside herself. The plate in front of her was a symphony of southern goodness: smoked trout with fingerling sweet potatoes, all swimming in fresh peas, carrots, mushrooms, and artichokes, dressed with some kind of sauce.

"This looks delicious." She picked up her fork and went straight for the trout.

"I'm glad." She could feel him looking at her, watching her reaction before he started his own dinner. She wanted to change the subject, talk about something besides herself. "So why did *you* choose Agora?"

"Well, I'm a data scientist. Where else would I have access to such large and interesting data sets?"

"Of course."

"Plus, I love the South, and I love this city."

That's strange, she thought. He doesn't look or sound southern

"Yeah, I didn't even apply to jobs out of state. I wanted to get out of my small town, but I couldn't bear to be so far from my family."

For one brief moment, they looked at each other, and she knew he understood what she was saying. She savored every bite of the meal. It just might have been some of the best food she'd ever had, other than the restaurant at her family's inn, of course.

He leaned forward and hushed his voice slightly. "Do you think you'd ever leave Agora?"

She laughed. "Leaving Agora would be career suicide. There's nowhere else to go but higher within the company."

"Not necessarily, maybe it's not about going higher."

"Oh, I agree. For me, the work has to be meaningful." *God, I hope he doesn't think I sound like a rank-climbing Charley.*

"Objectively or subjectively meaningful?" He ran his finger around the rim of his now empty champagne glass.

"What do you mean?"

"Well, a lot of work is objectively meaningful to society, right? The mail has to be delivered, trash picked up, food grown, delivered, and sold. All those things keep the world moving. So is it more about what work subjectively means to you?"

She thought about this for a moment. She didn't necessarily consider the kinds of jobs he mentioned as meaningless. She had worked various student jobs on campus, and the work she did at her parent's inn seemed meaningful to her. In school, she'd had several friends who worked at fast food restaurants or in retail positions that had been miserable.

"Hmm, what about salespeople? Or people who work at fast-food restaurants? I bet they don't necessarily think they are making the world a better place," she countered.

"Touché! I guess that depends on what they believe about fast food."

"And do you think fast food in general makes the world a better place?" Eleanor gave him a firm look across the table. She was animated by the conversation.

"No, I don't," he conceded. "But that work might be subjectively meaningful to them in that it provides the money they need to survive."

She considered this. "But I dream of a better world for everyone, even those who can't dream it for themselves." She felt something welling up inside her, but she didn't understand what it was.

Across the table, Kitt parted his lips slightly, and his eyes locked with hers. "I've never met anyone quite like you."

She blushed, and inside, her pulse raced. Her knees felt a little weak too. "The food was wonderful. Thanks for bringing me here."

"You're welcome." He popped his last potato in his mouth then pushed his plate away.

It's like his natural state is smiling. How can one person be so happy?

"So, other than grappling with life's biggest questions, what else do you like to do?" he said.

The two talked about various outdoor activities as the check came and went, Eleanor insisting on covering half but Kitt refusing. Her promising to get the next one.

"So that means there will be a next one?" His eyes glowed from the flicker of candlelight.

"Yeah. If you'd like to."

She looked at her shoes as they walked back to the car. When she reached for the door handle, she found Kitt's hand there instead. He pulled her in for a kiss.

"I would love to see you again." He nuzzled her forehead.

Her face brightened as she looked up. "Good."

When she got back to her apartment, Emily was waiting to drill her for details. Recounting the evening, she was warm and happy, and when she finally dropped into bed, she drifted off to sleep right away.

NEW DIALOGUE

Kitt Berkeley
<Data Scientist @Agora>

Amazing dinner at **The 404 Kitchen** tonight with a fascinating person.

---

22 ❣ 98 ⚜

Comments:

Jean
Omg how did you get in there?

Kitt
Know the chef ;-)

9

A week later, the SmartData features were implemented in production, and before Eleanor had time to be upset about it, she was assigned a new annoying task.

"Hey, Eleanor!" Bethany the Engagement Engineer waved big, jingling her bangles as she walked over to her cube. "I'm *so* excited to be working with you!"

Eleanor took off her headphones and gave a short head nod.

"I hope it's okay to just meet at your desk like this. I *hate* conference rooms."

"Works for me." Eleanor had to agree with her on that.

"Okay," Bethany sat down in the chair next to her, "let us commence the first meeting of a super exciting new project..." She let loose with a metallic-sounding drum roll on her laptop. "Plaza 2.0!"

"2.0?"

"For lack of a better name at the moment." Bethany let out a laugh as silky as her coral-colored blouse. "My team has a ton of fun new features we're workshopping to make the experience on Agora more engaging, but the first priority is building and testing some changes to the Plaza because that's where Patrons spend the most time."

"All right, that sounds cool. It *is* the gathering place, after all." Eleanor thought, *This might be okay.*

"Yes, exactly! Daryl said you'd be excited to work on this since it relates closely to your Inner Circle feature."

Eleanor smiled just a little. "Okay, so what am I building?"

Bethany opened her laptop and began clicking the keys. "Great energy. This is gonna be *so* fun." She pushed some more buttons on her keyboard. "Okay, I added you to the relevant stories and a brainstorming document we've put together. This is very experimental, but the general idea is similar to the feature you've been working on which is that everything users currently see in the Plaza is just chronological. So that one girl you went to high school with posts five times in an hour? Your Plaza —flooded."

Eleanor returned a bemused smile.

"We gotta make it more dynamic, so we're going to test out a ranking system. Most importantly, we want this to be something our team can adjust without having to push out new code."

"You want me to build a kind of dashboard with some variables you can manipulate, and those variables change how the Plaza appears?"

"Yes, exactly! So, here's what we want to be able to toggle for this feature." She pulled up a document and turned her screen, allowing Eleanor to see. "The three variables we're looking at are how much Cor a post has been awarded, how long since it's been posted, and the number of comments."

Eleanor leaned forward and nodded quickly. "Okay, that makes sense."

"We also want some data points collected: impressions, clicks, comments, and time spent in a session."

"Okay, what do you want me to do with those points?"

"Glad you asked! For now, we'd like a simple reporting view along with the dashboard. There's an example in the tracker story I'm adding you to."

Eleanor picked up her notebook and began jotting down some notes. "So how does my Inner Circle feature calculate into this?"

"Ah!" Bethany broke eye contact. "Well, that's gonna stay chillin' in the icebox for now. We're going to be doing a bit of testing and experimentation with this for right now."

"Alright." Eleanor tried not to take Bethany's patronizing dismissal as a personal affront.

"Okay, well, great! Do you have any questions?"

"No, seems pretty straightforward." Eleanor set her notebook down.

"That's *so* awesome!" Bethany snapped her laptop closed. "You wanna grab some lunch together?"

Just to feign polite interest, Eleanor glanced at her clock. "Oh, sorry, I've got another meeting in a few minutes. Next time?"

"Sure. See you later, Eleanor!"

After Bethany was out of sight, Eleanor grabbed her laptop and went down to Kitt's floor for their, now quite regular, lunch meeting. He gave her his best nerdy, toothy grin and took his headphones off.

"I just met with our *engagement engineer*," she said, using air quotes.

"Oh yeah. *Them*. We've got some work with them in the pipeline too." He pulled an empty chair closer to him, and she plopped down in it. He'd already gone to the café and picked up today's lunch special for them: Greek chicken gyros.

"Thanks!" She bit into the soft, warm pita bread. "How's your morning?"

"Crazy busy. Now that we've gone public, we're really ramping up the advertising efforts on the platform, and that's about all my work has been lately." He started on his wrap, and feta cheese crumbled out of the back. "Kinda boring."

"Yeah, I hear that." She detailed to Kitt what Bethany had asked her to work on.

"Well, at least that's a real feature of some kind, makes Agora more interesting to use."

"True. I'm just annoyed. I was already working on something similar, and now it's getting scrapped for this."

"Yeah, I get that. I think things will continue to be a lot different here now that we're growing so fast."

She could see the terminal on his computer scrolling rapidly, and as soon as she finished eating, she opened her laptop. She wanted to talk to him about her Hacking project, but he had another idea.

"Let's do something fun this weekend." He spun around in his chair.

"Like what?" She didn't look up from her computer.

"I don't know. What do you do for fun?"

"Nature," she said as she typed rapidly.

He laughed. "Oh yeah? Tell me more about this *nature* activity of which you speak."

She looked up from her computer and smiled playfully. "Very funny. You know, just get out of this city, away from these screens, and breathe some fresh air."

"I agree, let's go do some hiking."

"Sounds good." She momentarily lost track of what she was doing.

"You've started working on something for content moderation?" He straightened up as if they were in a meeting now.

"Oh—yeah! I'm working on a tool that could precede the human moderators, and you know, only images for now but something that can catch all the most obvious stuff and remove it right away. Then if it can't reach an answer, send it to a moderator."

"That sounds great."

"I'm just getting started, and I was hoping to build a model beginning with the breastfeeding photos since that's front and center right now."

"Very sensible."

"Well, I'm using an open-source image processing tool, and I've set up a simple decision-tree algorithm to start. I've written some rules, and now I just need some data sets to train with."

"So *that's* the reason you've come to me." He made a pouty face.

"Among other reasons," she teased.

"Okay, so what do you need?" He turned back to his computer and began typing.

"Ideally, a large set of photos, ones that were approved to stay up as well as those that were removed, but I need to make sure that I create labels based on the new rules we've established."

"Okay, so maybe just pull from the past couple days?"

"Yeah, I think that should work."

"Okay, you got it." They both worked quietly for a little while until Kitt smacked the enter button and said, "Done!"

"Yay! Thanks." She closed her laptop with a short huff.

"Okay, I've got a one o'clock I gotta go to." He picked up his laptop and gave her a wink.

"All right, see ya later." She returned to her desk and spent the rest of the afternoon working on the new features for Plaza 2.0, thinking occasionally about Kitt's goofy grin or where they might go hiking this weekend.

CODE COMMIT BY E.CRAWFORD

```
branch: develop-feature#2834
    Notes: Created framework for Plaza 2.0
    public class PlazaRank extends Plaza {
    //TODO add modifiers to Post class
    private int numAwards;
    private int numComments;
    private int postAge;
    private int priority;

public int getNumAwards() {
    return numAwards;
    }

public void setNumComments(int numComments) {
    this. numComments = numComments;
    }
```

10

———

Over the next few days, Eleanor stayed busy coding Plaza 2.0, and by Thursday morning, she was mostly finished and had begun testing it before the demo she was scheduled to present that afternoon.

Planted at her desk with her headphones on, she was running her code locally and using her Plaza as a testing ground. She had it open in one window and the dashboard visible in another. It showed the three different categories: time, comments, and awards. For each, you could add a new weight parameter—entering the target value and the rank value it received.

Eleanor entered some values like, a post with more than five comments would get plus two rank and a post less than six hours old would get plus-three rank.

All the potential posts that could be in her Plaza would run through her algorithm, receive a ranking, then populate by highest rank first. She simply had to give higher rank values to those items she wanted to prioritize and lower ones to those she wanted fewer of.

Eleanor saved the values she had entered then refreshed the Plaza page.

Where before, she just saw everything people in her Circle had posted in the past few hours, now she saw a much busier public square. Photos with numerous awards—there was one her sister had posted, a drawing Eleanor hadn't even seen yet. *Cool!* Buzzing Dialogues with many comments and conversation.

Instead of having to scroll through a bunch of stuff she wasn't interested in, it now seemed like everything was worth looking at. She went back to the dashboard and readjusted the values a bit, giving more weight to comments and awards and allowing a greater time span.

She refreshed the Plaza again and was able to see what could be considered the 'best' posts from her Circle over the last few days. There was a Dialogue from Kitt with over a hundred awards. *Popular kid.*

An Observation from Emily standing thumbs up next to a lineup of expensive-looking champagne bottles.

A photo of a guy she went to college with showed him wearing dark sunglasses and looking away from the camera off into the distance.

Then she saw a Dialogue with only a few awards but a ton of comments, so she clicked on it.

> Is anyone else tired of hearing about these wraps?!

Eleanor laughed. The latest multi-level marketing product was some kind of weight-loss belly wrap, and she'd seen plenty of people she went to high school with talking about them and trying to sell them. She scrolled through the comments, enjoying the spats that resulted from those who agreed and those who tried to defend their product.

"Hey, Eleanor!" Avi's voice broke into her reverie.

"Oh, hey—"

"Didn't mean to interrupt."

"Oh, you're good! I'm just testing out Plaza 2.0 before the demo this afternoon." She leaned into a stretch and shook her wrists out a little.

"Great! Everything working all right?"

"Yeah, I think so."

"Cool. We're planning to go live with it tomorrow, so I wondered if you could be on call this weekend in case anything breaks?"

"Yeah, of course." It was her code after all.

"Thanks." He looked at his watch. "Time to grab some coffee?"

"Sure." She stood up and locked her computer.

They headed towards the café, and Avi asked, "So, how was the first content policy meeting?"

"Oh, good—I forgot to fill you in. I think we found a pretty good compromise on the photos, and—"She smiled in his direction."—I've been working on something with my Hacking hours."

He raised his eyebrows in mock surprise. "Of course you are. What is it?"

"Just trying to get some automation in place to help the process." They reached the café and ordered lattes.

Avi smiled as if that were precisely what he expected her to do. "Good idea—I heard they just took on a third-party firm to help with moderation."

"Wait, what? They didn't mention anything about that in the meeting."

"Yeah, it's been too much, and they needed more help ASAP."

"So they outsourced it? To more... *people*?"

Avi nodded as they grabbed their drinks from the barista.

"Why not use software?" She shook her head back and forth, trying to get a handle on what he was telling her.

"Oh, I'm sure there will be a lot of interest in what you're working on, especially since this doesn't seem to be a popular project for people to join." He chuckled. "But in the meantime, they have a PR issue that needs attention right away. This is more like a team of firefighters than a long-term solution, I believe."

"I guess that makes sense." She felt more of an impetus to work on her project than ever before. They started to walk back in the direction of their desks. "I was actually wondering if you could give me some feedback on what I've got so far."

"Yeah, of course. After the go-live though. Just put some time on my calendar."

"Awesome, thanks!"

"Okay, see you at the demo later. Good luck." He picked up his laptop and headed off to another meeting.

She sat back down and opened up her calendar. His schedule was packed, so she grabbed some time on Monday.

She was going to do a little more testing of her feature, on Acropolis now, which is what she would be using for her demo. She went through a similar process, toggling values and refreshing the page, enjoying, of course, getting to scroll through the master feed so much.

She couldn't help thinking how great it would be if anyone could customize their Plaza this way. She knew it might be too much to hope for right now, but, man, it was really something she'd like to work on at some point.

She decided to test some edge cases next and put a really high weight on comments. This resulted in a Plaza full of Dialogues with large discussions and/or arguments. *Not necessarily a bad thing.* Next, she put a heavier weight on awards, and the Plaza took on a different look entirely. Now, it was mostly dominated by photos rather than Dialogues, and as she scrolled, a surge of curiosity captivated her attention.

A photo of the President and First Lady captioned "Four more years" had over a million Cor.

A black and white cat squeezing through a small hole in a box. Eleanor couldn't help but smile.

A tropical island with sparkling blue water and seaside cabanas captioned "Who wants to be here right now?" She could almost feel the sunshine on her.

There was a man in a military uniform sitting in an airport holding his newborn baby, hands over his eyes. Two million Cor. Her eyes prickled.

Her heart skipped a beat when she saw a golden retriever puppy cuddled under a fluffy white comforter.

As she did this, she wondered if she should put in some limits— maximum or minimum values that could be set so that the content wouldn't be too unbalanced. But she hadn't been asked to put any limits in place, and this was experimental, after all.

After lunch, Eleanor headed to the Apollo conference room a little early to get set up for her demo. She plugged her computer into the cable that snaked from the center of the table, and her laptop screen appeared behind her on the larger display. She placed the dashboard and Acropolis side by side.

Bethany came in first, followed by someone else from her team, Eleanor assumed. "Hey Eleanor! We're *so* excited to see this and start using it." Bethany had on a satiny maroon blouse and mauve lipstick.

"Hey! Yeah, this has been great to work on."

Daryl came in, nodding a quick hello, then sitting and typing rapidly on his phone.

Finally, Avi and the rest of her team trickled in, and Daryl closed the door to indicate the meeting could begin.

Eleanor explained how the dashboard could be manipulated, looking at Bethany and her teammate, then gave a brief overview of the technical implementation to her team. Finally, she scrolled through Acropolis, changing the values a few times and refreshing the page as she'd done earlier. When she finished, she nodded at Daryl to indicate she was done.

"This looks great," he said.

Bethany looked like she might actually clap her hands. "Absolutely! This is *exactly* what we were looking for!"

Eleanor's confidence soared. "I think there's a lot of potential for user customization going forward with this approach." She made direct eye contact with Bethany. "Do you think that's something we might implement at some point?"

Bethany nodded breezily. "Anything is a possibility in the future, but for now, we're focused on curating an engaging experience *for* people."

Daryl gave a dry laugh. "If I had asked people what they wanted, they would have said faster horses."

Most of the room laughed along with him. *Scyophants.* She decided not to mention that the difference between Henry Ford and Daryl was that one of them actually had something useful to contribute to the world. Her cheeks growing warmer, she snapped her laptop closed. "So, any questions then?"

Bethany finished a dainty little simper then turned to Eleanor. "How do we access the dashboard?"

"I'll send you a page of documentation and a link."

Bethany gave a thumbs up and typed something on her computer.

Daryl stood and gathered his laptop. Eleanor knew he was talking to her even though he wasn't looking in her direction. "Go ahead and send a pull request to Avi to merge into develop, run your tests again, and we will push to prod tomorrow morning at 6:00 a.m." He finally glanced at her. "You're on call this weekend?"

Eleanor nodded.

"Okay, great." He rushed out of the room.

"Thanks *so* much, Eleanor!" Bethany smiled brightly.

"Will there be any more features for this going forward?" Eleanor asked.

"Possibly. Currently, we're working on spinning up a dedicated team for Plaza 2.0, but we wanted to get something going. I do have some time on your calendar next week to work on some other features though."

She jingled a wave as everyone filed out of the conference room. Eleanor walked back with her team, and Avi gave her a light elbow tap. "Good job."

"Thanks." She smiled reluctantly.

The next morning, the code was pushed out into the world. Now Eleanor would have to wait and see what they did with it.

NEW DISCOURSE

Anne
Hey! Are you guys making some changes to the Plaza?

Ellie
You noticed? Lol

Anne
Everyone did haha

Ellie
We're testing some new things, yeah

Anne
Well, I like it. First time I logged in and didn't see 3 straight rants from Aunt Lily.

Ellie
😁 That's not all it does

Anne
Do tell

Ellie
Wellllll things with more comments or Cor
will get boosted

Anne
Oooh does this apply to Gallery too?

Gonna get my art boosted

Ellie
Not yet

Anne
Boo

Ellie
Glad you like it tho

Anne

Ellie
Oh btw, I'm not gonna be able to come to
dinner tomorrow

Anne
What! Why?

Ellie
Sorry, I'm on call in case anything with the
new feature breaks

Anne
It's sacrilege to work on Sunday you know?

Ellie
HA true

Anne
Ok fine but you better not even think about
missing Thanksgiving.

Ellie
I wouldn't dare

11

———

On Monday morning, Eleanor walked into the office oscillating between relief that there were no production issues over the weekend and disappointment she'd missed hiking with Kitt and dinner with her family.

Going through her email, she noticed a last minute meeting invite for the Content Policy Committee. After her stand-up, she made her way over to the Atlas conference room again.

Jeff, the board leader, had already started explaining the issue that prompted today's meeting. "… shouldn't be too much disagreement… as it pertains to Assemblies."

Eleanor tuned in, hoping she hadn't missed anything important.

"Our platform hosts a number of parenting-focused Assemblies, which is a wonderful thing, but we've had an uptick in reports about a certain type of content in these groups. Now, we're not dealing with photos this time but rather a lot of conversation suggesting that parents shouldn't vaccinate their children."

A few eyerolls and sighs went around the room. Eleanor had seen this already in posts from people in her hometown about the *believed* negative side effects of vaccinating their kids, but she always assumed it was just the occasional uninformed sort having a rant. It wouldn't really catch on.

"For the most part, moderators have been leaving it up because, of course, we don't have any rule about it. But with increasingly more of them, I'd like to nail down a clear rule."

He began to scroll on his laptop and shared his screen on the projector. "Here's an example of what we're seeing. There's a combination of sharing articles or blogs on the subject but mostly personal anecdotes and quarreling."

He pulled up screenshots of a couple of different posts:

> "God gave us an immune system for a reason!"

> "The measles was actually just a result of chemical exposure! The highest mortality rates were actually in areas where vaccine distribution was the highest. Do your research!"

> "I've been trying so hard to convince my sister not to get the MMR vaccine for her baby, but she won't listen to me. Advice?"

> "Believe in parents' right to choose? Come join us over in our new Assembly: Vaccine Truths!"

There was some mumbling throughout the room as everyone read and reacted to them.

"So, how should we handle this?" Jeff looked to the room for a solution.

"This kind of feels like coordinating harm, does it not?" someone said.

"They're just expressing differences of opinion though, even if we don't agree."

"If we're seen as a company that frequently censors people, they won't use our platform," someone else agreed.

A mumble of agreement went through the room, but Eleanor was still thinking quietly. When people gathered in real physical places, there wasn't anyone to censor their conversations—except perhaps a police or military force. Agora certainly didn't want to be seen as some military force hushing the population.

The same woman who had advocated for leaving up the breastfeeding photos at the last meeting spoke up now. "But isn't it about intent? These groups aren't working on the intention of causing harm like a terrorist group would. They believe they're keeping people *from* harm."

"Yes, but the underlying motivation of most terrorists is something they believe is good or right. That doesn't make it right." A younger guy wearing an Agora hoodie and jeans scratched his nose.

"But there are, even if rare, occasions where vaccines *do* cause extreme negative reactions, or they are recalled," the breastfeeding advocate shot back.

"There are people who shouldn't get them, like those with autoimmune disorders."

Someone Eleanor assumed was from Advertising stood up. "There is also a significant revenue stream associated with these groups."

"It's true. It's not a black and white situation." Jeff seemed to be taking a moment to think, then his eyes widened. "Let's try a little test. For each of these posts I've got up here, you all will vote whether you would remove it or leave it up, and we'll see if we can nail down a pattern."

Everyone nodded approvingly, and Jeff said, "Okay, so the first one—the one about God giving us immune systems—raise your hand if you would remove it."

I feel like that really isn't implying or saying much, Eleanor thought as she decided to keep her hand awkwardly in her lap.

Jeff nodded. "Ok, number two, the one about measles."

Eleanor put her hand up right away. *This feels like blatantly false information,* she thought, pleased to see that a majority of the hands in the room went up too.

"Three?"

Eleanor left her hand up, as did many others. *She's directly trying to influence someone else's decision.*

"And number four?"

There was a good bit of hesitation on this one.

"Sounds like this one is advertising a whole group dedicated to this. We can't ban the group, can we?" Eleanor asked.

"Depends on the group, but if it's not currently banned, then I don't think removing posts that invite people to the group would be right." Jeff ran his hand along his jaw. "There seemed to be a consensus about two and three. Let's talk about those."

Opinions started coming in from every corner of the room.

"Well, that third one feels like a direct attempt to influence someone's decision on the matter."

"Number two just feels like a conspiracy theory."

"The thing is," Jeff began, "Content Moderators aren't fact-checkers. We just want to keep people safe. An individual can decide what they want to believe or do with information, but feeling coerced or forced to see gore is another thing."

Hoodie guy was tapping on his keyboard, probably coding during this conversation, and spoke without looking up. "So, maybe we should only remove posts that specifically instruct people not to get vaccinated?"

Eleanor felt herself agreeing with this. Some heads nodded throughout the room, and no one else added anything to the debate.

"Let's take a vote then." Jeff clapped his hands. "Those in favor of only removing posts that advise not vaccinating?"

The majority of hands went up around the room. Eleanor was nervous. She wasn't sure this was the best solution, but it was also better than doing nothing, so she raised her hand too.

"Very well, we will treat posts that direct others not to get vaccinated under the 'coordinating harm' rule. I'll update our rules. Thanks, everyone."

As Eleanor walked back to her desk, she felt unease at the idea of labeling these people as "trying to coordinate harm." As she saw it, they were just afraid, and sometimes fear clouds judgment. Silencing an entire group who was afraid of something wasn't going to make them not afraid of it anymore. In fact, it may make them more afraid. They would feel threatened or like their voice was being silenced. The whole point of Agora was to give *everyone* a voice. She wondered if they had made the right choice.

When she opened up her laptop, she had a new Discourse message from Bethany: "Eleanor! Average Session engagement time is up 3 minutes since Friday!"

"Awesome!" she typed back, rolling her eyes.

Avi popped his head over the divider. "Hey, Eleanor—want to grab some lunch?"

"Yes!" she sighed with relief. "But let's go off campus. I need some fresh air."

"Sounds good."

As they walked over to a sandwich shop a little ways up Peachtree Street, Eleanor filled him in on the Content Policy meeting.

"Sounds like a sensible start, but I think this is gonna come up again," he said thoughtfully.

"I agree. It's kind of overwhelming how many angles there are. Plus I'm just trying to work on handling photos; the complexity of what people are saying will be harder to deal with in code."

They sat down at a corner table with their sandwiches.

"Speaking of which, let's talk about your Hacking project."

She explained what she had done so far. "What do you think?"

He swallowed a bite of his pesto panini. "First, I think this is a fascinating project, and I'd be interested in working on this some too, if you're okay with it."

"Of course, I think we need lots of people working on this." she quickly agreed.

Avi nodded, looking pleased. "Cool. I think you're off to a great start. The decision-tree is a good choice for something with dynamic rules, and it might even be a good idea to keep the rules in a database so they can be added and updated more frequently."

"Oh, good idea, and I could make a dashboard for them to be entered."

He smiled through a mouthful of food then took a sip of iced tea. "Great—okay—back to the implementation. I think we need to be careful. It's easy to let our own opinions and biases slip into this."

"How? I'm creating a rule set based on specific examples."

He frowned. "You should know by now from your policy meetings that it's not that simple."

"True, but it's still better than a bunch of different people making their own decisions."

"That's somewhat true, but I actually think those decisions are really valuable, and we should be collecting some data on that as soon as possible."

"Like what? Can we do that?"

"Well, I'm imagining that when a moderator chooses to take down an image, they can pick a reason why they did it, which can help us build up a database of images *and* keywords to match with."

Why didn't I think of that! "Avi, that's brilliant! But can we still use a database with images and keywords right away? I've already got some training data to use from current photos."

"We could still do that and keep adding to it, but I think there's real value in collecting the decisions of lots of moderators—like an average of lots of opinions rather than just a few of them."

Eleanor thought about this for a moment as she pulled a long string of mozzarella cheese from her bread. "I think you're right, Avi."

He smiled, and they both finished the last few bites of their paninis. "Would you want to take some weekend time to work on this?" he asked. "I know we don't have a ton of free work time right now."

"Sure, that could be good." Her heart pounded with excitement, but she calmed it by reminding herself there was lots of work to be done and more obstacles to face before their project would really be usable.

"Awesome." He checked the time then leaned back in his seat. "Any plans for Thanksgiving next week?"

Her eyes began to sparkle. "Oh, yes! Thanksgiving is a big event for my family—there's a huge party and dinner at my parents' inn that's second only to Christmas there."

"Sounds fun."

"How about you?" She emptied her water cup and crinkled up the paper wrapping from her sandwich.

"Just enjoying a day off mostly, not a holiday I'm used to celebrating, really."

They continued to talk for a while about family holidays, podcasts they'd been listening to, and what their current favorite software was. It was well after one when they saw the time and decided to walk back up the street to Agora.

NEW DIALOGUE

Anne Crawford
<Senior @ Aska Valley High School>

Comment if I show up in your first 10 posts 🏆

---

27 ❣ 60 ⚜

Comments:

> **Eleanor**
> ME!

> **Benny**
> ME!

> **Ethan**
> Mine of course

> **Lily**
> Yes

Anne
Wow, so ajnjsnd–

Marie
What?

12

Georgia weather in November usually isn't much colder than fifty or sixty degrees, just right for a sweater or light jacket. But the next morning was unusually chilly, and the few minutes Eleanor spent running back to her apartment for a warmer coat meant she reached Agora later than usual. Nevertheless, she'd already gone through her regular morning routine when her phone began vibrating on her desk.

She normally ignored her phone during the workday. That's why, as a rule, she usually kept it in her desk drawer, but for some reason, today she hadn't. Something subconscious had told her to keep the phone where she could get to it quickly.

She flipped the phone over. Her father.

Her pulse raced. Dad never called in the middle of a workday.

She answered right away. "Dad?"

"Ellie?" There was some scuffling on the other end of the phone, " Your sister…was in an accident."

"What happened? Is she okay? Where is she?" Eleanor's thoughts tumbled over themselves.

"She's in intensive care. We're on our way to the hospital. Can you come home?"

"I'll be there as soon as possible."

"I love you…" Then he somberly added, "Drive safe."

"Love you too, Dad." She tapped the big red "end call" button.

Tears welled up behind her eyes, and her chest squeezed against her ribcage. The clicking of her teammates' keyboards surrounded her. She had to find a place to be alone.

She walked quickly to the bathroom, locked herself in a stall and leaned against the door, trying to catch her breath. *Get it together.* Her sister, her parents, needed her now. She dabbed her eyes on her sleeve.

She'll be okay. Everything will be fine. She wasn't convincing herself.

Leaving the stall, she saw herself in the mirror—cheeks flushed and her eyes red and damp, her brunette hair tied in a half-up bun looked ruffled and messy. She tried to smooth it over some. For once, she was relieved to work with men. No one would come after her in the bathroom.

She exhaled deeply. She had to inform Avi and Daryl that she was leaving for a family emergency and might be out the rest of the week. Leaving the bathroom and starting in the direction of her desk, she saw Avi waiting for her in the break room. *He would have known.*

"Is everything okay?" he asked, his voice gentle.

She could see he was trying not to look at her red eyes, but she knew he could tell. She wasn't even sure how to form the words. She opened her mouth to speak for a moment, but nothing came out. "My sister's been in an accident. I have to go to the hospital."

Avi's face showed concerned lines around his eyes. "I understand. Don't worry about anything here. I'll take care of everything." He seemed to anticipate her concern. "Really, everything will be fine here. Do what you have to do."

She whispered a thank you and felt her eyes watering up again. She looked down at the floor, and before she knew it, her laptop was in her bag, and she was outside.

She practically ran back to her apartment, feeling the cold more intensely than before. When she unlocked the door and walked in, she was acutely aware of how quiet it was. She wasn't used to seeing what it looked like at this time of day. The morning sun was coming through the windows, but the place was cluttered with clothes, shoes, books, and dirty dishes. She set her work bag on the couch and looked out the window at the gray clouds and the washed out buildings. *How could so much gray be in one place?*

She walked through the kitchen. Emily was bad about leaving dishes, and Eleanor hadn't even been there several nights this week. The days she had been there, she had worked late, come home, thrown her clothes on the floor, and eaten some take-out at her desk. Most of her clothes were dirty.

She found herself picking up trash and filling a laundry basket. Cleaning up took all her focus until she remembered why she had come home early. *What am I doing?* She had to leave.

She switched to a duffel bag and started shoving things into it: phone charger, makeup, jeans, shirts, leggings, jacket. In ten minutes, she was back out the door and taking the elevator to the parking garage, where her beat-up old sedan was waiting. She tossed the duffel into the back and slid into the driver's seat.

Without much thought, she auto-piloted towards home. Not her apartment, her *home*. The place where she was from, where her mom and dad and sister were waiting for her.

She navigated to I-75 North, and her chest plummeted to her stomach as she accelerated up to speed. A sense of urgency spread to her fingers and toes, and she drove awash in a flood of white noise from the road, avoiding any stimulation from the radio for about an hour. The long, straight road took her away from the city, away from tall skyscrapers, clogged roads, and rushing people. She watched the number of cars and buildings dwindle around her.

She shifted the radio station, then plugged in her phone and tried listening to an audiobook, then music when she couldn't focus on what the reader was saying. Finally, the highway narrowed down to just two lanes. She was getting close to home.

There were no more exits—just road, trees, and fields of grass. The occasional town rolled by. Occasionally, she had to double take to make sure the small clusters of restaurants and grocery stores she passed weren't Aska Valley.

She picked up her phone and opened the Agora app to check her team Assembly. She saw notifications for a few code pushes but not much talk between teammates. She expected to see conversation about who would pick up her tickets. She sensed Avi's work here. He must have talked to the team and organized everything. He knew she would feel bad about leaving her work for someone else to do. And she did.

There was a message from Avi. "Please let me know if there is anything I can do."

She felt bumps underneath the car warning her that she was veering off the road, and she quickly jerked back into the lane, her chest pounding. She had forgotten what it was like to drive on winding roads. She put her phone down and breathed a sigh of relief.

Her stomach growled, yet the thought of eating made her feel nauseous. Suddenly, she remembered that she had made plans to eat lunch with Kitt. She grabbed her phone again and opted to call him rather than text. He answered after two rings.

"Hey! Are we still meeting for lunch?"

"Sorry, I can't today. Can we reschedule?" She wasn't sure what to say really. The professional answer just came out.

"Reschedule?" He laughed, "Sure. Is something wrong?"

"I'm not sure why I said that... I got a call from my dad. My sister got into some kind of accident. I'm on my way home now."

"Shit, why didn't you just say that. Are you okay?" All the playfulness went out of his voice.

"I mean, I'm freaking out, but I don't even know what happened yet." Saying that gave her some relief. Maybe it wasn't that bad.

"Okay, well, let me know if there's anything I can do... and text me later."

"I will, thanks." She hung up the phone.

She drove in an uncomfortable silence for the last ten minutes of the trip until, at last, her car inched up a steep hill that revealed her town to her. She called her dad to let him know she would be at the hospital shortly. He gave her the room number.

She pulled into the Aska Valley Hospital complex, which was

smaller than most of the medical buildings in Atlanta, parked, and walked towards the entrance, looking for the sign to the intensive care unit. When she found it, she followed it along the hallway.

Car accidents happen. She'll be okay.

Fluorescent lighting stung her eyes, and she held her breath to avoid the antiseptic scent that was covering up other, more unappealing smells. Worse than that was the feeling of pain, suffering… Her head spun as she approached the room number her dad had given her.

She pushed the door open and stepped inside. The room was dark except for the glow of several monitors attached to the equipment keeping Anne alive. She could hear the slow, rhythmic chirp that indicated the beat of her sister's heart. Everything else in the world melted away.

She approached the bedside and looked at her unconscious sister. Anne's hair was matted and tied into a loose ponytail on one side. There was a respirator over her mouth and stained gauze wrapped around her head, covering her eyes as well.

The kind of cold she associated with a fever—a chill that makes the body tremble and hands clammy—took over her body. She grabbed on to a chair and eased into it. She couldn't even remember what her sister's face looked like. It was as if she had never known an Anne who didn't look battered and bruised.

Eleanor closed her eyes and tried to remember the last time she had seen Anne. Today was November 18th. When did she last take time off? She dropped her head into her hands and sighed. Family dinner? But not last weekend. She'd missed it. Must have been the one before. *Yes, that was it. We talked about her art class and her portfolio.*

Anne had always been more creative than Eleanor. She'd taken an interest in drawing at a young age. Their home was situated on fifty acres of land that was shared with Grayson House, which, for kids, seemed like a whole world. They would spend hours romping around in the woods, searching for cool places to hide or something new to be discovered. Eleanor would bring a book to read, and Anne would bring a sketchbook and pencil.

Anne would draw the trees, leaves, flowers, nuts, and animals they came across. At first, her drawings were childish, the way a little girl's efforts should be. But over time, they started to get better. From Eleanor's perspective, Anne didn't learn how to draw—she learned how to see.

She would spend a long time observing whatever it was she planned to draw—looking at it from different angles, in different lighting—then, she would look at the subject more than the paper as she drew.

Once she got better at drawing singular things, she started to take on larger scenes. The whole landscape of the woods or a view of a mountain range. She loved drawing nature, but eventually, she realized she needed an even greater challenge.

Eleanor remembered one particular day when she was eighteen and Anne was thirteen. Anne had asked if she could sketch Eleanor, and she'd agreed. They'd sat in their favorite place—a part of the woods that dipped between one hill and the another—a spot where a river could or maybe at one point did run across but now hundreds of ferns sprouted everywhere. The trees were tall, and the sunlight dappled through, spotting the ferns all over.

With all this draped behind her, Eleanor had sat on a blanket and read for hours, keeping as still as she could, and occasionally had looked up at Anne to see her working with intensity. Determined to be a good subject, she'd focused on her book, *The Secret Garden*, a favorite of theirs. Anne had thought it would suit the drawing entirely.

After several hours, as Eleanor was finishing the book, Anne had looked up and smiled, clearly pleased with herself. The drawing was done.

When Eleanor looked at it, she'd only been able to raise her eyebrows in amazement. She'd never thought of herself as beautiful as she looked in this drawing, nor did she think anyone but Anne would see her that way. But the drawing was clearly her. Anne had captured all her features, the book cover, even the fern garden behind her. More than anything else, the drawing had captured Anne's love for her sister.

Recalling that memory, Eleanor could not keep the salty tears, which she hated to let fall, from leaking down her cheeks.

The sound of her father's voice startled her out of her weepy state. "Ellie, you're here." Her mother walked in behind him, her eyes cloudy and a hand fumbling with the gold cross around her neck.

She put an arm around each of her parents and wrapped them in a hug, wiping her tears on her mother's shirt, just as she'd done numerous times as a child.

"Anne's not going to be awake tonight," her father whispered, "let's go down to the cafeteria, and we can fill you in on what we know."

"Shouldn't we stay with her?" Eleanor didn't want to leave her sister's side.

"They're about to close the floor for shift changes. We're allowed back after that," he reassured her.

The three of them walked quietly down the bland, white corridors. Eleanor thought for a moment that it might be nice to eat something, but the idea of hospital food made her stomach turn. They found a rickety plastic table and sat down.

Her dad looked at her and sighed. "It happened this morning. Anne left for school but was runnin' a little late."

Eleanor knew her sister drove the family's old Chevy Trail Blazer, the same one Eleanor had learned how to drive on. She considered the winding roads that led to their house and how she herself almost veered off the road on her way here. A shiver went up her spine.

"It was a foggy morning… and with the cold snap too…" her father continued. "She probably hit a patch of black ice. You know how the end of fall is, all the leaves on the road. Luckily, there was someone behind her when it happened. They saw the car veer off the road but didn't see why exactly."

He took a deep breath. "Unfortunately, she didn't quite regain control of the car after swerving. She slid off the road and rolled down the side of a small embankment. The driver behind her stopped and immediately called 9-1-1, but the car was upside-down."

Eleanor felt cold in her core. She wished she could wrap a blanket around her whole body to block out the harsh lighting and overpowering smells and sounds around her.

"He stopped to see what he could do in the meanwhile, but Anne was unconscious. The ambulance and fire truck arrived and got her out of the car and rushed her here. Luckily, Cousin Benny was on duty and called us right away."

"God bless the person driving behind her." Her mother let out a little sniff, holding back tears.

"So what is her current condition?" Eleanor stammered.

"She has suffered severe head trauma, broken ribs, broken wrist, and lots of bumps and bruises." Her father looked uneasy. "Then there's this…"

Eleanor's mom reached into her purse and pulled out a ziplock bag. Inside was Anne's phone covered with dried blood.

"The police officers gave it to us… They found it when they got her out of the car and that—" he stopped for a moment— "they said… she was probably using it while she was driving."

"How do they know that?" Eleanor went on the defensive. Anne knew better… but then she thought about how she almost swerved off the road on her way here.

"They say the injuries… on her face… the broken right wrist, and the amount of blood on it… all add up to her using the phone when it happened."

No one said anything for a bit.

Eleanor's mind went to an Agora post Anne made that very morning. It couldn't be… right? But now she couldn't get the thought out of her mind.

She withdrew inside herself, searching for some kind of answer or understanding. She had trouble putting all of this together in her mind. She understood feeling confused and afraid. But there was a faint feeling of something more intrusive… *guilt.*

NEW DIALOGUE

Bethany Dawson
<Engagement Engineer @ Agora>

Big shout out to the mobile app team, especially their lead @Avi and superstar @Eleanor! Their work has helped us increase engagement time drastically! ☆

---

270 ♥ 600 ⚜

13

After sitting with Anne as long as the hospital would allow, the Crawfords headed home to try and get some sleep. For a moment, she was glad the road that led her home was paved with chunks of granite rather than asphalt. It forced her to slow down, take in the trees, and breathe. The grumbling and crunching of gravel underneath her tires welcomed Eleanor to the hand-hewn log cabin she'd grown up in.

She parked her car beside her parent's truck and turned the engine off. She paused in the cool dark night, listening to the crickets, but mostly the silence.

Can you hear quiet? she asked her steering wheel.

Serenity and isolation surrounded her like a bubble. She got out and gazed up at the clear, moonless sky and realized she saw stars for the first time in a long time. Hundreds of them. They twinkled and sparkled and whispered to her that she was small.

She grabbed her bag and crunched up to the front door. It was unlocked.

Once inside, she tiptoed to her childhood bedroom. It looked mostly the same. She'd never taken any furniture from the room, but some things here and there indicated the space was occasionally borrowed. A storage box here and some paint supplies there. Her mother was creative too, often restoring furniture or creating decor for Grayson House. Likely where Anne got it from.

Eleanor changed into leggings and a t-shirt and sighed, peeling back the patchwork quilt that seemed stuffed with more memories than cotton now. This blanket was once a shield to her from the monsters of the night as a child, then concealed her with a flashlight and a book late into the evening, or as a teenager texting in T9 on her flip phone. It contained her physical world so that she could unleash the vast one of her imagination.

She sank into the bed, the blankets stiff from their recent lack of use. Curled up tight, she could feel tears welling up in her eyes.

Isn't it the way? she thought. *Life moves along just fine, then something hits you, and suddenly, it's all different. Nothing can be the same again.*

She lay in the dark room, unable to fall asleep. She felt alone. Everything that was so important to her just eight hours ago seemed so distant: Agora, content policy, Kitt, her messy apartment. She remembered the message from Avi she hadn't replied to. Pulling out her phone and opening her work chat, she read it again: "Please let me know if there's anything I can do."

She was surprised to see that his status was showing online still. She checked the time. It was after eleven. Was he waiting to hear back from her?

She typed "Thank you" and hit send, but it felt awkward. What should she say? Then she saw that he was typing: "Is everything … okay?"

Avi wasn't Daryl. Of course he'd be more concerned about her than the work she was missing. She could tell he was trying to be kind and offer help without prying. She decided to give him some facts, not too many, and withhold emotion. She didn't want too much of her personal life to flow into her Agora persona.

"I've been to the hospital, and I'm at my parent's house now. She's still in intensive care and unconscious." She pressed send.

Eleanor noticed she was just staring at the screen, waiting to see what he would write back. Perhaps he wanted to know when she would be back without seeming rude.

She quickly typed another message: "I'm not sure when I'll be back in the office, but—" she began to write that she had her work laptop with her, but then realized she didn't. *Shit.*

"I'm not sure when I'll be back in the office yet." She sent it.

He started typing right away. "I'm not worried about that… I just want to make sure you're okay."

She smiled for the first time all day, suddenly not feeling quite so alone. She wanted to express this, but she always found it strangely difficult to convey by text what she was truly feeling. She swiped through the list of emojis to find the right one to put in her message: "🙂 I appreciate it. I will feel better when I learn more about Anne's condition tomorrow."

Another message came across. "Will you let me know?"

Where her blankets felt cold and crunchy before, now they registered as a soft, warm hug. "Yes, I will."

"Good, now try to get some sleep."

"Thanks. You too!" She briefly felt young again, texting under the covers at night, but a shadow hung over it all that had never been there before. She tossed and turned until she finally reached some fractured state of sleep.

The next morning, the scent of breakfast wafting down the hallway woke Eleanor with a turn of her stomach. She came into the kitchen to find her dad making eggs, bacon, and a fresh pot of coffee. "Thought we'd have a little something to eat before we go to the hospital."

"Alright." Eleanor poured herself a cup of dark black coffee. "When will we know more about Anne?"

"Well, I called this morning to check in, and they said they're going to keep her sedated today and run a few more tests but that she's in stable condition. We can come visit this afternoon, but she won't be awake. The doctor wants to talk to us."

"So she's… okay then?" She slid into a barstool at the counter.

"She's out of the worst of it, sounds like." He placed applewood-smoked bacon on a plate lined with paper towels.

"What does that mean?"

"Well, I really don't know. That's what the doctor wants to talk about with us this afternoon. He said that she is out of the worst of it and will recover but that her life may not be quite the same again." He sighed.

"In what way?" Eleanor's heart began to race. "What a thing to say to people that are scared!"

Her dad slowly placed scrambled eggs onto three plates, then exhaled deeply. "I'm not sure… He said to try to be relieved with where we are now, and he will be more confident after they run tests this morning."

"Will she be moved out of the ICU?"

"Probably tomorrow after she wakes up."

"Well, that's good then. One step at a time." She tried to sound cheerful, but her concern was palpable. Her dad offered a slight smile, and she noticed the lines around his eyes: He was tired and worried too.

He gave her a hug. "Yes, one step at a time."

Her mother came down the stairs, still looking comfy in a matching pink flannel pajama set. Eleanor grabbed two plates, handed one to her mom, and automatically headed to the table for breakfast.

The three of them sat down to eat, but it was as if a dark veil had been placed over the table. For most of her life, this table had been the site of lively conversations, but today, nothing. The family feigned interest in eating for a short time before getting up to get dressed to leave for the hospital.

About an hour later, the Crawfords were back at Anne's bedside. In the daylight, Eleanor noticed the room was full of flowers, balloons, and gifts from friends, family, and people in the community who were concerned about Anne.

Her parents were sitting in padded metal chairs uncomfortably, and her mom was alternating between twisting her hands and rubbing them together, trying to warm them. Her eyes were cast down and red.

There was an old TV in the corner of the room—a square plastic box rather than one of the more modern flat-screen varieties. To Eleanor, it represented the technological lag of her small town. The news was on, and she chose to preoccupy herself with it.

There was footage of the royals and their new baby—beautiful, happy, smiling. She almost laughed, thinking of what Anne would say if she were watching this with them now. She'd often talked of wanting to visit Britain to sketch the landscapes ornamented with castles, a realm of fairy tales and princesses. Just the kind of whimsical wonder Anne would crave to show people with her art.

Then, Eleanor remembered something Anne had said to her once. "Art helps people see chaos in the world as beauty."

I will take her there when she gets better, Eleanor promised herself.

The newsreel shifted to something less cheery. "Two measles outbreaks in New York State have been reported..." the news anchor's voice bounced around the room.

Eleanor wrapped her arms around her waist and slouched back in the chair, suddenly aware of how cold the twelve-by-twelve room was. Everything in the world felt horrible and dreadful. She reached for the remote and clicked the TV off.

All that remained was the rhythmic beeping of Anne's heart and hissing of the ventilator. Her dad glanced at his watch and made an uneasy attempt to smile at her.

The sudden tick of the door opening made all three of them start. The doctor mumbled a quiet good morning and sat on the stool in front of the computer monitor. He squinted slightly at the screen, the aged skin crinkling around his eyes as he reviewed Anne's information. Without looking away from the screen, he delivered his report. "Her vital signs are stable today. She's suffered a concussion, which is why we weren't sure at first about..." He swiveled around slowly to look at the Crawfords. "She sustained significant damage to both her retinas. Your daughter likely won't see again."

Marie dropped her head into her hands and began to sob while Eleanor's father wrapped his arm around her and pulled her close.

"Is there any chance… when she wakes up?" Eleanor didn't even know what she was asking.

"The damage is visible on the CT scan. We reduced the sedative some last night and performed a visual field test. It is quite certain." He let out a dry cough.

The room was dead silent for a moment, then only her father seemed to be able to speak. "She's going to be okay other than this?"

The doctor moved his head up and down exactly twice. "We'll keep an eye on the concussion, and she will need time to recover, some physical therapy, but she will be fine in most senses, sure," he replied cautiously.

Okay? How is this okay? She's an artist who can't see. Eleanor was sinking deep into the quicksand of her mind and desperately wanted to be alone to process everything.

No one spoke for what felt like a lifetime, and the doctor looked back to the monitor—smacking on the keyboard and clicking the mouse. Eleanor's hands tightened around the arms of the chair.

"We should be able to stop administering the sedative tomorrow and let her wake up. We'll be moving her out of the ICU as well. I'll make sure the nurse gives you the new room number. It would be good if you all were here with her. It can be a bit shocking to wake up with vision loss. We'll need to take it slow."

"We'll be here." Her father nodded. "Thanks, doc."

"Of course." The emotionless doctor shuffled out of the room, likely off to deliver more horrifying news.

"She's alive. We still have her. We will get through this," her father said, seeing the look on Eleanor's face.

"What will she even do?" Eleanor's voice cracked. "She's supposed to go to art school!"

"There's time to figure all that out. She's still Anne."

She wasn't in the mood for her dad's optimism. She stood up, ready to flee.

Her father pulled her and her mother in for a hug, and they all turned to face Anne. He bent down to kiss her forehead. "Anne, we'll see—" he stumbled over the word— "we will all be together again tomorrow."

NEW EMAIL
SUBJECT: CHECKING IN

Eleanor,

I understand there is some kind of emergency that has resulted in your absence. Please provide an update on your expected work attendance.

Thanks,
Daryl

14

Eleanor was just driving.

She didn't really know where, only somewhere quiet and away from everything. She couldn't imagine what it would be like to suddenly lose her vision. How could life move on for her sister?

She gripped the steering wheel hard as she twisted it around the curving country road. She knew these roads so well and drove without thinking about it.

Browning leaves swished in the air as the car traveled through piles of them. She looked at endless fields of grass, losing their green, seeming to roll past her even though it was the other way around.

Grayson House, a place so full of memories for her, appeared then disappeared on her left. She imagined all the happy families enjoying a vacation together right now, soaking in the last remnants of a beloved season before winter settled in. Maybe the recent cold snap disappointed some of them. It had already been bitter enough to frost. Not knowing how dangerous that ice had made the roads.

She kept driving.

Before she knew it, she was pulling off the asphalt road onto a dirt one, faint with the pattern of car marks. This was a place she knew—a lesser-known trail that led to a serene spot with a view of the wide blue sky and a lake.

She pulled herself out of the car and started walking down the path, relieved to be wearing jeans and sneakers. She found the deafening silence of the forest just as overwhelming as the roar of the city but in a cleansing way. She crunched on the leaves, taking deep breaths.

In this place, I can think. The chilly wind blew through her hair.

She considered what the doctor had told them: "Significant trauma… probably won't see again."

"This can't be happening," she shambled along, attempting to explain to nature.

A small river joined her along the path, its edges decorated with red and orange leaves, melting into a glaze of rippling honey.

She followed this trail for some time. Occasionally, she closed her eyes, trying to imagine what it would be like to be blind, but she'd quickly stub her toe on a tree root or almost fall over.

She turned away from the stream and climbed a steep, stony slope that ended at an overlook. Out of breath when she reached it, she sat down on a large rock and observed the looking glass of the forest. Ducks landed in the lake, blending the perfect reflection into a watercolor canvas. *A whole world that lives and even thrives without the presence of humans.*

That's how alone she felt. She closed her eyes and listened to the symphony of nature all around her. Her body tensed. She rolled onto her back, the cold slab of granite chilling her spine. She stared straight into the sky, letting it swallow her whole.

She believed that wandering into a forest meant stepping out of time altogether. It just didn't seem to matter here. So maybe if she stayed, the clock would stop moving.

A subtle vibration pulsed in her pocket. The brief digital sensation reverberating through her body reminded her that this brief moment of listless abandon was transient. *Real* life was calling; the *real* world needed her.

She pulled her phone out, and the screen lit up. Its harsh blue light came across as alien compared to the wash of natural sunlight.

Though phone service was spotty outside of the main part of town, she apparently had just enough bars at this peak to transmit the onslaught of alerts the device hadn't received down below. Her screen was full of notifications for emails, text messages, Agora, Twitter, Tinder, missed calls from her mother and… Daryl!

The rage Eleanor felt surging through her was like no other. She gripped the phone tight and stood up, stepping her feet near the edge of the cliff.

Here she was in a sacred place, then all of a sudden, this horde of banners and variable ratio messages emerged with no purpose other than to draw her away—enticing her to simply tap or pull like the lever of a slot machine. Not to deal with what was right in front of her.

This power, she realized now, had the strength to convince people to look even at times when they shouldn't. Like behind the wheel of a car. The rush of dopamine and fear of the world moving on without you became worth risking your life.

"And I have helped build it!" she cried.

Tears began to run down her cheeks.

In her grip, she attempted to crush the seven ounce portal that lead anywhere and nowhere—disgusted by anything she felt it had to offer. Her fingers turned red as the muscles in her hand strained against the unyielding aluminum.

She felt her arm begin to rise above her head then, with all her strength, she launched her phone towards the lake. She watched in a state of shock as it arched into the sky, the forbidden fruit with its missing bite on the back catching one last glint of sunlight before it plunked into the water.

MOBILE APP TEAM PROJECT TRACKER

@Eleanor - You have been tagged in a ticket

> Type: Bug
> Reporter: @Daryl
> Assignee: @Eleanor
> Priority: High
> Click <u>here</u> to view the ticket.

15

___

When Eleanor woke up the next morning, she groggily reached over to the nightstand and felt a sudden burst of panic. Nothing was there. Oh, yeah, the phone she had expected to grab was now at the bottom of a lake.

She looked around, wondering what time it was. No alarm had awakened her, and there were no antiquated analog clocks anywhere. It was just a room. The house was quiet.

Eleanor was truly alone, with no connection to the outside world, for the first time since... well, she couldn't even remember when. Maybe childhood. Sometime before her first cell phone had been cautiously placed in her eager hands. It was just Eleanor and her own mind.

I could be the only one left in the world. She let out a deep sigh, falling back into the pillows with a sense of overwhelm at the flood of emotions moving through her.

She lay there for several more minutes unsure what to do with herself, feeling at war with her own mind. Her fingers twitched for something to do. Part of her wanted to savor this moment of just being. Frustration and boredom nagged at her though. Her brain was fully aware that it had been forcibly unplugged from the hive.

She wanted to read news articles and know what was going on in the world. Had anyone tried to contact her? She'd never updated Kitt—was he worried about her? What was going on at work? Did they need her? And her sister…

A tugging sensation from somewhere deep inside her tried to pull her away. *Look away. Don't think about it. Distract yourself. Just tap and scroll.* Without this tether, she was disconnected from humanity.

I am still human without it. Life is still happening. Why do I feel this way?

Eleanor slipped on leggings and tennis shoes and ran out the door. She took off down the gravel road, hoping to outrun her discomfort. Where before she felt the heavy pain of what happened to Anne, now she was forced to stare it right in the face. There was nothing else to look at. She had no music, no podcasts, no Emily gabbing in her ear—only the conga of her own thoughts. Anxiety began to drip down her skin.

In her rush to get here, she had forgotten her laptop, so she was out of touch with all her workmates. Her parents weren't home and no longer kept a landline phone; it had stopped making sense. She had no means of contacting anyone.

If I injured myself right now, I would have no way to call for help. I could only yell out and pray someone would hear me and hope they weren't stupid enough to throw their phone in a lake. Thoughts like those pummeled her head as the exertion increased her heart rate, her breath coming out in puffs in the cool morning air. She was used to jogging on the flat concrete sidewalks in the city, and she felt her calves burning from the steep inclines.

She rounded back to the house and went to clean up, jumping in the shower while the water was still cold. "Shit!" She danced back and forth on her toes as the frigid drops ran over her. She let out a scream then a fit of hiccups took over. Maybe she was going insane.

She delighted at the raised bumps covering her body from the cold water. She savored how her leg muscles pulsed from her run. When she got out, still dripping wet, she stared at herself in the mirror. She really looked at who she was instead of feeling inadequate based on the constant barrage of more beautiful women or avoiding her reflection entirely.

She embraced a moment to experience the cotton of her leggings as she pulled them on, then sauntered into Anne's bedroom to borrow a wool sweater. She wanted to be warm, and she craved to experience everything fully. She slipped into the scratchy-soft fabric and wrapped her arms around herself, breathing in the smell of Anne.

She couldn't avoid it anymore. Real life was waiting. She had to go to the hospital. Hopefully, Anne would wake up and could come home soon.

When Eleanor arrived at the hospital, she realized Anne probably wasn't in the ICU anymore, so she backtracked to ask the receptionist where she'd been moved to.

She turned down the hallway labeled with the new room number and saw her parents standing outside the door talking to the nurse.

When her mom made eye contact with Eleanor, her face instantly bore an exasperated look. "For heaven's sake Ellie, we've been trying to call you. I thought I was about to have two daughters in here."

"Sorry. I, uh, lost my phone." She was embarrassed to tell them the truth of it all, and her guilt at having worried everyone threatened to overwhelm her.

Her father spoke before her mother could say anything more on the matter. "Anne should be waking up soon."

The three of them made their way into the new room. It was larger than the last and had two beds in it, the other empty. Anne seemed to have regained some color and looked more like she was taking a light nap rather than lying unconscious. She was breathing on her own, and the bandages had been removed. This was less than reassuring. There were bruises and cuts around her eyes and on her face.

Eleanor felt a lurch in her stomach that might have resulted in vomiting if she'd eaten anything.

"Oh Anne…" her mother whimpered.

"Hey, sweetie… We can't wait to talk to you again." Her dad pulled up a chair alongside her hospital bed.

The nurse was sitting in front of the computer, keeping tabs on Anne's vitals. "If she goes into too much shock, we will have to put her back under because of the concussion. So we'll take it slow. Talk to her. Comfort her."

Eleanor went to the other side of the bed and held Anne's hand, which was also bruised and cut. She thought she may need her own heart rate monitored. It felt as if the floor was moving beneath her feet.

They sat for some time, saying gentle things to Anne, trying to have normal conversation and watching her occasional twitches with held breath until she finally made a few soft sounds and started to stir. Eleanor squeezed her hand harder.

"Time to wake up, you sleepy head," her mom said as if it was a lazy Saturday morning.

"…Mom?" Anne's voice was raspy and came out in little more than a whisper.

"We've missed you, Anne." There was a slight crack in their father's stable optimism.

She opened her bruised eyes slowly. Eleanor could see her sister's pupils attempting to scan the room, and, for a moment, she closed her own eyes and prayed that the doctor was a moron.

"Why is it so dark in here?" her sister said hoarsely, "Dad?"

Eleanor let all the breath leave her lungs and fought back the tears welling up in her.

"Anne, we're right here with you." Her dad stroked Anne's hair, his hand shaking.

Anne tried to move her hands to her eyes, but Eleanor held one and her father grasped the other. They could hear the heart rate monitor beeping quicker now.

"Sweetie, you were in an accident, we're at the hospital." Motherly affection filled the room, but her voice quivered.

"But why don't they have the lights on?" Anne took shallow, short breaths.

Their mother was barely holding it together.

"Anne, it's not the lights..." Their father, the hard-working, encouraging man who had raised them, was faltering. He couldn't find the words to tell his own daughter that she could no longer see.

The nurse helped them out. "Honey, you suffered a lot of injuries in your accident. One of them was your vision."

The look of panic and horror that was painted on Anne's face would remain burned into Eleanor's mind for a long time. Her heart twisted with pain and pity.

Anne heaved and moved her head around quicker as if the vision might come back that way. "No... That can't..." She didn't understand why she was waking up in a world of darkness, but she wasn't willing to believe that it was real.

"Anne, it's me, Ellie. I'm here with you." Without thinking about it, she put Anne's hand to her own face.

Anne kept opening and closing her eyes, and tears began to stream down her cheeks. "Ellie? Why can't I *see* you?"

"You're going to be okay. We're all here with you." Eleanor couldn't hold her tears back any longer.

"But I want to *see* you!" She was sobbing.

The nurse checked the monitors. "I think we're through the worst of it," she said quietly. "Her heart rate is mostly stable. She'll likely fall asleep again with little warning because of the concussion. This is very exhausting for her."

Why do they keep saying that? Through the worst of it? What does that even mean? Eleanor wanted to be angry at something instead of sad.

The room was quiet except for the sound of Anne's whimpering as she reached out to touch all her family, trying to take in the reality of what had happened. They all held her close, trying to reassure her everything would be okay.

Eleanor thought she might be saying those words to comfort Anne rather than truly believing them herself. Would it really be okay?

She imagined it like one of those nights when you wake up and everything is dark—groggily you stumble into the bathroom, and you're almost moving from muscle memory, but as you become more awake, you panic because you can't see anything. You wonder where you are or if you woke up somewhere else, some place outside time. You desperately look around for anything that might cast light, or you blink and squint, and eventually your eye catches some little thing like a crack of moonlight streaming through a window or a blinking LED on the TV. Suddenly, your brain begins to construct the world around you again, and you think: "Ah yes I'm safe. This is my world."

Then you carefully tiptoe back to bed, tripping over some clutter and reaching out for things until you're there. You feel safe. You wake up the next morning, and the room is bright and sunny. You can see the world again.

But what if one day you woke up and it was dark, and you never did find that blinking TV or the full moon? And what if you just kept squinting and blinking, hoping and praying to see something, but you never did? You're just there in the darkness. Eleanor was watching Anne experience this, and there was nothing either of them could do.

NEW DISCOURSE

Avi
Eleanor, I'm sure you have a lot going on. I just wanted to check and see how you are doing.

Avi
Also, please don't worry about work, that's not why I asked.

Avi
Just update when you can.

16

After Anne's turbulent awakening and her subsequent return to a peaceful doze, the Crawfords found themselves exhausted, standing in the hall outside Anne's room.

Her dad finally broke the silence. "I've got to check things at the inn for a bit. Thanksgiving preparations are in full swing." He turned to his wife who looked tired and withdrawn. "Marie, why don't you go home and rest some?"

She nodded slowly but didn't lift her gaze.

"Ellie, you'll take her?"

She linked her arm through her mother's. "Of course. Need me to come help out after?"

"If you're up to it." He seemed relieved at her offer.

"Definitely." She wanted to check in with Avi as well, but without her laptop or phone, she wasn't sure how to do so.

She and her mom drove home in a dreary silence. Eleanor imagined that her mother was experiencing all of the pain of Anne's situation. Deep down, she too felt helpless and pessimistic about Anne's condition but didn't want to let it show.

"How about some tea?" Eleanor asked as they pulled into the driveway.

"Sure, sweetie… thanks. I think I'll take a shower." She forced a slight smile in her daughter's direction.

In the rustic, woody kitchen, Eleanor picked up the old cast iron kettle her mother had used since her childhood, filled it with water, and put it on the stove, clicking the gas igniter until blue flames appeared underneath. She took out her mom's favorite tea cup and sorted through a box of sachets on the counter, deciding on a sleepy chamomile lavender. She waited impatiently for the water to boil, pacing the kitchen.

The image of Anne's terrified expression flooded her mind. *What can I do? What's going to happen?* Finally, the kettle whirred, and she grabbed the heavy pot with a hot pad and poured the water over the tea. The steam prickling her face induced a slight calming effect.

She'd always thought her mom a bit silly for having such a slow and dated process for making tea. Eleanor owned an electric tea kettle that would heat to a specific temperature in less than a minute. But today, it all made sense to her—the thick cast iron rooting her to the ground, the excessive heat just on the other side of the potholder. She popped open the jar of local honey their neighbor gave them for Christmas every year. Breathing in its sweet scent, she stirred the liquid gold into the cup, the spoon clinking the sides of the ceramic.

She carried it up to her mother and kissed her on the forehead as she tucked her into bed. They both smiled at each other, appreciating the role reversal.

"I'm going to help Dad for a bit. Try and get some sleep."

"Thanks, sweetie." Her mother gave her a feeble hand squeeze.

Eleanor tip-toed down the stairs back into her childhood bedroom where she began sifting through some of her old belongings until she found what she was looking for—a treasure from her teenage years that she'd refused to get rid of—her very first cell phone. It had a number pad on the front and flipped open sideways with a QWERTY keyboard. Many a night she'd spent under the blankets clicking away with her thumbs on the miniature keyboard, sending messages to her friends and crushes.

Her lips turned into a smile. "I wonder if it still works."

She dug around some more and found the charger that went with it, plugged it in, and waited. Sure enough, it turned on, the logo pixelating on the tiny screen on the front. On her way to Grayson House, she stopped at the Verizon in town to see if it could be activated. Then she could call Avi and let him know what was up.

She walked up to the only employee and placed the outdated device on the counter. "Can I get this activated?"

He raised an eyebrow and looked at her like she might be joking. "You want to use *that*?"

Even in this small town, it probably would still be uncommon to see something like this, especially for someone Eleanor's age. Who didn't have a smartphone nowadays?

"Yeah. I, uh… lost my phone." She bounced her toe on the ground.

The employee put on his best salesman voice. "Well, we're having a sale right now if you just want to replace your phone. Did you have an iPhone or Android?"

"No," Eleanor stopped him in his tracks, "I really don't want that at the moment. I just need to be able to make some calls." The shortness of her words surprised even her. She knew she was being ridiculous, but she didn't care. *I just want to be away from that world right now.*

"Okay, do you already have an account with us?" he scoffed.

Eleanor gave him her info, and after some struggle finding a SIM card that would fit the old phone, he had it working with her number. Any calls or messages she missed, however, could not be retrieved. *No problem,* Eleanor reassured herself.

The employee was able to pull some of her contacts from her account, but she realized she didn't have a phone number for Avi or work. She'd always used Agora or email.

"Um, one more thing, if you could. I need the phone number for my work." She waved the device around trying to make light of the situation. "I don't have a way to look it up."

He shot her an "I told you so" kind of look and an "I bet you can't last one day" kind of eye roll. "Of course, ma'am, where do you work?"

"Agora headquarters. The one in Atlanta," she said.

The haughtiness drained from his face as he searched for the number and wrote it on a sticky note for her. "Anything else I can help you with today, ma'am?"

"No, that'll do it. Thanks!"

Back in her car, she sat in the parking lot as she dialed the number, pressing the tactile keys with a certain amount of delight. She was greeted with an automated line and fumbled through the options until she could ask to be transferred to Avi Kumar. Luckily, he was actually at his desk and answered on the second ring. "Avi speaking."

"Avi, it's Eleanor."

"Eleanor, thank goodness! I was starting to worry."

"I'm sorry. I…" She hesitated. "I threw my phone in a lake." For reasons she didn't quite understand, she felt compelled to tell Avi the truth.

"You what?" He laughed in his "Avi way," and she found herself smiling at her steering wheel.

"Long story."

"Is everything okay, though?" His tone grew serious.

Eleanor briefly filled him in on the situation.

"I'm really sorry, Eleanor. Is there anything I can do?"

"Well, I'd like to stay up here until after the Thanksgiving holiday, but I forgot my work laptop at my apartment."

"That's fine. I'm not worried about that. Is there anything I can do for *you*?"

She wasn't entirely sure how to respond. "I'm okay for now. I appreciate it. You can text or call this number, but I won't have access to Agora or email. If you could send me a message so I have your number, that would be great. I had to go through the front desk."

"Sure, okay. Seriously, don't worry about things here. Work will still be here when you get back, and I'll talk to Daryl."

"Thanks, Avi."

She then called Emily and Kitt to update them on the situation, and they both reminded her to let them know if there was anything they could do. Kitt even told her that he missed her, which gave her a nice warm feeling. With her calls done, she drove to the inn.

As she pulled into the long, tree-studded driveway of Grayson House, she was overcome with nostalgia. She stopped for a moment, taking in the view. The passageway of trees was vibrant with reds, oranges, and yellows. A place she had seen so many times before, but in the dusk of late fall, and maybe today especially, it took her breath away.

The rolling green lawn disappeared into white columns, and picture windows glowed from the joy inside. The rocking chairs on the porch were framed by azalea bushes. She recalled swaying back and forth with a sweet tea in summer. It seemed clichè to her now, but it was still home.

She pulled into the parking area around back and caught a glimpse of the garden that was kept to make fresh farm-to-table meals at the restaurant. She felt a flicker of uplift when she remembered that Thanksgiving was coming. The dining room would be fixed with all the rustic wooden tables pushed together in one long communion of families—laughing, telling stories, passing food around.

She breathed in the cold air and crunched up to the back door. As soon as she stepped inside, she could hear people in the dining area, clinking glasses and silverware, the murmur of conversation and happy memories being made. She walked down the hallway to the manager's office and found her father sitting at a desk stacked with papers and folders. "Hey, Dad."

"Oh good, you're here." He squinted as he looked away from the computer. "We're at max capacity for Thanksgiving."

"That's great!"

"Yes, well, I'm glad, believe me, that business is good. But Anne usually works after school and your mom, of course, so we're a bit shorthanded. I'm relieved you're here." He smiled at her.

"Of course. I'm here for whatever you need."

"Okay, let me introduce you to the new assistant manager we hired a couple months ago. He's been a great help."

"You hired a manager outside the family?" Eleanor was surprised despite knowing that she was the reason that would be necessary.

"Ellie, your mom and I aren't getting any younger, and she's been teaching more painting classes lately. We never wanted to force you or Anne into anything. I myself didn't particularly want to take over the family business at your age either." He sighed. "It just made sense to get some more help and maybe have someone in mind to take over running the place someday."

"I understand," she reassured him. "Well, let's meet him then!"

They walked out to the lobby, and her dad pointed to a tall, lanky guy about Eleanor's age working at the front desk. "That's him."

His slacks and polo shirt seemed to hang off him a little, and he had dark hair that he kept as tidy as he probably cared to. His skin was heavily browned by the sun.

"Emmett, this is my daughter, Eleanor. She's going to be helping us out some, so feel free to give her the hard tasks!" Her dad winked at her.

Emmett stuck his lean arm out and gave a droopy handshake. "I've heard a lot about you. Appreciate the help." He didn't offer a smile of any kind.

"Nice to meet you too." She thought him a bit rude.

"You're good with computers, right? Can you get the menus made up for Thanksgiving dinner and sent to the printers?" Emmett continued to flip through the papers in front of him.

Good with computers… How old is he?

"Um, sure." She bit her lip and looked at her dad.

"You can use the computer in my office," her dad said. "I've gotta talk with the gardener." He turned back towards his office.

Eleanor hurried to keep up with him, and, once there, plopped into his squeaky leather chair. "Well, he's… interesting."

"He does good work but not much of a talker. Had a rough time of it from what I heard."

"As long as he's not rude to customers." She logged into the computer.

"All right." He put his hand on the back of his neck. "I'm going outside."

She nodded and set her focus on the outdated computer to type up the menus. She found a paper in Anne's handwriting with careful instructions on how to edit the template she'd made. Eleanor knew her sister had been learning how to make digital art, but when she saw the cute fall-themed border with alternating pumpkins and turkeys in a hand-drawn style, it was all she could do not to burst into tears.

Will she be able to do any of this anymore?

The ache she felt in her chest drained her of any energy she'd had when she arrived. She sent the file to the printer and leaned back in the chair. The flip phone buzzed in her pocket, and she pulled it out. The text message was from an unknown number. With childish curiosity, she flicked it open to read: "It's Avi :) Let me know if you need anything."

She clicked her thumbs over the keys. "Any plans tomorrow?" She propped the phone up on the desk, contemplating her own question.

A little envelope popped up on the screen a few minutes later. "No, why?"

"You wanna come to Thanksgiving here in Aska Valley?"

She suddenly missed those three little dots that indicated someone was typing a response and confirmation of the messaging being read. Why hadn't she thought to invite Kitt? She just knew she already missed talking to Avi about work or grabbing lunch with him.

The phone buzzed with a response. "Sure! Sounds fun." She could imagine his dry laugh and wry smile.

She slowly typed out the address then clicked the phone shut. As she put it back in her pocket, her breath felt as if it was stuck in her chest.

Time to get to work.

AGORA ASSEMBLY
CONTENT POLICY COMMITTEE (PRIVATE)

Welcome to the group, everyone! This is a place for any and all Agora employees who are interested in free speech and keeping Agora a fair and safe place for everyone.

Next Event: November 21st, 10 a.m. in Hypatia Conference
Room
6 going, 10 invited

Comments:

Jeff:
We've had some questions coming up about
one of our recent policy decisions that I'd
like to revisit with you all.

17

───────

On Thanksgiving morning, Anne was discharged from the hospital along with an overwhelming number of instructions from the doctor: "Take it easy, don't overexert. Lots of rest until the concussion heals. Formal eye exam. Someone will need to assist her with a lot of things, in the meantime… Braille… white cane… screen readers. Once she's a bit stronger, a trip to the Center for the Visually Impaired in Atlanta is recommended."

One directive in particular stood out to Eleanor: "Counseling is recommended. She may find it difficult to adjust… Her life won't be the same. Watch for signs of depression." The three of them nodded their heads in earnest.

Anne groaned about having to be discharged in a wheelchair. "My legs still work just fine. I'm tired of laying around."

The Crawfords hovered near her anxiously as she hopped out of it the moment they were outside and took off walking on her own, reaching her hands out in front of her. She stepped off the edge of the sidewalk, stumbling a little, and three sets of hands reached to catch her. Eleanor knew her headstrong sister didn't like the idea of needing so much help. She gave Anne's hand a gentle squeeze, and with a sigh, she took Eleanor's arm as they walked to the car.

Her sister had insisted she still get to attend Thanksgiving dinner as the Crawfords would do every year. "What's the alternative? We have a dreary day at home with me lying in bed?"

No one saw any reason to deny her that, so they drove straight to Grayson House from the hospital.

"I can't wait to eat some real food." Anne fiddled with the scarf around her neck.

Eleanor was amazed at her sister's ability to be positive. But then again, optimism was a notable trait of their fathers and perhaps both of his daughter's as well. "Anne, are you sure you wouldn't rather go home and rest?"

"Ellie—no way, I've been laying in a hospital bed for days. I can't take it anymore. I've got to do something other than lie around."

"Okay, okay." Eleanor conceded. "But tell one of us if you get too tired."

When they pulled into the parking lot, Eleanor saw Avi leaning against his blue BMW talking on the phone. He was dressed the way he would be for an important meeting at work—a stiff white dress shirt and tie. Eleanor couldn't hide her smile at how out of place Avi looked at this southern country inn.

She waved at him as she helped Anne get out of the car, and he crunched over the gravel with his dress shoes. "Did you know there's a Confederate flag along the main road?" He laughed nervously.

Something about the way he enunciated con-fed-er-ate made it even more absurd than it was. "Old bonnie blue flies forever here," she said matter-of-factly as if it wasn't ridiculous.

"Just tell me I'm leaving this place alive."

This was an element of her hometown she never quite knew how to reconcile. It could be a comfortable and welcoming community to some, yet hostile and unapproachable to others.

She could see that Avi, having never left Atlanta, had never experienced this element of the South. "You'll be okay. Avi, this is my sister, Anne, and my parents, Ethan and Marie."

"Nice to meet you all." He was surprisingly cool and calm,

showing no awkwardness about Anne's situation or the accident. He politely shook hands with her mom and dad.

Eleanor caught her mother giving her a strange look and whispering something to their dad as they walked towards the building, but she chose to ignore it.

"This place is impressive." Avi took in the large, old house.

"It was built after the Civil War by Grayson Crawford, who was my great-great-grandfather, I think." Eleanor began reciting the history as she would to inquiring guests. "It's a stunning example of Greek revival architecture. Grayson also built several mills along the Toccoa River and made most of his fortune by supplying the lumber needed to rebuild during Reconstruction."

Avi raised his eyebrows. "You don't think about the history so much in Atlanta. It's mostly just a modern city."

"True, but not even two hundred years ago, we fought and killed our own…"

In the town where Eleanor was born, where she was raised and where she dreamed of leaving, many of the citizens were uneducated. It had one of the lowest high school graduation rates in the state. Some harbored a generational love for the Old South and probably dreamed of the day that it would rise again. She thought about how her high school history class taught that the Civil War was about State's Rights, completely glossing over the dark truth.

With a cringe, she recalled going to football games in high school, where kids would paint their bodies and run back and forth with Rebel flags to the band playing Dixie, the fight song. She often wondered if they realized what it meant to do such a thing. How was it even allowed? But it was a small town that lacked diversity. Who would complain?

She noticed Avi smiling at her, likely aware of the rumination going on in her mind. "Thanks for inviting me. I've never experienced an American Thanksgiving."

"You're welcome." She smiled as they approached the white columns as large as trees and entered through the thick, oak door. The elegantly decorated lobby was full of guests mingling and waiting for dinner to be served. Soft music drifted from the

Chickering piano in the corner of the room, and the smell of cornbread and pecan pie floated in the air.

Anne was smiling, but Eleanor could see her tugging at the sleeves of her jacket and the skin around her eyes tightening as she took in all the smells and sounds. She was clearly trying to convince her family that letting her come was the right choice. Eleanor grabbed onto Anne's arm, and they walked past the sweeping marble staircase and into the dining room. It was exactly as she had always remembered it on Thanksgiving—all the heavy wooden tables pushed together to form one long table that would seat about twenty, formally set with forks, spoons, knives, and porcelain plates. A fire crackled in the stone fireplace.

Waiters bustled around with armfuls of bowls and plates to fix the table family-style with pimento cheese appetizers, buttered rolls, cornbread dressing, candied yams, collard greens, and peppery mac-and-cheese.

Her father went to the head of the table, and everyone found seats according to their name cards. As the chef rolled a large golden-browned turkey out on a cart, her dad, as host, rang a tarnished silver bell to gather everyone's attention.

"I want to welcome you all to the 43rd annual Thanksgiving celebration at Grayson House! Today we are all family as we give thanks and enjoy this feast together." He ceremoniously carved the turkey.

"I can feel the warm, happy energy of this room." Anne whispered to her sister.

Their father presided at one end of the table and their mother at the other—Anne at his left and Eleanor on his right. Eleanor had placed Avi's name card next to her own, and a few moments later, Emmett came and sat down next to Anne.

As conversation rumbled and filled the room and bowls were passed around filling up plates, Eleanor tried to be happy. Across from her, she watched her dad put food on Anne's plate. She observed Anne's slow movements, reaching for a fork, feeling the edge of the table and plate with her fingertips before trying to put any food on her fork. Eleanor couldn't help notice looks of pity coming from those around her. Emmett occasionally leaned over to tell her what dishes were being passed by or catching food she spilled.

He seemed a bit nicer now than when she'd met him yesterday. She looked down at the freshly carved turkey and steaming vegetables on her plate then noticed Avi's hand in her periphery—his warm skin tone standing out amongst all the white linens—passing a bowl to her. Their fingers met momentarily under the dish, and she noticed he was glancing at her with a calm, reassuring look, and Eleanor smiled gratefully in return.

Conversation went on all around her. Talk of sports, seasonal activities, and the Mars Rover, which Eleanor would have gladly discussed on any normal occasion, but today she couldn't bring herself to join in.

"Okay, this is the best mac-and-cheese I've ever had." Avi scooped more onto his plate.

"Wait till you see dessert."

Made from scratch pecan and pumpkin pies circulated the table along with hot cups of coffee, and the white noise of conversation dwindled. Everyone was full and happy, including Eleanor.

"I don't think I've ever eaten so much food." Avi chuckled.

After dinner, some people gathered to play board games or cards. Eleanor twisted her arm into Anne's, and they went to sit out on the porch, like old times.

With Anne wrapped in a blanket, rocking back and forth, they talked about dinner, Avi, mom and dad, and the mysterious Emmet. Anne didn't know much about him other than that he didn't seem to have any family.

Some silence. The sky was turning orange and yellow, and the temperature was dropping.

"I'm scared, Ellie," Anne whispered.

There was nothing but the squeaking sounds of the rocking chairs until Eleanor said, "What part is the scariest?"

"I don't know… dying… or living really."

"Well," Eleanor started, unsure of what to say, "you just escaped death."

"I wish I hadn't, sometimes. Not right now… but when I first woke up I did." Anne's voice quivered.

"Don't even think that." Eleanor said firmly. She turned to look at Anne then felt a hollowness when her sister didn't look back.

"I feel so horrible. I've done a terrible thing, and I'll always be a burden now. How will I take care of myself?" Tears started to roll down her bruised face. "How can I… draw anymore? What about college?"

Eleanor couldn't hold back her tears either. "Anne, we will figure everything out, I promise. You are alive. We all love you no matter what."

Anne pulled the blanket tighter around her. "I know you got rid of your smartphone. It's because of me too. I don't even remember exactly what happened, but I *know* what happened. Everyone knows."

"Anne… It was an accident. It could have happened to anyone…"

Her sister didn't acknowledge this offer of comfort. "You know the sickest part of it Ellie? I miss my phone. I miss talking with people and knowing what's going on. I feel so out of the loop."

Eleanor shivered. "I know. I do too." She reached out to grab her sisters hand. She couldn't even think of any other comfort to offer.

It was quiet as the sun started to fade away, and after a while, Eleanor noticed that Anne had nodded off to sleep. Her parents came out to check on them and decided to take Anne home.

"I'm going to stay and hang out with Avi a bit." Eleanor whispered as her father led a groggy Anne towards the car.

Her mom nodded, gave a sly smile, and then walked to the car before Eleanor could say another word. She sighed and went back inside.

The gentle mumble of happy, likely slightly intoxicated voices hit her as she searched for Avi then found him mingling with the only Indian couple there. *Funny how we do that.*

"Hey, thought you might like to take a walk," she said.

"Ya, sure." He said goodbye to the couple as if they were all old friends then stood up and followed Eleanor out the back door.

The sun was set now, but the path down to the river was lit with lanterns that hung from the trees. It was cold enough that Eleanor could see her breath, but she didn't feel chilly. Rather, this place felt like a warm bubble of tranquility in the world. The crickets chirped as the stars started to twinkle one by one.

"When I'm here, I don't know how I manage to live in the city." She looked back at Avi. He seemed out of place in his dress clothes, but his face was at ease.

He was looking up too but somewhere much further away, she thought. The sound of the crunching rusty gravel gave way to flowing water—the Toccoa River. She watched his face as his eyes met the stream. Light, seeming to glow from the bedrock, illuminated and colored the currents—places where the water tumbled over rocks gurgling blue or pink and swirling eddies of ethereal yellow.

She approached the creek and slipped her shoes off, stepping onto one of the large flat pieces of bedrock shooting up from underneath, the icy water flowing around her ankles like liquid diamonds.

If yesterday she had lost her tether to the digital world, today she reconnected it to the natural one. With lanterns lighting up the orange, red, and yellow maple leaves and the rush of cold water from the mountain ahead of her, she felt completely whole.

She turned to Avi and smiled. "What do you think?"

"I've never seen anything more beautiful." He moved carefully towards the river.

Despite the frigid water, her cheeks were warm. She gestured at his feet and laughed as he clumsily took off his dress shoes and socks then rolled his slacks up. She grabbed his hand, and the two of them slowly stepped over the large rocks crossing the river—the rest of the world light-years away.

He didn't let go of her hand after their wet feet landed on the dirt path on the other side, and she didn't let go either. The sound of flowing water was loud, but the thumping of Eleanor's heart was louder.

They landed on an old, creaky swinging bench with ivy growing along its posts. The only light was from the river and the stars.

They looked down at their wet, dirt-covered feet, laughing and swinging the bench slowly.

"Aren't you cold?" He pulled at his jacket with a shiver.

Her hand was still in his; it felt warm. "No. I don't know." Her deep exhale filled the air with frozen particles.

He looked at her. "I like seeing this side of you."

"I'm still me." She pulled at a loose string on her knit sweater.

"Yes, but you're… more you, I think."

She swayed her legs, trying to dry them off and pushing the swing a little more. "This is all a dream, though, and I'm going to wake up soon. And when I do…"

"Anne won't have been in an accident?" He squeezed her hand.

"Yeah…" She rubbed her feet together, the dirt falling off them. They were quiet for a few moments. Eleanor felt that her entire relationship with Avi had changed in one night. Or perhaps she was just seeing it in a new light.

"Why did you throw your phone in a lake?" He leaned his head back and looked up at the stars.

She turned to look at him, surprised. Never had she seen him so relaxed and at ease, betraying his usual formal posture, yet still confined to his starched white shirt that hugged his broad shoulders.

"I don't know really… The doctor said Anne was using her phone when the accident happened. I just suddenly hated the thing."

He turned his head over his shoulder to face her. "And you felt guilty?"

"Maybe." She flushed from his steady gaze. "How do you know?"

He inhaled deeply and spoke softer. "You know, you don't have to carry the entire world on your shoulders, Eleanor."

"If I contribute to something that hurts people, how can I not think about that?" She sat up straighter.

"You're just one person."

"One person who wants to do *something* good for the world." Her heart beat even faster now, and she let go of his hand.

"But nothing is completely good or bad. There are other factors to consider."

He's so laid-back, so even-tempered, why can't I be like that?

"Yes, but if the bad outweighs the good, then it might no longer be a good thing." She shook her head.

"And those who build that thing carry the responsibility?" He loosened his tie a little.

"Some of it, yeah. We shouldn't blindly build things without thinking about their impact." They rocked back and forth for a few moments while he seemed to consider what she said.

"You know what I like about you?" His eyes reflected the glint of the stars. "You project this calculated and reserved outer appearance; it's almost intimidating. But hidden underneath is the biggest heart I've ever seen." He paused. "It's so much more obvious to me now… tonight… that you would want to protect that with heavy armor."

Eleanor didn't think she'd ever felt any warmer on a cold night than she did right now.

Avi leaned in closer, and she felt herself relax into his shoulder. "I want to be part of that armor," he said, "to help shield you while you're busy worrying about others… busy solving problems."

His arms wrapped around her like ivy, and no words came to her, but she felt calm and rooted. Avi seemed to understand her better than she did herself. He saw something in her that she'd never noticed.

This must be a dream.

She felt his chest moving up and down, and the smell of his cologne made her dizzy. She looked at him now, his eyes kindly waiting for her to say if this was okay.

A tingling sensation swept from her chest to her face and with it arose a reassuring smile. She leaned into his gravitational pull as he kissed her. The rushing of the river seemed to match the rushing of her heart as she kissed him back. He pulled her in closer and held her tight as they rocked back and forth to the sounds of the forest, late into the night.

NEW EMAIL

SUBJECT: HAPPY THANKSGIVING

Happy Thanksgiving Agora family!

I hope you all are enjoying a relaxing long weekend with your families and friends. I always like to take this time of year to be thankful for the amazing family I have here at Agora that are working hard every day to connect the world.
It's also in this spirit that I'd like to announce that, in order to better support our communication practices, Agora will begin issuing company phones to select teams including engineering, IT, and business intelligence. See your manager for details.

All the best,

Matthew Erickson
Agora CEO

18

Eleanor awoke the next morning in a daze, trying to distinguish dream from reality. She rolled over and noticed the flip phone sitting on the nightstand.

Oh yeah. That part's real.

She picked it up and flipped it open. There were several messages to read through. Kitt and Emily both wondering if she was okay and when she was coming home. Nothing from Avi, though.

Maybe it was a dream. Or maybe they weren't going to talk about it. She shook it out of her head. *I'll deal with all that when I get back to Atlanta. For now, I have two more days with Anne.*

Eleanor would definitely have to get back to work on Monday. She had missed enough already. Anne was out of immediate danger, and Eleanor could come up on weekends.

She threw her feet over the side of the bed and padded to Anne's bedroom. She was still asleep. Eleanor went out on the back porch and found her mom painting with watercolors. "Morning, Mom."

"You got home late." She looked up from her painting with a smile.

"Mm… did I?" Eleanor plopped into a chair and flipped her phone open again, checking for a message.

"What kept you?" her mother pried.

"Oh, I just hung out with Avi… showed him the river LEDs."

"Ah, yes, those were a great idea. Very romantic."

Eleanor didn't say anything and clicked the phone shut again. She knew her mom was giving her *the look*. "So tell me more about your *friend*."

"Avi is my colleague. He had never experienced an American Thanksgiving, so I invited him."

"Well, that was nice of you. He seemed to have a good time." She clinked her brush in a mason jar with water that turned blue.

Eleanor changed the subject. "I'm going to have to get back to work on Monday. Are you and Dad going to be okay with Anne and the inn and everything? I can come up on weekends."

"We'll manage. Now that we have Emmett, I can be home with Anne most of the time… There's physical therapy, and we'll probably have to find a tutor or something to help get her finished with school." She sighed. "I'm not sure about college."

"Let's just take it one step at a time. I'm sure there's a way…"

"Yes, you're right. We can think about it more in the spring when acceptance letters come in. If she can finish high school in time, that is."

"Don't say *if*, Mom. Anne is smart and strong. We can get her through this."

"I know you want to believe that, Eleanor. But there are a lot of challenges… We have to be practical…" She lay her arms helplessly in her lap.

Eleanor got up and pulled her into a hug. "I know, but I have to believe in her. We all do. She needs us."

Her mother gave a watery-eyed smile. "I know. Let's go check on her."

When they went inside, they heard some loud banging in the bathroom and rushed towards it. Anne had knocked over some bottles in the shower. Their mom tapped gently on the door. "Sweetie, do you need any help?"

There came the sound of frustrated muttering and a loud "towel!" Eleanor grabbed one, and when the water shut off, handed it to her sister behind the curtain.

"Ellie, can you get me some clothes? Something comfortable. I don't feel like fumbling through the drawers…"

"Of course." Eleanor came back with some sweatpants and a t-shirt and helped her sister put them on. Eleanor's stomach twisted at the sight of all the bruises and cuts on Anne's body.

"So embarrassing," Anne huffed.

"I didn't look."

Anne crumpled her towel and tossed it on the floor. "No, just not being able to wash or dress myself."

Eleanor lifted the shirt and positioned the neck opening over her sister's head. "Are you hungry? What would you like?"

"No…"Anne grumbled. Then, when the t-shirt was over her head, she gave in. "Maybe a little."

Eleanor and her mother got Anne situated on the sofa with some warm soup in a mug. She asked to listen to the TV, so they complied, exchanging awkward glances. They then spent a few hours *Anne-proofing* the house—removing breakables from ledges, things that stick out in walkways, and applying small tangible stickers on appliances or food items as identifiers.

"She's going to start physical therapy in about a week. They will help her learn how to use a white cane to get around. We'll just have to be careful in the meantime," her mom said.

Eleanor took special care with Anne's bedroom, gathering up all her laundry and washing it. She organized her dresser and closet in a more streamlined way, grouping shirts together on one side, then dresses on the other, jeans in one drawer, shorts in another. *These are the last articles of clothing Anne will ever own that she will truly know what they look like.*

When she approached Anne's desk, she lost her momentum. It was cluttered with pencils, papers, and various sketches. Some of her drawings were entire scenes and landscapes. Others featured figures darting around the terrain. She had gotten so much better since they were kids. Eleanor gathered them all up and stacked the sketchbooks off to the side.

How will she ever do this again?

She noticed a sticky note stuck to Anne's computer that read, "Art is not what you see, but what you make others see."

Eleanor pulled the note off and stared at it for some time. Anne's looping handwriting faded in and out of her vision as her eyes watered.

She sniffed and dried her eyes then folded the note and slipped it into her pocket.

The sound of the front door opening got her attention. When she went into the living room, she saw her father was home, and Emmett was with him.

"How're you feeling?" she heard her dad ask.

Emmett was awkwardly holding a box from the inn's restaurant. "The chef made your favorite—tiramisu."

"Hey, Ellie." Her dad noticed her enter the room. "Emmett's gonna join us for dinner."

"Oh, great. I'll set another place."

Her mom was in the kitchen taking a casserole out of the oven. Eleanor warmed some rolls and made a salad. "Does he come over often?"

"Sometimes. He's taken a liking to your dad… and to Anne. Like a big brother."

"Interesting," Eleanor said absentmindedly.

"I don't think he has any siblings." Her mother hushed her voice. "He's never mentioned any family or brought any around."

The five of them sat down to dinner, Eleanor feeling at home in the same chair she'd had so many childhood meals in. Anne looked tired and frustrated.

"Thanksgiving was a success. Now we get to start preparing for Christmas!" Her dad was as animated as always about the holidays. "We have a small reprieve at least. All the Thanksgiving parties will be heading back to the city."

Emmett looked at Eleanor. "You'll be goin' with 'em?"

"Um, yes." She was surprised by his direct question. "Gotta get back to work."

Her dad shook some pepper over his plate. "We're going to miss having you around."

"I can come up on weekends, and I'll be back for Christmas, of course." Eleanor smiled.

"You better," Anne said halfheartedly.

"This time of year goes so quickly," their mom said gently. "Anne, why don't we invite some of your friends over tomorrow?"

"Nah, that's okay." She started to get up from the table clumsily, and all four of them jumped up to help her, but she put up her hand in protest. "I'm going to go lie down for a bit. I'm tired."

They all exchanged concerned looks as Anne walked slowly in the direction of her bedroom, hands out in front of her moving along the wall.

After dinner, Eleanor volunteered to do the dishes, a chore she strangely enjoyed in this old house that didn't have a dishwasher. She loved the large farmhouse sink as it filled with warm water and steamy bubbles. She took pleasure in systematically filling all the cups with soap and water on one side of the basin while soaking all the silverware in their own tub on another. Then she washed all the plates and lined them up, one by one, on the bamboo drying rack.

Looking out the window as she worked, she let her mind wander. She was going to have to leave all this. Atlanta seemed so far away, but her life was waiting for her there. Growing up, all she'd ever wanted to do was leave this town. To go and be where something was happening, but now she felt torn in two directions.

Her mind drifted to Avi. The oven clock said it was six. She imagined him probably in the office, even though it was a holiday, sitting at his cubicle—slowly pecking on the keyboard, responding to emails—doing Eleanor's work that she was missing so the team's productivity didn't lag. He would work overtime to make it look like no absence in the team had occurred. She scrubbed a particularly crusty plate.

After the dishes were done and the kitchen dark, she slipped out to go for a walk. She wanted to enjoy as much of the quiet as she could before she left. The cloud cover hid most of the stars. She walked along in the shadowy moonlight, her mind ruminating over ways to help Anne.

Her heart jumped when she came upon a figure sitting on a log in the clearing ahead of her. It was Emmett.

"Sorry. Didn't mean to scare you," he said awkwardly.

"I thought you left."

"Just felt like walkin' some." He started to get up to leave.

"Oh, you don't have to go." She began to walk past him, but something stopped her. "It was… nice of you to bring dessert to Anne… and check on her."

He looked surprised but nonchalant. "All of us over there're worried 'bout her." His accent came out thicker than it had previously.

Eleanor smirked. "It's a challenge to hide that accent when you're working, isn't it?"

She noticed some of the tension leave his shoulders as he almost cracked a smile. "I reckon it is, although I'm not fixin' to change it permanently."

"Meaning?" She sat down on the log next to him.

"I mean, I haven't decided if it matters, I guess. It's a southern inn, why shouldn't I talk southern? It's who I am."

Eleanor sympathized with his struggle. "I can't say I understand it, but I went through it. Most people associate a southern drawl with a lack of intelligence."

"Well, I'm not like you." He stood up, his scowl returning.

"Thus proving my point." She looked at him, amused.

"Some of us just want to do honest work."

"What the hell does that mean?" she scoffed.

"You act all high and mighty, working for that technology company, but you're not doin' anything so great."

"That's bullshit! People are more connected than ever before thanks to the internet *and* Agora." Eleanor was losing her cool. "What, you still want to be writing letters to your *pa* on the battlefront? Waiting weeks or months to know if he's still alive?"

"Sure, you might be able to communicate faster now, but what are we trading for it? People miss everything right in front of their faces because they're too busy looking at everything they wish they had *out there*." He waved his arm outward.

"People have always looked towards things they wanted but couldn't have." This was an argument Eleanor felt she couldn't win because she wasn't even sure she was right. Her eyes went to the old phone protruding from her pocket.

"You know I'm right. Why the hell else would you be pollutin' our lakes with that shit?"

"How—" Eleanor's face was red with frustration.

"Your city-slicker pal mentioned it."

She couldn't think of anything to say. She felt silly and immature, and she didn't like it. Having this near-stranger shout at her that her work didn't matter or that it was making the world a worse place was infuriating.

When he turned to walk away, she yelled, "You're too simplistic. You can't stop innovation."

He didn't turn back around though. She stared in that direction until she was sure he was gone, then stomped back up to the house.

FORUM
CONTENT MODERATORS ANONYMOUS

Viusting
What's the most fucked up thing you saw
today?

BomberClone
Blown up heads

Born2Moto
Bro are you new here?

Viusting
Thats light you're not going to make it here

BomberClone
4rl?

Born2Moto
Welcome to life as one of the garbagemen
of the internet

19

Sunday came, and Eleanor gave long hugs to her mom, dad, and Anne, reminding them to call whenever they needed her. Pulling out of the driveway, seeing her family and home in the rearview mirror, she couldn't help feeling sad. On the long drive back to Atlanta, she finally allowed her mind to think all the negative, hopeless thoughts she'd buried for Anne's sake.

How cruel the world seemed. How complicated life was. She thought about how much she didn't understand in the world and how much she never would. Her mind turned to what Emmett had said to her, then to Kitt and Avi, and at some point, she just got tired of thinking and decided to listen to whatever was on the radio.

As she re-entered the city of Atlanta, she found herself turned around in the spaghetti network of roads. She never drove anywhere there without using the GPS on her phone. After living there all this time, she still wasn't confident navigating the mess of one-way streets and narrow side roads. *How could I get lost in my own city?* she thought.

Finally, noticing a landmark that guided her to Peachtree Street and then to her apartment, she was glad to leave her car in the parking garage. Her apartment was dark and empty. Emily, no doubt, was at some social gathering or another. The sink was full of dishes, and her work bag was still sitting on the couch right where she'd left it.

She took her duffel bag to the washer and prepared to dump everything in it, but when she unzipped it, the woody, earthy smell of her home hit her. She suddenly desired to zip it tight again and keep the aroma in there. She went to her room and plopped on her bed.

Using the front of the phone, she slowly clicked a message out to Kitt using t9: "I'm back in ATL"

Why hadn't Avi messaged her? She would see him at work tomorrow and had no idea how to act. No response came from Kitt, and Eleanor felt bored and lonely like there was nothing for her to do.

She lived in a huge building full of people, but she knew none of them. She had never felt more disconnected in her life than she did right now, without being plugged in to the fiber-optic ether that ran through the city like blood.

She took her phone out again and clicked a message to Emily: "Meet me at Vivo whenever you can."

She responded a few moments later: "Okay, I'll be there in about an hour."

Eleanor let out a deep sigh and decided it was time to find out what she'd been missing at work. She grabbed her laptop bag, slipped on some sneakers, and walked up the road to one of her favorite coffee shops—Vivo Espresso Bar.

She ordered a hot latte and settled into her favorite window seat with its view of both everyone in the coffee shop and everyone walking by outside. While she normally would have been looking at her phone or hunched over her laptop, she watched the world instead, sipping her drink slowly, feeling it kindle her entire body. The whir of the espresso machine filled her ears.

When was the last time she just sat in a coffee shop and relaxed?

Most of the others in the cafe were working on laptops with their headphones on or slouched in chairs looking down at their phones. She stared at a girl taking a selfie with her coffee held up in her left hand so a large diamond engagement ring was visible in the photo. When the girl noticed Eleanor staring and flashed a smile, Eleanor quickly opened her laptop to blend in. She continued to observe her surroundings though.

There was only one couple sitting and talking with each other. Eleanor studied them for a while, noting several occasions during which the conversation lagged and they would both look at their phones for a bit.

How different this was compared to Thanksgiving dinner. This passed for normal life here, but had it fully seeped into Aska Valley too? Why hadn't she noticed it before?

It was like the slow rise of sea levels but with occasional large waves—the radio, television, personal computers, smartphones… What next?

A moment of boredom prompted withdraw from the physical world into the digital one. Eleanor knew the feeling. *I can't look now at the world because I will miss something else, something more important.* But what could be more important than the real world right in front of us? The people right in front of us?

No, this is Emmett making me think this way. Coffee shops are places to work.

She logged into her computer and began to read all the emails and messages from the past few days, rolling her eyes at Daryl's emails, then stopping to reread the one from the CEO on Thanksgiving.

Company Phones? Do we have to….?

One week ago, Eleanor had been no different from anyone else here. This was just modern life, or so she'd thought. But the image of 20 strangers gathered around like family on Thanksgiving glowed in her mind. This was the world she knew… or wanted to know.

She had been coming to this same coffee shop for over a year now and saw most of the same faces behind the counter, yet she didn't know their names. She'd never seen any indication that they recognized her either.

In Aska Valley, she knew most of the people working at the grocery store or shops around town and would chat with them;

many of those working at the local coffee shop had been her schoolmates.

She returned to her laptop and reflexively started doing work tasks until the sound of Emily's voice pulled her back. "Working already, are we?" Emily scooted into the window seat and gave Eleanor a long hug. "How are you? How's Anne?"

Eleanor gave her all the details, clicking the flip phone open and closed as she talked.

"Oh, Eleanor, I'm so sorry." Emily squeezed her tight again.

Eleanor let herself be comforted, her eyes watering a little. "Thanks, Em."

"Of course." She smiled then pointed to the old phone. "You gonna tell me what's up with that?"

Eleanor laughed. "No, I better not. But…" She stopped, wondering if she should even mention it.

Emily blinked wide. "Don't do me like that!"

So she explained what happened with Avi at Thanksgiving. "What do I do?"

"Girl, you got more drama than me for once! What about Kitt?"

"I don't know!"

"Have you talked to Avi?"

"No."

"Are you going to?"

"He's my team lead. I'll have to talk to him at work tomorrow." She pulled her legs up and crossed them.

"Well, what do you want to do?"

Eleanor tucked her head into her knees and thought, *I really don't want to deal with any of this.* Instead she said, "Work on my Hacking project, I think."

"Oh, *lord*!" Emily was wearing a blue gingham dress, probably having been at some ritzy brunch.

Eleanor looked out the window somewhere far away, then something occurred to her. She began typing rapidly on her laptop.

"I'm gonna get a coffee then," Emily said with a lighthearted laugh.

When she returned, Eleanor raised her eyebrows and nodded at her computer with a smile. The terminal was scrolling rapidly with white text.

"Yeah, I don't know what that is, sweetie." Emily sipped an iced macchiato.

"Training data!" Eleanor felt energized from the coffee or maybe the code. Probably both. "I realized something wrong with my moderation algorithm and fixed it."

"That's wonderful." Emily swirled her drink before taking another sip.

"Well, that's going to take a while." Eleanor leaned back, looking at her friend. "I think I'm gonna keep using this phone for a while." She held it up with a smile.

"If that's your way of coping, then go for it."

"Life has felt quieter... more peaceful."

"It's also boring and stupider without this." Emily held up her own battered, well-loved smartphone.

"Maybe, but we treat it like a second brain. We stop remembering things because we can look it up like that." She snapped her fingers. "We stop making concrete plans because something better could always come up."

"But you love knowledge! That's, like, your schtick." Lines of concern formed around Emily's perfect no-makeup-look eyes.

"That's true, but I like having knowledge in my own brain. I like *understanding* it. Maybe it's better not to be connected to it all the time." Her mind was swimming with thoughts. *How do we know what decisions, thoughts, or wants are our own anymore? We don't spend time reflecting and forming our own opinions because we can instantly adopt an expert's views as our own and feel superior. Why ever be wrong when you can always be right?*

"Ellie, why don't we head back home? You look like you really need some rest. We can watch *Office Space* if you want?" She cracked a smile.

"Yeah, okay." She closed her laptop and got up, feeling dizzy. Deep down, she knew there was no coming back from the cliff she had jumped over. She could never see the world in the same way again.

But I won't be like Emmett either.

Eleanor still believed the world was a better place because of technology and innovation, and it was possible for the world to continue to improve.

Good and evil didn't exist. The world was more complicated than that, more nuanced. There was always more to the story, more information, a different perspective, more research to be done.

That's what Eleanor would do. She would dig deeper, try harder to see what was really going on. There was still good to be done, a chance to correct. She would make her voice heard.

SMS CONVERSATION

Eleanor
I'm back in ATL

Kitt
Hey! Sorry, I was mountain biking with some friends. Want to come over?

Eleanor
No worries. Feeling pretty beat probably wouldn't be much fun

Kitt
Ok, Wanna do lunch tomorrow then?

Eleanor
Sure

Kitt
Ok I'll come get you around noon

20

Eleanor arrived at the office the next day with a renewed sense of purpose, which she used to form a protective barrier around herself. There were many things she was going to have to face, and as she sat in her cubicle trying to perform her usual routine, something didn't feel right. The office seemed noisier than usual.

She set her old flip phone on the desk and stared at it in all its out-of-placeness, Emmett's words echoing in her mind. She sighed, opened her email, and tried to go through the 88 messages that had come since she was gone. Every time someone walked by, she would get distracted. She peeked over the cubicles; Avi wasn't there.

She read the high priority emails first, but nothing seemed relevant to her anymore. Every one of them had a response from Avi swiftly resolving the issue.

Then she saw Daryl walking through the hallway with his usual look of rushing around keeping busy with nothing specific and offering expertise to no one but wholly believing that he was.

He noticed Eleanor in her cube, probably actually looking for her, and rushed over. "Hi, glad to have you back." His fake grin indicated he didn't *really* care, but it was his job to pretend he did. "I'm sorry about your family situation."

Eleanor nodded but didn't say anything.

"I understand this was an emergency scenario, but please try not to be without your work laptop for extended periods of time. Your skills are sometimes needed in emergencies here too."

"Yes, I'm sorry." Eleanor stared straight into his eyes with a look that let him know she wasn't sorry at all, but she was pretending she was.

He turned his mouth up in a way that made Eleanor think he actually enjoyed her stubbornness. Maybe it made his job more interesting. "And did you see the email about company phones? I'd like you to get yours activated today."

"Uh, yes, but is the company phone a requirement?" She groaned internally.

"Yes," he said plainly.

"All right. Where do I go?"

"Just talk to Employee Care. They'll help you out." He started to walk away. "Oh, and say hi to Kitt for me."

"I'm sure you can tell him yourself at the bar later." She swiveled her chair around, feeling as if she'd won something, but she heard a deep sigh as he scurried off to his next confrontation.

She spent the morning getting caught up on work, starting on a feature marked "high priority" by Bethany.

She read the task summary:

We're introducing two new kinds of awards for posts in the Plaza. If a piece of content meets the requirements below, it will receive the award, which will give the post a special banner (see attached assets) for twenty-four hours. The user's Persona Photo will also receive a special banner for that period.

—Socrates Award: When a post has more than 10 comments, and the initial poster responds to at least two of them.

—Aphrodites Award: When an Observation receives more than 100 Cor.

She got started and worked till around lunch time when she got a calendar alert for a team lunch that she had no idea was happening. *Oh, shoot.*

Having been out for nearly a week, she knew skipping it was not an option. When she walked into the pizza place outside Agora headquarters, she saw most of her team milling around and talking, including Daryl and Bethany, and her heart bounced when she saw Avi talking with them. It quickly dropped again when she saw Kitt too.

Daryl was the first to make eye contact with her, and that one look let her know it was him who had invited Kitt, likely for the sole purpose of getting back at her for earlier. Kitt looked over and smiled when he saw her. "You said we could have lunch, remember? So Daryl invited me. I'm glad you're back!"

"Of course." She smiled, the corners of her eyes tightening.

Bethany threw her long arms out for an awkward hug. "Eleanor, I'm *so* glad you're back! It's been no fun without you."

When her eyes met Avi's, she knew everything that had happened at Thanksgiving was in fact real but that he was also trying to do the "right" thing and pretend nothing had. Or was he?

"Hey, Eleanor. We're glad to have you back." Avi spoke in that lyrical way with the roll of a long 'r' at the end of her name. She knew he meant it. "Even Daryl is glad you're back. He scheduled this lunch just for you." He smiled at Daryl.

"Oh, thanks." Eleanor was embarrassed by this, mostly because she didn't believe Daryl's intentions were good unlike Avi. She felt even more awkward when she found herself seated at the end of the table between Avi and Kitt with Daryl at the head. Charley and Reed sitting across from her had decided not to share their opinions on her return.

The general small talk of team lunches ensued, and knowing Daryl was watching her, Eleanor did her best to remain professional and indifferent to the men on either side of her.

"Oh, Bethany, I got started on the new award feature this morning," she said.

The bangles on Bethany's wrist clanked together as she stuck her fork into a bowl of leaves. "Isn't that *so* fun! I can't wait to see how our users like it."

"How is your sister doing?" Avi asked her at one point.

She made sure to answer in a way that didn't reveal he had already seen how she was doing. "She's having a hard time, but she's also stubborn about everything."

"I can't imagine just waking up not being able to see one day," Kitt said.

"It was hard to watch." She sighed, looking at her plate suddenly uninterested in the third piece of pizza she had put on it.

"It would probably be hard to work without vision," Daryl added, clearly not giving much thought to what they were talking about.

"You know, they've done studies on people who win the lottery or lose an arm, and they all return to their previous baseline happiness after a year." Kitt said. Eleanor decided to give him the benefit of the doubt. Maybe he was trying to be comforting.

"Oh, yeah, I think I've heard that." Eleanor briefly noticed Avi's hands tightening their grip. *Could this be any worse?*

"Daryl, what are we going to do for the holiday party this year?" Avi changed the subject.

The conversation went on from there until a few people at the other end of the table started looking at their phones, and the rumble of conversation grew followed by the pinging sounds of alerts. Eleanor watched everyone down the line tumble into the portal of their devices, their faces glowing with blue light as something viral began to unfold.

"What's going on?" She was completely out of the loop with no smartphone to check.

"Who knows." Avi was the last to take out his phone.

She leaned over to look at Kitt's screen and saw the headline: *NSA Is Collecting Information on Millions of Americans Daily.* She thought the National Security Agency was supposed to protect American citizens from foreign threats. What on earth did they want with millions of ordinary citizens' information?

Louder conversation began to erupt, and Eleanor felt instant tension around the table. Without her own screen to hole her gaze, all she could do was observe the mob response.

"A traitor… putting America's safety at risk," Charley said.

"We're practically living in a police state!" Reed agreed with him.

"Oh, no," Avi exhaled. She looked over at his phone and read a different headline: *Secret Program Gives NSA Backdoor Access to Agora Data.*

"Oh, shit." Eleanor knew that a headline like that with Agora's name in it was a big deal no matter what the truth of the situation was.

"What is the big deal exactly?" Kitt scratched his head.

Avi showed him the different headline they were reading. "Ah, well, a headline like that won't be good for business." Kitt seemed the least concerned of anyone at the table.

Everyone was reading a different news article with a different bias or information in it, and there was no way to know what the person next to them was reading.

"How could Agora let this happen?" Eleanor said.

"Maybe they didn't know?" Kitt suggested.

"I don't think the NSA could access Agora's servers without *someone* knowing," Avi replied.

Eleanor was eager to get back to her computer so she could see some of the news headlines for herself. Daryl didn't seem too thrilled and had a look that indicated he was more bothered by the stress and lack of productivity this situation would bring than anything else. "All right, everyone, let's get back. They will probably call an all-hands meeting," he huffed, waving the waitress down for the bill.

Eleanor excused herself from the table and rushed back to the office. While walking to her cubicle, she noticed everyone on the floor milling around, talking about the news. Finally alone at her desk, she opened several different news sites and skimmed all the articles they were headlining.

She felt like she was getting the general idea. Someone who worked for the NSA leaked a bunch of documents about a program focused on getting data from internet and communications companies, collecting everything from audio, video, and photos to emails, texts, and documents. The leaker claims the companies participated willingly.

One quote stood out to her: "Even low-level analysts are allowed to search and listen to the communications of Americans without court approval and supervision… They quite literally can watch your ideas form as you type." *What the hell, no way.*

Eleanor thought of every weird thing she had ever Googled and picture she had sent and felt a gross sensation at the idea that some stranger out there was sitting and looking at it. This sensation only grew as she read an account about how agents all sat around a table looking at women's nude photos.

Several of the companies, including Agora, had already released statements saying that they knew nothing about the program nor did they provide any government organizations with direct access to their servers.

Eleanor really hoped that was true. *To think that Agora would agree to that, or even help build the backdoor.* She shuddered.

A high priority email came across her screen inviting her to a mandatory meeting, as she expected. She clicked to join the live stream but didn't put her headphones on. Instead, she looked at the CEO she had been so taken by—he looked stiff and annoyed by the situation he'd been forced to deal with.

Eleanor could tell he was now giving one of his impassioned speeches about Agora's purpose to connect people and assuring them this current disturbance was merely the action of a rogue agent. At least that's what she assumed was being said, but she didn't care. She wasn't buying it this time.

She saw Kitt walking her way. "Looks like we're not getting any more work done today." He plopped into a chair with a relaxed smile. "Wanna go get a drink or something?"

"No…" *How could he just ignore this?*

"Well, duck out early and go hang out? The atmosphere is weird right now."

Confusion flooded her mind. "Aren't you bothered by this?"

"Should I be?" He didn't seem to be giving it a second thought.

"I don't know… I feel like this is pretty bad if it's true."

He shrugged. "We're already collecting and selling a lot of this data anyway."

"Yes, but isn't that anonymous? What they're saying the government is collecting is tied to each individual, to you and me. We'd no longer have any private life."

"If you have nothing to hide, why should it matter?" He ran his fingers through his hair.

"You don't really think that," she scoffed.

He thought for a moment. "No, you're right. I don't. But I also don't see what say I have in it. Someone else will fill my chair and do the work if I leave."

He had a point there. There was a perpetual cycle of people that would be so excited to work for Agora that they'd jump at the chance, no matter what they were asked to do. Like she had done. Some of them would eventually realize what they were doing, but most would probably never understand or, even worse, care. But she didn't think she could share this with Kitt, so all she did was sigh. "I just worry that we're not helping people but instead… using them for something."

"Isn't that how business goes?" Kitt seemed to be growing impatient.

"I don't think that necessarily has to be true. I mean, doctors aim to help people, not use them."

"I'm talking about corporations. Name a corporation that isn't exploiting people somehow to make their bottom line."

There was a time she would have had a simple smug answer: Agora. But she wasn't sure that was true anymore. Retail companies used factories, most of them full of people making things and working long hours for very little money. Then there were warehouses where people exhausted themselves in often dangerous conditions.

He continued, "At least now, workers have rights, salaries, vacation days, health insurance. Hell, I bet your distant relations owned slaves on that large property of yours up there."

"You mean workers in the US or Europe? There's tons of places still where people don't have that." She felt her voice rising. "Even if the quality of life now is better than it was 200 years ago, you're conflating the matter at hand."

"So what is it then?"

"That it's wrong to use people as a means to an end. People only have those rights because the companies are meeting the bare minimum requirements of regulations, not because they value the human beings doing the work. That's why they build factories in other countries, to get around those regulations. Then they use all their wealth to lobby the government to minimize those regulations."

"Yes, but isn't that the way human societies have always worked? There have always been people who manage to access more power and wealth than others."

"You're okay with maintaining that status quo? Shouldn't we all be working to make the world a better place for everyone?"

Kitt smiled at her now, in a way that implied that she was being adorable but naive. "Your brain is like that little Dig-Dug character from the arcade game, just digging deeper and deeper into things. But, Eleanor, the deeper you go, the more the falling rocks hurt."

This frustrated her rather than amused her. "So I'm wrong then?"

"Why does it have to be right or wrong? At some point, you have to take a break from debating good and evil and just enjoy the life you have."

She let out a long sigh and slumped back in her swivel chair.

"So what do you say? Let's duck out early and go have some fun?" He looked extra charming in a way that made her want to say yes, but she just couldn't.

"Sorry, I'm just not in the mood."

"All right." He looked genuinely disappointed, so Eleanor forced a reassuring smile as he waved goodbye.

She turned back to her computer, put her headphones on, and opened the code editor. She didn't want to think about all this right now, and the best way to divert her attention for hours was in code, solving problems.

People bustled around her or left the office early in little cliques, talking about the news, but Eleanor was there in the middle of it all, clicking away on her keyboard. She fixed several bugs and finished a small feature that she'd been working on.

Before she knew it, the whole afternoon had passed, and the office was dark. The grumble of her stomach convinced her it was probably time to quit. As she packed up her stuff, she noticed a message from Kitt blinking on the old flip phone. She ignored it, tossing it in her bag. As she started to leave, she spotted someone sitting in the cafe near the elevators. It was Avi.

"You weren't waiting on me, were you?" she said

He smiled, closing his laptop. "I was actually, but I didn't want to interrupt that crazy work ethic."

"I got a lot done."

"I know. I kept seeing those ticket complete emails popping up on my screen."

She smiled too, feeling the tension of the day start to melt away. "Well, I'm starving now."

"Let's go get something. I'm hungry too." His voice was warm and comforting.

NEW !!! HIGH PRIORITY EMAIL
SUBJECT: NEWS HEADLINES

Agora Family,

Regarding the slanderous accusations that are dominating the news channels today, I wanted to remind you all of a couple things.
Our customers' privacy and rights are of top priority.
It is advised that you **do not** speak to press for any reason and simply say "no comment" if approached.
Let's keep doing what we do best. This is just a minor stick in the path of our goal to connect the world.

Stay the course,

Matthew Erickson
Agora CEO

21

Avi and Eleanor made their way out into the cool winter evening and walked up the street to a place that served affordable, fast-casual Greek food. She ordered a platter that came with the works: Greek salad, a gyro, fries covered in feta cheese, hummus with olives, and pita bread.

While Avi gave his order at the counter, Eleanor slid into a booth and slipped her shoes off, tucking her feet underneath her legs. The place was more of a hole-in-the-wall than a top destination, but she loved that she could relax here. It seemed like every restaurant in town nowadays had large flat-screen TVs plastered on every wall, brightly flashing and inviting people's eyes to look at it instead of the person across from them. Thankfully, this place didn't have that.

Avi edged into the booth across from her. "This place is so cheap!"

"I told you! It's good food too. What'd you order?"

"Greek salad."

When their food came, they both chewed silently for a few minutes. Maybe he was as unsure as she was of how to begin.

"Well," Eleanor started, "what do you make of the big news today?"

"Not sure yet. Don't think this is the last we'll hear of this issue." He crunched on a mouthful of romaine lettuce. "There's stuff like it in India, but people want to think of America as much freer. We also don't have the largest Internet companies in the world on our soil."

"So you think it's true?"

"If you're asking if I think it's true the NSA is conducting surveillance programs, I wouldn't be surprised if they were. Now, whether Agora and all these other companies agreed to participate to this extent, I don't know. I'm not sure the NSA could get access to the servers on their own, so even if most of the company doesn't know, someone likely does, but I doubt we'll hear it from them."

"It just seems like people aren't concerned about it... or they're more concerned about the company's image or its stock value rather than such a huge infringement on people's privacy." She dipped warm pita bread into red-pepper hummus.

"When people are afraid, they will do anything to feel safe," he replied.

"But this doesn't make me feel safe. And it doesn't feel right to use Agora for that purpose."

"I really don't have many answers for you." He took another big bite before continuing. "But I think asking these questions and thinking about it is the right thing to do. I don't agree with what your—" He hesitated, and she realized he must have overheard her conversation with Kitt, "—friend said."

Her cheeks flushed slightly. "Yeah, neither do I."

"But learning to accept things as normal is another way we protect ourselves, I think."

Avi's mind never ceased to surprise her—always trying to empathize with people and find some good in them. It wasn't because he wanted something from them; it was just that he seemed determined to find a reason to treat everyone with respect, even those people Eleanor was convinced didn't deserve it. *Is there anything in the world he wants other than to help others?* she thought.

They continued eating until their plates were mostly cleared. The discussion they were both avoiding inevitably had to come up.

"Eleanor…" He hesitated. "I'm not sure how to approach the topic."

"I know… Me either." She smiled. "I thought I may have dreamt it at first."

"If you want to forget it happened, we can." His voice was steady, and his eyes communicated he was more interested in her happiness than his own.

This pained Eleanor more than she thought it would. "Is that what you want?"

"No…" He shook his head. The long 'o' sound of his speech lingered in the air.

"I don't either." The words were out of her mouth before she had a chance to think about them.

A slow smile crept across his face, and the way his happy eyes looked directly into hers made Eleanor's heart skip.

"But," she continued, "I don't want to have to change teams."

"Ya," Avi seemed to have already considered the dilemma. "In general, two people under the same manager can't be in a relationship."

The idea of Daryl finding out about her and Avi made the blood rush to her ears. There was no question he would use any drop of information at his disposal against her.

Avi folded his fingers and rested his chin on them. "This certainly places me in an unexpected ethical gray area."

Join the club, Eleanor thought. "I don't really know what to do, but can we just agree not to say anything to Daryl for now?" she pleaded.

"Yeah… okay," he said, reluctantly.

"I mean we don't even know if…" she stopped.

"It would go anywhere?" He understood her thought process.

"Yeah…" She looked away, thinking she'd said the wrong thing.

"You're right." He smiled. "Practical Eleanor."

She didn't feel at all practical just now. She had made no accommodations for the awkwardness that could ensue if she and

Avi didn't wind up becoming serious. What if someone were to find out that they were a couple? Worse, what was she going to do about Kitt? Not that they'd agreed on any kind of formal relationship, but still. She pushed all that out of her mind for now. "So we play it cool?"

"Sure, let's just see where it goes." He began to clear the table, stacking up all their plates and silverware.

Leaving the restaurant, they stepped back out into the cool, December evening. She shivered in a stream of wind that howled between the tall skyscrapers. They began walking up Peachtree Street in the direction of their apartments.

The sky was clear of clouds, but the city's lights were too bright for her to see any stars. There was a new moon, and as Eleanor looked up into the black sky, she realized it was so different from the one she'd looked up at in Aska Valley. She felt like she was wandering around in the dark with no light to guide her. She stuck her hands in her jacket pocket and stared at the ground instead.

"In all the chaos, I forgot to ask how your moderation project is coming." He wrapped a plaid scarf around his neck.

She'd almost forgotten. "Oh, yeah! I actually had a breakthrough with it yesterday. I've been feeding it training data. I haven't had a chance to test it yet though."

"Awesome. Don't give up on it," he reassured her.

When they reached her apartment, she let her eyes meet his. "This is me."

His breath was puffing into the air. "I hate the cold." He laughed lightly into his wool scarf, and his quilted down jacket brushed against her arm. He always dressed so nicely.

"Me too..." She continued to stand there instead of going inside.

He took off his scarf and wrapped it around her, his familiar woody smell enveloping her, the wool soft on her cheeks. All that had happened today slipped out of her mind as she reached out for Avi's hand, giving him a look that said *don't go*.

He leaned in to kiss her, gently in a way that said *I have to*. But she kissed him back, wrapping her arms around his neck, feeling the transfer of heat between them. He put his arms around her and held her tight before picking her up lightly and setting her next to the door. "Goodnight, Eleanor," he whispered as he pulled away.

She watched him walk up the street before heading up to her apartment and collapsing into bed, exhausted.

AGORA COMPANY CELL PHONE POLICY

For the purpose of this policy, the term "cell phone" is defined as any handheld electronic device with the ability to receive and/or transmit voice, text, or data messages without a cable connection. The Company reserves the right to modify or update these policies at any time.

Use of Cell Phones

While at work, employees are expected to exercise the same discretion in using personal cell phones as with company phones. Excessive personal calls during the workday, regardless of the phone used, can interfere with employee productivity and be distracting to other employees.

Employees should restrict personal calls during work time and should use personal cell phones only during scheduled breaks or lunch periods in non-working areas. Other personal calls should be made during non-work time whenever possible, and employees should ensure that their friends and family members are instructed of this policy.

To ensure the effectiveness of meetings, employees are asked to leave all cell phones at their desks. On the unusual occasion of an emergency or anticipated emergency that requires immediate attention, the cell phone may be carried to the meeting on vibrate mode.

Company-Issued Cell Phones

The Company may issue phones to employees whose jobs require them to make calls while away from work or require them to be accessible for work-related matters. Cell phones issued by the Company are Company property. Employees must comply with Company requests to make their Company-issued cell phones available for any reason including upgrades, replacement, or inspection.

Employees who leave the Company for any reason must return their Company-issued cell phones.

Personal Use of Company Owned Cell Phones

Company-issued cell phones are to be used only for business purposes. Although occasional, brief personal phone calls using a Company-issued phone are permitted, personal use that exceeds this standard will result in discipline up to and including termination.

Security of Company-Issued Cell Phones

Employees are responsible for the security of Company-issued cell phones and the information stored on them. Always carry it with you; never leave the cell phone unattended. If lost or stolen, you must immediately notify the same to the Company.

Effect of Policy

Violations of the foregoing rules will be considered a serious offense and may result in the imposition of discipline up to and including termination.

22

———

Over the next few days, the NSA leaks continued to dominate the news as the person responsible came forward to speak out against the mass surveillance operation. The office buzzed with the topic every time a new article came out, and Eleanor had no doubt there was a dip in productivity the rest of that week. Daryl walked around looking annoyed, and the large conference rooms were regularly filled with C-Suite executives engaged in tense-looking conversations.

Eleanor remained in her corner, trying to work and hoping to avoid most of it. She checked in on the news occasionally because she was curious. In fact, she was convinced she was more intrigued by the topic than most of the Agora staff, whose interest, she was pretty sure, was to gossip for gossip's sake.

She watched the leaker livestream a speech from a Russian airport and found herself moved by his words. He seemed just like many of the guys she'd worked with—casually dressed, well educated, and a little awkward. He didn't seem at all like a person who would want fame and certainly not the kind that drove him away from his home and family. Eleanor saw him as a person who had acted out of a deep sense of morality and a desire for a better world, even if his life would never be the same. Not everyone felt this way, of course.

While she was listening to him talk, she took out her notebook and wrote down something he said: *I don't want to live in a world where everything I say, everything I do, everyone I talk to, every expression of creativity and love or friendship is recorded.*

Eleanor felt the same way, and suddenly all her fears about contributing to the opposite washed over her again. Her calendar chimed an alert for her monthly one-on-one meeting with Daryl, and she sighed, collecting her laptop and making her way to a small conference room. She hated these rooms. They were boxy and claustrophobic.

Daryl was already there waiting, so she closed the door and sat down across from him with a bland smile. He was clacking away at his keyboard in a hurried kind of way, and when he finished whatever communication he was working on, he looked up and greeted Eleanor.

"So how's it going?" he said.

"Fine, just trying to stay busy among the chaos." She didn't often say much in these meetings. Any real problem she would take to Avi. This was all required protocol.

"Ah, yes." He rolled his eyes. "Been quite the week. You attended the meeting about it on Monday? You're clear on everything?"

"Um, yes, I think so. I am concerned, though." The words came out before she knew what she was saying.

"Regarding the media approaching you? Yes, there have been some press outside the building."

"No, about Agora giving all its data to the government. It doesn't seem right."

"Rest assured, this is just a publicity stunt. Agora values the privacy of our customers and does not give direct access to our servers to anyone." He sounded like he was speaking from a script.

Eleanor noticed his statement didn't really cover the protection of people's privacy despite its claim to. She also knew this conversation with Daryl wasn't getting her anywhere. He seemed to have completely bought into Agora's narrative and would do anything to protect it.

"Okay." She gave a fake smile.

"Moving on, I have some good news for you actually!"

"Oh?" She shifted in her seat a little.

"You're being promoted to Senior Developer. Congratulations." Daryl straightened his tie.

Eleanor felt a sense of pride mixed with confusion, but seeing Daryl's eyes close in on her, she quickly corrected her reaction. "Wow, that's amazing!" She smiled like it was the best news she'd had in a while, and maybe it was.

"Well, you've done great work with Bethany, and Avi's told me about your Hacking project, so good job. You can talk to Employee Care about the details. Any questions for me?"

Eleanor said she didn't have any and thanked him again as she knew it was expected, and they parted ways, him scurrying off to some other meeting.

Leaving the conference room, she saw Kitt sitting in a large pod chair waving to her. "Hey!" He looked chipper. "So, what's the good news?"

"What?" Eleanor said absentmindedly.

"Your promotion, of course. Didn't you just come from talking with Daryl?"

"Oh, yeah." *I got a promotion. Shouldn't I be happy?*

"He told me. Hope you don't mind. I'm really happy for you!"

"Thanks." Bewildered, she sat down across from him.

"God, I'm so glad it's Friday. Where you want to go tonight?"

She tilted her head sideways feeling all the conflicting thoughts roll to one side.

"We have to celebrate, of course."

Eleanor couldn't help thinking this next ascension up the corporate ladder wasn't as fulfilling as she'd hoped it would be. This was another box she could check, and yet she wasn't feeling the satisfaction she normally felt with her achievements.

"Hey, Kitt, the other day you mentioned we're selling our user data. What exactly does that mean? Who do we sell it to?"

"*That* again?" She could tell he was only acting annoyed as he actually enjoyed talking about his work. "Well, surely you know ads are one of the main ways we make money?"

"Yes, I mean, I get the main idea. Someone looks at shoes on another website, and we show targeted advertising for that product, the creepy stuff following you around thing. But where exactly does that data come from?"

"Well, the more data we have, the more specific and personalized the ads can be, which generally makes them more effective, and then we can charge more. So this is something I've been working on actually. It's called the Agora Beacon." He set his laptop aside and leaned forward a little. "Well, it's a bit of code that other websites include that sends us information about what people do on those sites. That's why if you look at a pair of shoes on one site, you might get an ad for them on Agora."

"You're telling me the shoe store website adds the Agora… Beacon thing to their site so they can better advertise on Agora?"

"Basically."

"But how do they decide who sees what? They can't just show someone every shoe they look at."

"Bingo. This is where my specialty comes in. Predictive analytics." His face was growing more animated.

Eleanor nodded for him to continue.

"Well, the simplest explanation is that using all this data we've mined, I can build statistical models of people's behavior that predicts what they might do. So I can create groups of people that are most likely to buy said pair of shoes, and the shoe company purchases advertisements for that segment."

"And how do they buy these… groups of people?"

"Well, there's a marketplace for advertisers basically. Anyone from small businesses to larger companies can use it. They can use keywords to find the right demographic in their budget."

"But anyone can use this? For anything?" Eleanor tied her hair back in a bun.

"I mean, I suppose, yeah."

"So I could start a website all about how The South will rise again, complete with rebel flags and Dixie playing, and then I could buy a rural southern demographic and market it to them?"

Kitt laughed. "Well, that would be an odd thing for *you* to do, but yeah, I suppose you could."

"But then what determines how the ads get shown to the user?"

"That's where the new Plaza 2.0 algorithm is going to come in."

"That's just a simple ranking system. I didn't include anything for ads."

Kitt looked surprised. "I thought Bethany told you. They spun up a whole team for that. Your feature was just a test. They're working on something much more complicated."

"Oh, I mean I knew that could be a thing, but I didn't realize it already was." *I was only gone a week.*

"Well, I guess you were out for a bit." He ran his fingers through his hair somewhat uncomfortably. "I'm sure you'll meet with them at some point."

"So how exactly does it work?" she asked.

"Well, I couldn't tell you all that. I'm a data wrangler." His hand had dropped back to his side, and he spoke with the assurance of knowing this was how things worked. "Often they're using keywords to search our database and find the most engaging content for each user—that SmartData thing you implemented a while back is part of it too."

She had almost forgotten about that. "What's happening to Agora?"

"It's growing, Eleanor." He tapped his foot, and she noticed he was wearing boat shoes without socks.

I actually liked this guy?

There was a gnawing feeling of resistance in her gut. "Growth doesn't have to be like this. And what about all the NSA stuff?"

He rolled his eyes. "Do you actually think there's *ever* been private communication, even before the Internet? Mail used to get opened all the time. Hell, postcards didn't even attempt to cover the writing. Phones could be tapped… The telegraph was like an open chat room, for God's sake!"

She blinked at him. "That doesn't mean we can't do better."

He leaned back in his chair and took on his trademark smirk. "You're so naive."

She was getting seriously irritated. It was like being back in college. The way he was looking at her was so reminiscent of the looks she'd receive from so many of the guys she'd been in class with. He saw her as entertainment at best and a nuisance at worst.

She stood up, clutching her laptop close. "You're so arrogant!"

He didn't budge. "We're *all* arrogant. That's why we're here. Only the best can do what we do." He crossed his arms over his chest, waiting to see how she would react to that.

But she wasn't going to concede. "Not *everyone* here is like that. Now, if you'll excuse me, I have lots of work to do."

She stomped back to her desk, cheeks burning, and spent the rest of the day getting her moderation tool polished and ready to share with the committee.

AGORA ASSEMBLY
CONTENT POLICY COMMITTEE (PRIVATE)

New Dialogue by Eleanor Crawford

Hi everyone! I've been working on a tool to help automate some of the content moderation and would love to demo it at the next meeting.

Comments:

> **Jeff**
> That would be awesome! Things are quiet right now, but we will definitely meet after the new year.

23

———

December passed quickly for Eleanor. Her new senior role brought more work with it. Her weekends were spent visiting Anne. In that time, she worked on task after task that Bethany brought to her, usually along with some kind of update she found exciting about the uptick in engagement time and interactions on the platform. "More than ever before!" Bethany had jingled her arms in excitement.

Eleanor rolled her eyes through meetings during which Daryl reported the increasing ad revenue the mobile app was bringing in. She spent every spare moment she had improving the algorithm on her Hacking project. Avi took his annual two weeks off to go to India to visit his family, and Eleanor had never been more uninterested in work.

Before she knew it, the Christmas holiday was finally upon her, and she couldn't wait to get away. Her duffel bag was stuffed with sweaters and scarves, and just like that, a flurry in the air swept her back home to Aska Valley.

She was sure a few days at home, at Grayson House, and all the holiday festivities were just what she needed to take her mind off Agora.

. . .

After work, she drove straight to Grayson House to see if her dad needed any help. As she pulled up the familiar driveway, the trees, now bare of leaves, allowed the great house to be seen in all its glory. Holly twisted around the large white pillars, and pots of poinsettias lined the porch.

In the lobby, the large Christmas tree they set up every year stood with its pine needles reaching out in all directions and the top almost touching the ceiling, but, so far, lights were its only decorations.

"Ellie, great!" Her dad pulled her into a hug. "We waited for you to get here before we decorated the tree."

"Thanks, Dad." She waved at her mom standing behind the front desk.

Anne was sitting in a chair near the Christmas tree, and Eleanor went to hug her as well. When she noticed that Anne's clothes didn't match, her dad chimed in. "Anne's been dressing herself this week. She's making great progress."

His look warned Eleanor not to say anything discouraging. "That's great. I'm so glad to be home for a few days."

The four of them spent the next hour hanging ornaments on the large tree, Eleanor and her dad taking turns placing the least breakable ones in Anne's hands and hovering nearby while she reached for a spot to hang each one.

"So, Ellie, did you invite your friend to join us again?" her mom asked.

"Who? Avi?"

"Yes, he's welcome to come to dinner again."

"Thanks, but he's actually out of town visiting family."

"Oh, how nice." She smiled. "Where does he originate from?"

"India."

A snort came from Anne, then Eleanor began to laugh.

Their mother simply blinked. "Well, I didn't want to assume."

When the decorating was finished, Anne and Eleanor found a spot on the couch in front of the fireplace.

"So how's it been going?" Eleanor asked.

"I'm like a toddler."

"I'm sure you're not. It's only been, what, a month."

"Well, I'm tired of sitting around in the dark. I can't do anything myself. I can't drive anywhere, cook for myself, draw, watch TV. I can't *do* anything."

"Anne…" Eleanor felt her heart racing at the thought of being in Anne's situation and felt she had no way to comfort her. She stared at the Christmas tree as its lights began to twinkle.

But then something occurred to Eleanor. "Listen, I know you feel this way right now, and it's completely justified. You may have lost a certain amount of physical independence you can't get back, but you haven't lost the independence of your mind. You can still think for yourself, and that's what matters. You are still Anne."

Anne scooted closer and rested her head on her sister's shoulder. After a while she began to doze off. Eleanor stared at the flickering flame and thought hard about how she might be able to help Anne. *I need to do some research.*

The next day was the Christmas parade and tree lighting festival in town, events that Eleanor deeply loved. The Crawfords, dressed in red and green sweaters, drove downtown together, singing Christmas carols. Anne looked happy to be taking part in something that wasn't a struggle for her.

Main Street was full of people walking around, tents set up with food and vendors. All the shops along the street were decorated with lights and wreaths.

Anne's art club from school had a fundraising tent selling hot chocolate, so they all stopped by and bought a cup. Her friends swarmed her with hugs and chatter.

"AP art just isn't the same without you." A redhead girl said, then immediately clamped her mouth shut as if mentioning art at all was wrong.

Another said, "Yeah, Mr. Bender doesn't even seem to know what to do without you there calling him out on stuff."

The pity on their faces was a bit too much to handle, and even though Anne couldn't see it, Eleanor figured her sister could sense it.

Since she still needed to do a little more Christmas shopping, she interjected with a wave and said, "I'm gonna walk around a bit I'll catch up with ya'll."

She walked past the fully decorated tree whose lights weren't on yet and began to go through the list in hear head. She always bought a book for her dad. *That's already done.*

She'd gone to a nice art supply store in Atlanta and bought some paints for her mom, and while she would normally have done the same for Anne, she knew that wouldn't work this year. She also wanted to buy Avi something, although she had no idea what.

First priority—Anne. She walked the familiar downtown streets with the merry refrains of "Silent Night" and "O Come, All Ye Faithful" around her, and she found herself humming along. She walked past the quirky pet supply store, a boutique with flowery dresses and gaudy jewelry, and a bookshop that specialized in rare old books on southern history.

She came across a stall with some handmade quilts, and one jumped out at her right away. Each square of the quilt featured a different flower or plant, but together they didn't form a flat pattern. They were made of unique, three-dimensional fabrics. She imagined Anne being able to actually touch the blanket and feel what was on it. Eleanor was certain Anne would love the distinctively textured designs, so she bought it.

Okay… now what do I get Avi? she thought.

She walked by the stalls, many of which had different types of art, but she didn't think anything like that was right. In one of the shops, she found herself looking at a merino wool sweater in a rich burgundy color. She imagined what it might look like on Avi and felt it was just the kind of thing he would wear.

A sweater could be kind of a lame, but Avi is practical and minimalist. He will like something he can wear, I think.

She bought the sweater and found her family by the large

Christmas tree in the center of town. Several people Eleanor knew were talking with her parents and giving hugs to Anne. It was almost dark now, and she could hear the marching band playing "Jingle Bells" as the parade moved by. It was the same as always, and yet, somehow, it felt different to Eleanor.

Growing up, she used to wonder if every place was like this—filled with old historical buildings, generations of families that all know each other, and people's beliefs unchanging.

But here were all these people gathered in one place to celebrate a holiday—those who had lived here their whole lives and those visiting from all over the world. It wasn't so small anymore, and it wasn't unchanging either. The coffee shop had free WiFi, restaurants were allowed to serve alcohol now, and there was a Starbucks in town.

Eleanor had always wanted the outside world to find its way to Aska Valley, but now that it had, she wasn't so sure it was a good thing.

Watching the twenty-foot Christmas tree light up the town, instead of being mesmerized by the lights and ornaments, she looked at the faces of the people around it. She couldn't imagine life without moments like these. The glowing faces of those sharing this moment gave her the sense everyone there felt the same thing. She took out her old flip phone and snapped a grainy, low-quality photo and sent it to Avi.

"You still using that old thing?" Her dad looked amused.

"Yeah." She stuffed it back into her jeans pocket.

"Seems like it might be sacrilege in your line of work."

"Maybe. Work actually gave me a phone, but I only use it when I have to."

His face grew serious. "Are you holding a grudge because of your sister's accident?"

The question took her by surprise. "Well, I hadn't thought of it that way but maybe."

"Don't be afraid of things… Be afraid of how people use things." He put his arm around her.

"That's exactly what I'm afraid of," she said, looking at the tree.

Eleanor spent Christmas Eve preparing for the Grayson House dinner—making up the menus and helping set up the dining room by wrapping tinsel around the chairs, stringing lights over the fireplace, and placing red bows and tall candles around the room. Every table had a vase filled with aromatic pine, bright white magnolias, and red roses. Eleanor felt like a Christmas fairy, dancing around, waving her wand to make the place a sparkling wonderland.

While her dad was out leading a hiking group, she went to his office to take a break for lunch. While she was eating, Emmett popped his head in the door. The embarrassed look on his face when he saw Eleanor made it clear he had been looking for her dad. She gave him a half-smile. "He's out with the hiking group."

"Ah, well—" He cleared his throat, "—mind if I join ya for a few?"

"Um, sure." *What does he want?*

He sat down across from her, looking a bit uncomfortable. "Listen, I wanted to apologize about our last conversation. It may have gotten a little out of hand."

Now Eleanor was the one embarrassed. She'd hoped to never think about it again, much less talk about it with Emmett. "No, you don't have to."

"I mean, I still think what you're doing is wrong, but I shoulda kept it to myself."

What an ineffective apology. "Does disapproving of someone's work mean you have to automatically disapprove of them?"

He rested his hand on his scruffy chin and thought a moment. "No, I s'pose not."

Although Emmett was supposedly near Eleanor's age, she noticed he looked a good bit older. He already had those little lines around his eyes that made him look tired and troubled. "Emmett, where did you work before you came here?"

"This is my first job out of college."

That's a two-year gap. "But you…"

"Yeah, I took some time off," he interrupted her.

She sat quietly, waiting to see if he would tell her more about it.

"I… was a bit lost after graduation, and I decided to hike the Appalachian Trail."

She had thought him awfully lanky. Walking 2,000 miles has a way of paring a person to their lightest possible state. "Really? That's amazing. I've always wanted to do that." She was impressed.

He let out a genuine chuckle. "A city slicker like you?" But he seemed happy someone was interested in this thing he had done.

Even though he was teasing, Eleanor felt compelled to say, "*This is my home.*" She gestured at the ground beneath her feet.

A look of mutual understanding passed between them, and some of the tension started to melt away. She peppered him with questions about what it was like to hike the whole trail through, and he seemed happy to answer them.

"There's just something about it… You have time to think out there. Just you and God's world."

"Yeah, it feels like no one spends time with themselves anymore," she agreed.

"You get a chance to figure out what really matters."

The trail always felt like this mythical entity to Eleanor. She knew it was a journey that lots of people chose to go on. Some didn't make it to the end, and some did. But mostly, she knew everyone had their own reasons for taking it on. "Why did you decide to do it?"

"Well—" He hesitated, "—it was after my dad died."

"I'm sorry…" There wasn't much else for her to say.

"My mom died when I was a kid, and my dad never really recovered from that." He stared out the window. "I had nothing left, so I walked to Maine."

"But you came back?"

He nodded. "I learned I could survive anywhere, but only this place was home. I came back, looked for work, and found the posting your parents put up. They didn't even know me, but they treated me like family right away."

She smiled. "I always thought that particular skill of theirs is why this place is so successful."

"I'm grateful to them. It made me feel like I can still have a family even though mine is gone."

"I'm glad you found that here," she said, and she meant it.

He looked back at her. "I guess I couldn't understand why someone would leave this." He tilted his chin up at her as if this were a question but not one he wanted to ask directly. "But we all have our reasons."

She had been thinking about it herself lately, but she didn't have a clear answer. "I don't know... I thought I had to. Staying in this town seemed like a kind of failure to me, I think. The world was happening *out there*, and I had to go be part of it."

"Well, you definitely are helping change the world, for better or for worse." She sensed the hints of disapproval seeping back into his speech. "So if that's what you wanted, then I say you're successful."

"Yeah..." She didn't feel successful at the moment. "I notice the older I get, the less black and white the world is. Everything is so complicated, it makes me dizzy sometimes, ya know?"

His shoulders rose with a dry laugh. "Yeah, I hear that."

"Well, I'd better get back to work." She picked up her now empty plate.

"Yeah, me too." He stood up. "It was... nice talking to you."

They both exchanged smiles that agreed on a kind of truce and went their separate ways.

By dinner time, pretty much everything was done. Eleanor looked out the window and saw the long driveway lit up with strings of lights hugging each tree. She and her dad drove toward home where they would all spend the evening making cookies and watching Christmas movies.

On Christmas Day, they woke up to find big, fluffy snowflakes falling from the sky and tufting on the ground. Eleanor looked in amazement. She only ever remembered having a white Christmas maybe once in her life.

When they were kids, snow meant school would be canceled, and Eleanor and Anne would twist their scarves on with their puffy coats and gloves and run outside to play for hours. In Aska Valley, snow was rare enough to be fun and usually not a pain.

This morning, they enjoyed the snow from inside, watching it from the tall picture windows while eating breakfast and exchanging gifts.

When it was time to get ready, Eleanor carefully curled her hair and slipped into a red sweater dress with black tights and boots. She loved getting all dressed up on Christmas.

Around lunch time, it was off to Grayson House to preside over the holiday festivities.

When the Crawfords arrived at the inn, Christmas was already in full swing. There were children outside playing in the snow, likely a welcome surprise for those that had never seen snow before. Inside, the halls echoed with jolly music, and there were even some couples dancing in the ballroom. The table for gingerbread cookie decorating was crowded with kids covered in icing while their smiling parents dabbed them with napkins.

Her dad was beaming. This was his favorite spectacle to put on every year. He bowed to his wife, offered his hand for a dance, and the two of them spun away.

Eleanor saw Anne smile and said, "Dad's having fun as usual."

"I figured. He's like a kid." Anne laughed.

"Well, what would you like to do?" Eleanor had her arm wrapped in Anne's.

"Let's see if there's a fire in the fireplace."

"Sounds good." The two sisters made their way to the dining room where the large stone fireplace was crackling with warmth. Eleanor carefully pulled up a chair for Anne and another for herself.

"Alright, Eleanor, you've been home all this time and barely told me anything that's going on in your life. Tell me about the world outside."

Eleanor stretching out a curl of hair. "Lord, I don't know. There's not much to tell. I mostly just go to work."

"Please, I know you've got a man in your life. Is it the one you brought to Thanksgiving?"

"Maybe." Eleanor took off her scarf, feeling warm from the fire.

"Well, I already know he likes you."

The music changed to "Jingle Bells," and Eleanor scooted closer so she could hear better. "And how do you know that?"

Her sister shrugged. "I can tell by the way he talks to you."

"You can? How?"

"It's my superpower now—hearing."

Eleanor frowned. "Really?"

"Yeah, I mean it's weird. I know it hasn't been that long, but I've been relying so much more on sounds that it's, like, stronger, I guess. And there's just something in his voice when he talks to you. It's very caring."

"Well, Avi is a kind person in general."

"Yeah, it does seem that way."

Behind them, the dining room was ready for the Christmas dinner that was set to begin any minute now. All the candles Eleanor had set out were lit, and the room had a joyful glow to it. There were Christmas crackers at each place setting above the gold-rimmed porcelain dinnerware.

Anne continued to press for information. "I think you like him too even if you won't admit it."

"I mean, I do, but he's my colleague and my superior, so it's tricky."

"Ah, I see. Poor ethical Ellie can't follow her heart." Anne gave her a teasing smile.

The volume of the music receded, and they heard their dad ringing the bell to announce dinner. Eleanor helped Anne to her seat before everyone crowded in, then country ham, mashed potatoes, butter beans, sweet potatoes, creamed spinach, yeast rolls, and sweet tea filled the table as quickly as the guests did. This time, their mother sat to the right of their dad, and Eleanor and Anne on the left.

She watched Anne eat and noticed that she'd already begun to move slower and more carefully. There was a grace to her movements she found beautiful in this moment, but she imagined it would grow tiresome if it had to be repeated in everyday life. Eleanor thought it might be like always having to walk through quicksand.

As the dinner went on into dessert, Eleanor felt a fullness in her heart that was warmer than the fire that heated the room.

NEW EMAIL

SUBJECT: HAPPY HOLIDAYS

Happy Holidays Agora Family,

No matter what you celebrate this time of year, I hope everyone is taking a little time off to rest, rejuvenate, and spend time with their families. Every day, I'm inspired by the work you do and the future we are building together.

Now for the moment you all are waiting for… the Agora Holiday Perk Pack! All employees will receive:

- A salary bonus equal to 5% of their annual salary
- Gift cards to local restaurants
- This year's brand new apparel item

And after the new year, we get back to connecting the world.

Matthew Erickson
Agora CEO

24

———————

When the Christmas holiday came to an end, Eleanor again found herself looking at Aska Valley in her rear-view mirror. Avi was back from vacation and had invited her to spend New Year's Eve together.

She'd carefully wrapped his gift and spent a little extra time getting ready. She didn't know exactly what he had planned, but she wanted to look nice. She chose a fawn-colored sweater dress with black tights, and since it was still rather cold, she pulled out the navy-blue wool coat from the back of her closet.

She placed a loose knitted hat, the same color as her dress, on her head, carefully tucking and fixing the curls. She dabbed some perfume on her wrists then slipped on her boots and was out the door. Avi had insisted on meeting her downstairs and walking over with her.

When she came out of the elevator and saw Avi standing outside, she felt a sudden flutter of anxiety about what she had gotten into. *I'm about to spend an entire evening with my team lead.* But then he waved at her, smiled in his relaxed way, and all her anxieties melted away. She stepped into the chill of the last night of the year. "Hey! Hope you haven't been waiting long."

"No, not too long." Avi was wearing a wool hat that covered his ears. The two of them set off up the street. "I can't believe I missed the snow." Some patches of ice and snow remained from the weather they'd had on Christmas, but the road and sidewalks were clear.

"Yeah, it was really pretty. My parents invited you to Christmas dinner, by the way." She stopped to push the button for a crosswalk.

"That was nice of them." They crossed the street, then Avi said, "Who do they think I am?"

"My colleague." She smiled. "But Anne's not dumb, and my mom suspects."

"Congrats on your promotion by the way. Sorry I wasn't there when he announced it."

"Thanks…" She looked up the road to the crowd gathered in Piedmont Park for fireworks and a block party.

"Alright, here we are." He gestured awkwardly toward the large building in front of them then opened the door for her.

Is he… nervous? She smiled to herself.

They rode the elevator up to the 25th floor, and Eleanor was happy to walk down a hallway that didn't smell like a frat house. He opened the door to a modest, single-bedroom apartment.

The place was spotless and minimalist. It seemed like the few things Avi owned were selected very carefully for their quality. She found herself enveloped in the same smell she associated with Avi but something else too.

"I'm making dinner." He took off all his outdoor winter attire and tucked it into a closet while slipping his shoes off.

Judging by how spotless the place was, Eleanor assumed she should take her shoes off as well. She unzipped her boots and set them next to his and placed the present she'd brought for him on the coffee table. "It smells great. I didn't know you liked to cook."

He went to the kitchen and put something in the oven. Then he washed his hands and began chopping vegetables. "Yeah, there's something relaxing about it."

"I mostly eat out." She slid onto a barstool at the counter. "Can

I help with anything?" A small dining table had already been set with plates, silverware, and candles.

"No, it'll be ready soon. So how was your holiday?"

"It was nice! The usual pomp and circumstance at the inn, and it was nice to spend some time with Anne."

"How is she doing?" He looked up from chopping.

"I don't know. She's having a hard time adjusting for sure. She was—well is—such an independent person. She feels she's lost that."

"She will find a way to have it again, and you'll help her. I know you will."

She gave a half smile. "I hope so. I feel somewhat helpless. I'm taking her to the Center for the Visually Impaired here in Atlanta soon though."

"I didn't even know we had one of those. What do they do exactly?"

"They just have a lot of classes and resources from what I understand. The doctor mentioned it might be a good thing to try. I figure at the very least, it will give Anne a chance to meet some other people who are facing her same challenges."

"I think that's a great idea." Avi smiled at her then began mixing up a salad.

A timer beeped, and Eleanor watched him take what looked like lasagna from the oven and set it out on the table. "I think we're ready." He said, bringing over the salad and a bottle of wine.

"This is lovely." She smiled as she sat down across from him.

"I'm glad to be home." He filled both their glasses with a ruby-red liquid and began serving the food.

Eleanor felt relieved to hear that this was where Avi felt at home. "Okay, tell me about your trip now."

"Ah, it wasn't too exciting really. Visited with my parents and some extended family. Went to a wedding."

"Oh?" She looked up from her plate.

"My mom was playing matchmaker too, of course." He looked amused.

"Classic."

"I told her I'm not ready to get married right now."

Eleanor raised an eyebrow, only thinking for a moment what that meant about her relationship with him. But then, she didn't want to get married either.

He gave a nod that seemed to understand her thought. "And Indian families don't exactly encourage marrying outside of our… culture." He let out a dry chuckle.

"Another universal truth," she laughed. "I don't think I want to get married anyway. It doesn't really make sense anymore."

"That's fair." His face showed no indication that he was in agreement or bothered by her thoughts on this. They both took bites of their dinner.

"This food is really good." It wasn't lasagna but was clearly inspired by it. "What is it exactly?"

"I'm glad you like it! It's my own creation. I love Italian food, but I also twisted some of my own cuisine in there."

"Avi! You're a food artist, and I didn't even know it." She ate every bite on her plate.

When they finished eating, he cleared away the plates, and she sat down on a black leather sofa with a second glass of wine.

He joined her, holding a small, wrapped box. "I brought something back for you."

"I got you something too." She handed him his gift.

Unwrapping the brown paper, she found a beautiful powder-blue pashmina scarf. *Thank goodness I'm not the only one who bought clothes.* She ran the luxurious fabric across her hands. "It's beautiful, thank you."

"I'm glad you like it. I know how practical you are."

She watched him open his present and was glad to see him smile. "We're such utilitarian gift givers." He held up his glass for a toast. "I love it, thank you."

"I was afraid of being *too* utilitarian." She laughed. "Speaking of which, you don't have a TV?"

"Eh, I just don't watch a lot of TV. When I do, I usually just use my laptop in the bedroom. I've moved around so much in the past couple years, it's just easier to have less stuff."

"That makes sense."

He ran to the kitchen and came back with a Lemon Lush dessert.

"Oh my gosh, that's beautiful!" It had a nutty shortbread crust and fluffy yellow mousse.

As unromantic as Eleanor figured it was, she decided to bring up what Kitt told her about Agora's Ad Market.

"Hmm…" Avi put his arm on the back of the couch and rested his head on it. "That's a bit different picture than what I had in mind. I mean, all the big companies have made their money with a targeted advertising business model, but I always saw it as an equal exchange. Like we were using their data to make a better product for them, or make their lives better."

"I did too, but, I mean… It's like everything I've been working on lately is to 'increase engagement' and collect more metrics." She jingled her arms, miming Bethany.

Avi let out a breathy laugh. "Yeah, working at Agora isn't quite as much fun as it used to be."

"But, like, what can we do?" She didn't just want Avi's validation. She wanted guidance.

He reached his arm around her and pulled her closer to him. She leaned into his shoulder and sighed. It was a moment before Avi spoke again. "I think your concerns are valid, and asking these questions is the right thing to do. If I've learned anything these past couple months, it's that there are things going on people aren't paying attention to. It's not enough to just build something. We have to do our part to see it's used for good."

She squeezed his hand. Eleanor felt so happy to have someone who understood her and even felt the same way. All her life, she had wanted to quietly fly under the radar to work hard, study, and learn. She drove herself toward prestige and success for no one but herself. She wanted to do work that mattered and solve real problems. But now she realized there had been a few problems along the way, and she wanted to do her best to correct them.

"Thank you," she whispered.

He wrapped his fingers in hers. "It's almost midnight."

They both looked out the large picture windows as bursts of gunpowder blew up the night sky, filling it with stars of a momentary life span.

I wish for the strength to be better this year, Eleanor said in her heart.

NEW DIALOGUE

Eleanor "Ellie" Crawford
<Software Engineer @Agora>

The problem with computing is that you begin to see the world as a series of inputs and outputs. Computers are like that but people aren't.

---

42 ❣ 58 ⚜
Comments:

> **Benny**
> Cryptic!

> **Kitt**
> The good outweighs the bad

25

The month of January was a blur for Eleanor. The only work she was able to do on her Hacking project was a quick demo to the policy team. Jeff, while impressed with it, asked for some changes before it could be used. Her team was preparing for a large code release that featured a significant redesign of the mobile app as well as all the features Eleanor had been working on. She barely had any time for anything but bug fixes, code merges, and conference rooms.

She sat through several tense meetings during which Avi argued with Daryl, pointing out that the team needed to transition to a more agile release cycle moving forward to avoid the current chaos. In early February, when the code finally went live, the team celebrated with beers and pizza.

The update would start using an algorithm from the new Plaza 2.0 team, but Eleanor had learned very little about what it actually did.

Now that she had some time, she decided to do her research. Bethany had told her who would be most likely to talk to her as well as who to avoid. "Russell doesn't think women should be programmers. Don't talk to him," she'd said.

Eleanor made her way to the corner where the team was located and scanned the cubicle names. "Hi, excuse me," she said to a younger guy in jeans and a hoodie who swiveled around to look at her. "I'm looking for David."

"That's me," he said with a relatively amused look.

"Um, Bethany said you might be able to help me out."

"With?"

"Well, I'm on the mobile dev team," She noticed his eyebrows raise ever so subtly. "And I wanted to find out more about how the Plaza 2.0 algorithm works."

"Well, what do you want to know, exactly?"

"I mean just a general overview of how it works, what kind of data you're using."

"Well, I'll tell you what I can, but there are about ten of us working on it, and some people know different pieces of it. The general idea is to show people what is most interesting to them. We started with a ranking system—"

"Yes, I coded the ranking system prototype."

He nodded. "Then you know the formula was the same for everyone, but the engagement engineers wanted it to be tailored to each person."

He paused to make sure she was following, and she nodded.

"So we were tasked with a machine learning approach, which basically means we take each user's data and give it to the algorithm to learn what they like and set personalized rankings."

"Yes, I know what machine learning is." She was impatient to make him aware she was smart enough to follow what he was saying.

"Great, so it's not exactly *one* algorithm curating the Plaza now, there's a lot of moving parts. Think of the Plaza like one contained application in itself that's specific to each user."

"That makes sense. So how does it work right now in production?"

"Basically, all the pieces of content you could see are given a relevancy score and sorted from most to least relevant. On average, and we've got data to show this, there are about 1,500 different pieces of content a user could see each day, but they typically look at only about 300. So we have to make that amount the most interesting so they keep coming back and seeing our ads."

Always with the ads.

David rubbed his hands together as if he especially liked the part he was getting to. "So the part I've worked on the most is what content you see from friends and family. We take things such as updates you like, who you are messaging... if you like a lot of photos from a specific person. So, if you like a lot of your ex-boyfriend's photos but not his text updates, his photos will get a higher relevancy score. So now photos might carry a different score for each user. But each piece of content has several factors that determine its total score, which is why it can get complicated."

"I'll say."

"And we're making changes to it a lot."

"Where—or who—decides the changes exactly?"

"A variety of places really. Engagement Engineering, of course. Advertising gets their say—they have their own contained algorithm within the Plaza—and, have you worked with the User Research team at all?"

She shook her head. "We get reports from them about stuff to fix, but I've never met with them."

"If you're still curious for more info, you might talk with them some. They run some wild studies over there with actual users about how engaging the content actually is, which informs our algorithms. That department is huge, but there they also have a dedicated Plaza team now." David grabbed a sticky note, wrote down the name of someone on the team and where to find him and handed it to Eleanor.

"Thank you so much, David. This was really helpful." she said, feeling a bit overwhelmed.

"Sure, no problem."

Eleanor decided to go down to the cafe on the main floor and take a break. She ordered some coffee and cocooned herself in an orb-like chair that was hanging from the ceiling. *I need to unpack all this.*

She was constantly learning how much she didn't know. It was part of her drive to keep working hard, but she couldn't believe how scattered the knowledge of Agora really was. *It seems like no one person understands all the moving parts.*

Already she had been shuffled around to several different teams to learn about just one small part of Agora's platform. She felt this overwhelming sense of amazement and concern that something so distributed like this could even exist and work.

But it also seemed completely obvious now how easy it was for things to go awry. One little bias programmed into the Plaza algorithm could have a global impact. Eleanor had, all this time, just focused on building a mobile app that worked and connected to these other parts.

She sipped her coffee and looked out the window at all the people walking by. Some talking on the phone, many looking down at their phones while they walked—scrolling, tapping, snapping selfies.

Her mind conjured an image of cattle being herded around. *These things tell us where to go, who to talk to, what restaurants to try, what events to attend.* Eleanor's favorite hole-in-the-wall Greek place would have never been found if she hadn't been wandering around the city. A small place like that wouldn't rank high enough in searches or reviews to be on the map, and they probably couldn't afford to pay to be on there either.

She was beginning to realize that Agora wasn't the free and open space to connect and share ideas that everyone wanted it to be. She was no longer sure there was anything she could do to stop it or that it could ever truly exist in the way she wanted it to.

NEW DIALOGUE

Daryl Abernathy
<Engineering Manager @Agora>

So proud of my mobile app team! We put out a huge new update with lots of great features along with @EngagementEngineering and @Plaza2.0 !

---

42 ❦ 58 ⚜

26

———————

On the last Thursday in February, Eleanor asked off from work. She'd done some research on the Center for the Visually Impaired and learned they hosted a monthly open house where people could take a tour of the facility. Her parents met her in Atlanta with Anne.

Eleanor was waiting for them in front of the building. "Hey, how was the drive?"

"Long. Dad can't drive in the city." Anne slid out of the truck, and Eleanor noticed that she seemed to be walking comfortably with her white cane. Her face had, for the most part, returned to its normal color.

"What? I can too!" He chuckled.

"We made a few wrong turns." Her mother put a hand over her mouth to cover her laugh.

"I still do that," Eleanor reassured them.

The family made their way to a small three-story building nestled between large skyscrapers. Eleanor wondered how long until it would be forced to grow taller as so many on this street had in the past few years.

An older woman greeted them at the front desk and told them

the tour would start shortly. Eleanor couldn't help noticing a strange chill in the room, the kind of sterility she now associated with hospitals.

A younger-looking woman with short blonde hair came into the room holding a clipboard. "Are you all here for the tour?"

"Yes, we are. I'm Ethan. This is my wife, Marie, and our daughters, Anne and Ellie."

The woman shook each of their hands, but her eyes lingered on Anne. "I'm Laura. I manage children and youth services here. Nice to meet you all."

Laura led them to an elevator in the hallway, and they all squished in. When they reached the third floor, she gestured them into a room with several tables and chairs and a projector screen set up. "I thought I'd start by giving you an overview of our services and a demo of some of the assistive technology that's available."

Laura sat down in front of an old, heavy-looking laptop, and the Crawfords filed into the first row of chairs.

"Here at the CVI, our mission is to empower those impacted by vision loss to live with independence and dignity. We support people of all ages and from all over Georgia. We have community-based rehabilitation services to aid with everything from personal care, cooking, communication, really anything to help you navigate your daily life. The youth program offers social, therapeutic, academic, and recreational services to school-age children."

Eleanor turned to look at Anne, whose face said, "I'm overwhelmed." Who could blame her. To have to relearn how to live at seventeen, just when she was on the cusp of really starting her life. Laura seemed to notice this as well.

"We can also provide guidance on which skills would be most helpful to the individual. We have a great community of volunteers and visitors. Do y'all have any questions so far?"

"Do you have other facilities in the state? We live a good ways away and wondered if there were any resources we might find a bit closer?" Marie asked.

"We are the largest provider in the state, but we certainly have some resources we can refer you to." Laura gave a polite smile.

"That would be helpful, thank you."

"Let's move on to the screen reader then. Proficiency with this is a skill we stress here, with how essential the internet has become to daily life. It allows for access to and navigation of websites and digital applications."

Eleanor had heard of screen readers before only in terms of the ALT text she had to code into the Agora app to meet legal requirements. For that, she just followed a list of guidelines but had never seen how it worked.

"Many devices are starting to come standard with screen readers. Your iPhone, for example, and many computers. There's also screen reader software with more features that can be purchased."

Laura turned up the volume on the computer and began navigating through a webpage using the tab button. A choppy robotic voice filled the room. "You-are-currently-on-a-toolbar-item-palette to-interact-with-the-item-on-this-toolbar, press-control-option-shift-down-arrow."

The voice-over spoke so quickly that Eleanor barely understood what it said. She noticed her mom glance in her dad's direction, and he put a hand on her knee.

Laura must have noticed their apprehension. "Sorry, the speed can be changed, let me slow it down some. It's a little overwhelming at first, but once people get used to it, they typically want it to talk faster. It does take some practice, and not all sites are easy to navigate."

The speech moved slower now, but only a little bit. "Chrome-Welcome-CVI-homepage-window-browser-tabs-toolbar-item-palette."

Eleanor watched as Laura tabbed through the main navigation items at the top but noticed she couldn't seem to access some of the options on the left side of the page.

Laura frowned. "See, our own website isn't even the most accessible."

The look on Anne's face screamed, "I am not using *that*," and Eleanor didn't really blame her. She didn't like the idea of this obnoxious digital voice yelling at her either. The vibe in the room was uncomfortable at best. Laura stood up and motioned to continue the tour.

They walked down a long, poorly lit hallway and were surprised when they entered a room that was set up as a kitchen. "We have cooking classes in here. On the counter, I've laid out some of the tools we use. We sell them downstairs as well."

Laura showed them a hand guard that could be used to safely chop vegetables and pointed to the microwave and stove that had Braille dots used to mark the different functions on them. There were also timers and measuring tools with Braille on them.

"How clever!" Her mom tried to be positive.

"We also have classes on navigation. Anne, I see you've started using a cane. Here in the city, we teach how to navigate crosswalks and public transportation. The city has been doing a good job transitioning to accessible crosswalks. You can see one up the road a little ways. It has audio readings, and you'll hear a chirping sound when it's safe to cross."

Laura led them back down the hallway again and down to the second floor. "Now in there is where we have Braille classes. There's one in session now."

The Crawfords peeked in through the window of the door to see several people holding some kind of board.

"Braille is another skill we recommend pursuing as soon as possible. On the other side of the hallway is where some of our community-based classes are offered. Is there anything specific you are looking for?"

The Crawfords were all silent for a moment, wondering if Anne might speak up.

"Well…" Anne began nervously, "do you offer any art classes?"

The Crawfords all held their breath, wondering if this woman would crush all of Anne's dreams in one quick sentence.

"Oh, yes! So art is your interest? We actually just did a collaboration with the High Museum for a youth program you would have enjoyed! One of our volunteers is a teacher at SCAD, you might want to meet her."

Did she say SCAD? Savannah College of Art and Design! Eleanor exhaled with relief as Anne's face lit up with more hope for the future than she had seen since the accident.

"Let's see if she's here. I'll introduce you." Laura scurried off down the hallway, and this time, Anne was first in line to follow her. Eleanor exchanged glances with her parents, who looked just as relieved as she felt.

Laura led them to a classroom cluttered with toys. It looked like a roomful of children must have just been there. A dark-haired woman who was tidying up turned toward the door when they came in.

"Hey, Mika, I have someone for you to meet." Laura introduced Anne, and Eleanor noticed Mika had a cane of her own.

The confidence in Mika's voice brightened the room. "I'm always happy to meet another artist. Welcome, Anne." Her smile took over her face. "What's your medium?"

"Well, I… used to draw." Anne's smile fell away.

"Used to? Well, we will just have to fix that!" Mika rested an affectionate hand on Anne's shoulder. "There are some tools we can use, and if you're interested in moving into painting, I teach a method at SCAD called raised canvas painting."

"That sounds amazing! I've actually applied to SCAD. I'm a high school senior."

"That's wonderful!"

The two spoke animatedly for a few minutes and exchanged information.

"I'll walk down with you. There's something in the store you might want to get." Mika smiled.

Back on the first floor, they walked into the center's gift shop, which was full of things like phones, remotes with large buttons, cooking tools, Braille equipment, and several gadgets Eleanor didn't even recognize.

Mika retrieved an item from the corner. "This is a raised line drawing board. When you draw, it imprints the paper so you can feel the marks you make. People used to scratch into surfaces with paperclips or knives," she laughed, "but this is a bit easier. I've seen some people use things like rulers and protractors to make raised outlines of the basic shapes of their work and then feel those while they sketch in the more traditional methods."

"That's brilliant." Anne looked giddy.

Mika's face grew serious. "It may be tough, but the vision loss forces us to think of more creative ways to express ourselves, and it can result in some really beautiful art." Mika wrote down the names of a few artists with visual impairments for Anne to research their methods and encouraged her to reach out to her when she started school. The Crawfords thanked Mika and Laura for all their time and then picked out a few more items to buy before leaving.

As they walked to the car, Eleanor listened to the sound of Anne's cane clacking with newfound vigor. She smiled to herself and began to wonder if there was any way to improve upon the tools available to Anne.

"I'm going to look into that screen reader thing some. There's gotta be something better." Eleanor's problem solving gears began to turn.

"Or I bet *you* can make something better," Anne said.

Eleanor hugged her family goodbye and walked up the street to her apartment. She spent the rest of the afternoon researching some of the things Mika mentioned and what other accessible technologies there might be.

ARTICLE
HOW THE EYES WORK

All the different parts of your eyes work together to help you see.

First, light passes through the cornea (the clear front layer of the eye). The cornea is shaped like a dome and bends light to help the eye focus. Some of this light enters the eye through an opening called the pupil. The iris (the colored part of the eye) controls how much light the pupil lets in.

Next, light passes through the lens (a clear inner part of the eye). The lens works together with the cornea to focus light correctly on the retina. When light hits the retina (a light-sensitive layer of tissue at the back of the eye), special cells called photoreceptors turn the light into electrical signals.

These electrical signals travel from the retina through the optic nerve to the brain. Then the brain turns the signals into the images you see.

27

———

It was a refreshing March morning, and Eleanor walked a little slower to work. Having stayed late the previous night, she was in no hurry to return. Little yellow daffodils were starting to pop out of the city's square shrubbery zones, and the trees were no longer naked of their leaves.

Eleanor couldn't help but dream instead of the wild mountain hydrangeas and rhododendrons that would be blotting Aska Valley. *Maybe I should go home this weekend,* she thought.

She was feeling increasingly suffocated by the city, and being promoted to senior had been no blessing these past few months. It mostly resulted in calls in the middle of the night to fix high-priority issues and more meetings to attend leaving less time during the day for real work. The worst part for Eleanor was that she only felt more pressure and responsibility rather than learning more or getting to solve more complex problems.

Every day felt like a fight to assert her own self or to quietly mold with the collective. What difference would it make if she left Agora or not or worked this place or that place? She was just one person, one cog in the machine called Agora.

But she was still a person. And if Eleanor believed that every single person mattered and had the opportunity to make a difference, then she had to believe this was true of herself too.

It was after nine when Eleanor finally got to the office. Avi gave her a formal greeting, and she smiled to herself. They'd been doing their best to act no differently at work.

Ever since she talked to David about the Plaza algorithm, she'd been thinking about visiting the User Research team to ask them some questions, but she'd been swamped. She had a lull in her schedule this afternoon, so she decided today was the day.

She went down to the floor dedicated to User Research, but since she wasn't exactly sure who to talk to, she approached the first friendly-looking woman she saw. This one happened to be sipping coffee in her cubicle.

"Hi, is this by chance the team that researches the Plaza?" Eleanor asked politely.

"Yeah, it is! I'm Jessica." She smiled brightly.

"Oh, great. I'm Eleanor. I'm a dev on the mobile team downstairs."

"Awesome, nice to meet you. What's up?"

"Well, I just wanted to find out a little about what your team does. Our team receives UX reports, but I've never really talked with anyone."

"But you're interested in the Plaza specifically?"

"I am." Eleanor tried to remain confident.

"Well, in general, the User Research team tests prototypes or even our current product to get feedback from actual users. Ultimately, our job is to advocate for the users. We find out how they interact with our product, pain points they may have, then hand that knowledge off for design and dev use."

"Okay, that makes sense." Eleanor smiled.

"My team in specific is newer, and we're focused on the Plaza, which is a big chunk of what users interact with, so there are several of us. A lot of our studies revolve around seeing how engaged users are with content to help inform the ranking system. Usually that means bringing users in to interact with their Plazas and collecting data about how long they are engaged as a whole and with specific content. Then they fill out a survey with questions about interest and satisfaction."

"That's interesting. What do these studies look like exactly?" Eleanor wanted her to continue, and the woman was happy to oblige.

"Oh! I'll tell you about a recent study we did. Since the election just happened, we were interested in studying voting behavior. We created a banner for voting day that showed up in users' Plazas."

Eleanor vaguely remembered seeing something like that in her own Plaza, and she nodded, eager to hear more.

"There were two groups. Each saw a banner with an 'I voted' button. But one group's banner also showed which of their friends had voted. It turns out, the banner that showed images of those in their Circle who voted received more clicks to the 'I voted' button."

Eleanor took a moment to process this. "So do you think the social pressure motivated them to click the button and share whether they had voted? Or did it change their actual decision to go vote?"

"Great question! You should join our team." Her eyes glowed. "We were thinking the same thing, so we used location data to determine if those users visited polling locations *after* seeing the banner and *before* clicking the button."

"Location data? You can use that?" *Creepy.*

"Oh, yeah, of course. They grant it to us when they download the app. I thought you would know that."

"I do, but I didn't think it could be used that way. On our end, we just use it if they want to share it when they post."

Jessica looked at Eleanor with a hint of skepticism. "It's very useful for our studies. I don't know what we would do without it."

"So what did this study conclude then, with the location data?"

"Right! We found more users turned out to vote *after* seeing the banner showing which of their friends voted."

Eleanor's eyes widened. "So you effectively manipulated voting behavior?"

"I wouldn't put it that way. It's more that the social pressure of their friends voting that motivated them to perform their civic duty."

"But it does prove that what we put in the Plaza can impact behavior?"

"Well, yeah, I suppose so." Jessica raised an eyebrow. "But even a news article could affect that. In fact, at any given moment, there are tons of things impacting our behavior."

"Yes, but couldn't political candidates use our marketing system to manipulate voting behavior?"

"How so?" Jessica asked.

"Well, the algorithm doesn't know if it's selling shoes or a political ideology."

"I see what you mean, but Agora isn't really a news platform. Hearing your crazy uncle rant on Agora or at the dinner table doesn't seem too different to me. Also, I think people are smart enough to use their best judgment about the content they see."

Eleanor thought for a moment. "Do you know how users feel about the idea that you're using their information like this?"

"I mean I think they *like* the idea of getting a better experience, especially for something that's free to them."

Eleanor smiled. "Very true." Not wanting to cause any suspicion, she cut the conversation off and thanked Jessica for her time.

Around 7:00 p.m., the office was mostly empty, and Eleanor was about ready to leave. She leaned on her desk with a sigh, staring at the blinking cursor in her code editor. Then she opened an incognito window and typed, "senior software engineer jobs."

She scrolled through job postings—a lot of contract-to-hire positions and postings from recruiting firms that refused to state the company they were hiring for. She rolled her eyes. *Why do they do that?*

She had been lucky to get directly hired at Agora, and looking at job postings made her heart race. Thinking of interviews, coding exercises, and whiteboard problems but also of leaving the place that she worked so hard to get to, it all made her feel like leaving was too big of a step to take.

She knew people with several years of work experience who'd struggled to land new jobs, mostly because the interview process was so skewed in favor of new grads. Sometimes just some random sorting algorithm or puzzle problem from college could trip them up.

Nowadays, it was common to get rejected for not being a cultural fit. Whatever that meant. Finding a job was hard enough. How did someone go about finding one that actually mattered to them?

Eleanor let out a deep sigh, closing the tab and smacking her laptop shut.

NEW DISCOURSE

Bethany
Hey Eleanor! I've got some really cool news!

Eleanor
What's up?

Bethany
I was telling my team about your content moderation tool, and we had some really good ideas for how we might be able to use it as well!

Eleanor
Oh really?

Bethany
What kinds of things can you make it recognize?

Eleanor
Really anything you have images to train it with.

Bethany
So could it recognize faces in photos?

Eleanor
Sure

Bethany
Ok, I'm going to schedule a meeting with
you to talk more about it!

Eleanor
Ok

Bethany
Thanks! :)

28

───────

A few weeks later, Eleanor was at work late in the afternoon when a high-priority email popped up for an emergency content policy committee meeting. It was unusual for these things to be called so last minute. Coming out of her state of flow, she looked around the office to see groups of people huddled around computers or phones. *Here we go again.*

She opened a new tab on her computer and typed 'news.' Several breaking headlines appeared on her screen.

"Terror in Boston."

"Terror at the Finish Line."

"Marathon Massacre."

"Deadly Blasts Rock Boston."

Eleanor was overwhelmed by the sheer number of headlines that contained the word terror. Almost as though it was a word guaranteed to get a click.

Some details were still unclear, but Eleanor gathered there had been two explosions near the finish line of the Boston Marathon. She wasn't sure if this was going to be relevant to the meeting, but she had a feeling it would—or should—be. She opened the live news coverage on her laptop, which she teetered on one hand as she made her way to the conference room. It wasn't the one they usually used. This time, they'd selected the largest one in the building, generally reserved for only the most important events. *I wonder if the CEO will be there.*

The room was filling up quickly, and Eleanor realized she'd broken a sweat. It suddenly became clear that this meeting would be filled with more gravity than any other she had ever attended at Agora. Should she really be here? Was she out of place? But she *was* on the committee.

As people poured in, their faces grim with concern, Eleanor tried to learn more about what was going on. The attackers were still unidentified and had not yet been apprehended. The bombs that caused the explosion had apparently been made with pressure cookers. Images of people fleeing the blast zone, some injured, were going viral on the internet. Including Agora.

Calls had been coming in from the content moderators about the sheer number of these photos they were deleting, per the policy: gore. An executive assistant came in and set up the large TV displays for the meeting. Jeff came in and set up his laptop with the Master Plaza on the screen. Almost all the content that appeared was related to the explosion.

One photo in particular seemed to be going the most viral of all —a man in a cowboy hat pushing a wheelchair with a guy whose face was painted a dusty ash and whose hair stood up straight. Most disturbing was that where his legs should have been, there was a bloody mess of skin, muscles, tendons, and bone.

Eleanor's stomach twitched and she looked away. Other members began to fill up the room, but it was quiet. Almost everyone was following coverage on their phones or laptops. When Matthew Erickson entered the room, everyone looked up in anticipation. Making no secret of his agitation, he took the seat at the head of the table, and after a few moments of uncomfortable silence, he began:

"In 1963, all of America huddled around their televisions, bearing witness to the assassination of President John F. Kennedy. Today, millions of Americans are gathering around their smartphones and computers, some desperately searching for news of their own loved ones, others just frozen with shock. Many will be unable to carry on their normal daily work because they can't stop imagining it being them."

All eyes in the room were on him as he gestured towards the stream of photos showing up on Acropolis.

"But here in this room today, we have a decision to make. Our goal is to connect humanity. Agora is the new gathering place for our age. Today, people all over the world are gathering over a tragedy, just as the ancient Greeks and Romans would gather to bear witness to political or social violence. But those of us in this room have the opportunity to decide if we think this violence belongs in *our* Agora."

There was something in the way he said *our Agora* that was unsettling to Eleanor. In that moment, she felt as if she were looking at a man who considered himself a god. Having the ability to censor two billion people might in fact make you a god. He looked now to his host for suggestions.

Opinions bounced around the room:

"We agreed no gore or blood already in the past. I think we should stand by that."

"So pictures of this are allowed if there's no blood in them? Look at that one?"

Eleanor looked at the monitor, but as the assistant scrolled through, there really weren't any that didn't have blood.

"What if the photos help someone identify their loved one? They can use our platform to find if someone's safe."

"People are posting updates, photos, and videos from the scene. There are too many posts. This topic is trending. It's everywhere else."

"We can't really shut down an entire event. Not one this newsworthy anyway. If this is dominating the platform, and we take it down, everyone will go somewhere else. That's tons of lost revenue."

"But we're not a news platform," someone protested, and a mumble of agreement went through the room.

"That's true. People can follow it on the news. We aren't a news network. People come to chat with long-lost friends, share a baby picture, and so on. They shouldn't have to see death and gore pop up on there."

Matthew stood up, bringing the room's attention back to himself. "This is not a decision to take lightly, and it certainly brings some fundamental ideas about Agora into question."

The discussion continued:

"This is about knowing what's going on in the world."

"Maybe we could link out to the content on other sites with a content warning?"

"Then we're just driving revenue to other sites."

"Or put a content warning on the photos?"

"But we've never done anything like that before. How would that affect everything else?"

"They can turn on any TV and see this right now. It's probably on TVs in restaurants and waiting rooms everywhere. It's already in the public square."

Eleanor decided to say her piece. "We've already decided this was not allowed on our platform. We made the rules for moments like this. Why would we make an exception now? It would be opening a Pandora's Box."

Some nods went around the room.

"I agree we're not stopping people from discussing the event or sharing news about it. We're just keeping people safe from violent images as we've always done," Jeff said to the room.

"So we continue to remove the photos per the *gore* policy?" Matthew looked around the room, and no one offered anything further. "Let's vote."

As thoughts and prayers flooded the internet, Eleanor Crawford, just a software engineer, voted on a crucial decision—one that could change Agora forever, or the world even.

This is not what Agora is for, she reassured herself.

Some hands went up right away in favor of removing the pictures, including Eleanor's. A few other hands went up, hesitantly. A heavy silence blanketed the room. As the last hand that tipped the majority went up, the meeting was over. The photos would be removed.

"Okay, the vote has it." Matthew said, nodding at Jeff. "Have the mods continue removing the photos."

"I'll make an announcement." Jeff began to type on his laptop.

Eleanor breathed a sigh of relief. She felt that her voice had mattered here, and *that*, she felt, was a victory. Maybe she could make a difference at Agora. She didn't have to give up.

She returned to her desk where Avi was waiting to hear what had happened. Like everyone else, he'd already seen the headlines, and news had rippled through the office that the content committee was voting on what to do about the photos.

After she explained everything, he smiled knowingly. "So your voice *did* matter."

"I suppose so… but do you think it was the right choice? I mean that's not what Agora is supposed to be." She looked down at her fidgeting hands.

"I think Agora is a platform, not a publisher. We are not subject to the same rules that news media is, and, therefore, we shouldn't be publishing news. I agree with you. Making this exception would mean changing the face of Agora."

She breathed a sigh of relief and smiled at him. "That's what I think too. I think we did the right thing."

Later that evening when Eleanor got home, she opened up Agora on her laptop, curious to see what was happening. She was shocked to see her feed was still full of the viral photos. She hit refresh. Still there. She logged out and then back in. No change.

Maybe the message hadn't been communicated to everyone yet? How could it not have been?

Emily came into her room, an uneasy look on her face. "I'm sure you've seen the headlines today."

Eleanor nodded.

"It's awful." She sat on Eleanor's bed. "But Ellie—" she turned her smartphone towards Eleanor to show her the Agora feed with the same viral picture of the man in the wheelchair, "—why is this on here?" Her voice dropped an octave.

"It's not supposed to be. We voted to take them down."

Emily left the app and set her phone down. Suddenly, the sound of Eleanor's old flip phone vibrating on the desk filled the room. It was a text from Avi.

Eleanor opened the message and read it out loud. "The committee was overruled. Someone at the top convinced Matthew to make an exception."

Emily's eyes widened.

"So that's why they're still up…" Eleanor stared intently at the 'G' key on the phone's keyboard.

Emily patted her on the shoulder then held up her phone. "We just won't look at that for a couple days."

Or ever again, Eleanor thought.

They said goodnight, and Emily went to her own room. Eleanor turned off her phone and shut down her computer. She was done with it for today. Instead of watching TV as usual, she just stared at the dark ceiling of her room.

All her former hope for the future of Agora—and her place in it —vanished. In its place was an ominous gray shadow. Eleanor believed the committee was an ethical stronghold for the company, a system of checks and balances. But if their choice could be overruled from the top, what other decisions were made without anyone to check them?

Her mind raced with thoughts, and she tossed and turned as she struggled to fall asleep, only drifting off when her brain finally seemed to have exhausted every path of worry and fear.

NEW !!! HIGH PRIORITY EMAIL

SUBJECT: MASSIVE TRAFFIC DIP

Matthew,

In the last couple hours, Agora has experienced the largest dip in traffic we've ever seen. What's going on?

Kelsey Tucker
Agora COO

Reply from Matthew:
We've been taking down all the photos from the bombing.

Reply from Kelsey
Why? A huge event is happening and people aren't gathering on our platform. That's not good.

Reply from Matthew:
The committee voted to continue removing gory photos per our rules.

Reply from Kelsey

Damn the committee, do you know what this will do to us? Agora will be seen as the gathering place for cat photos and what grandma ate today—not the important stuff.

Reply from Matthew:

I agree, the new public square should be dealing with something major like this, but I didn't think we would lose so much traffic just from removing those photos.

Reply from Kelsey

Well, let's tell content moderation to make an exception.

Reply from Matthew:

OK I'll let them know.

29

E*leanor walks down a dirt path, barefooted. The wind blows through the trees, rustling the leaves and swishing them all around her. She has the feeling she's been down this path a hundred times before, but something is different now. She notices every little pebble she steps on, every common dandelion, the pure white daisies that grow along the embankment.*

Tulips are springing up from the ground for no other reason than that she wishes them there. The sun dapples through the trees in a way that brings fairies to the forest. She can feel them all around her—dancing and playing.

Now she's laying on her back, looking up through the canopy, watching the tiny birds bounce from branch to branch, hard at work building their delicate nests or gathering food. If she lies still enough, she's sure she can feel the forest breathing.

Suddenly, she's running. Chest heaving, her body warm—the sun making her body perspire. All she can see is the blue of the sky and white, wispy clouds. Without realizing it, she's stopped. She can feel her toes hanging over the edge of a cliff, the rough dirt crumbling underneath her.

It's quiet. Her life hangs in a fragile balance; one swift wind could push her into a new world. She wants to leave this small forest in which she has lived her whole life. She closes her eyes and takes a few steps backward. In the distance, she can hear the leaves of the forest whispering to her, "Don't do it... We can't protect you there."

A strong wind taps her on the shoulder, and suddenly, she's sprinting to the edge of the cliff again, but this time, she doesn't stop. Her legs push away from the ledge. Dirt gives way from the spot on which her feet were once planted.

Her body feels free—suspended in time—her wild voice echoes throughout the mountains. An ocean of possibility is below her. She's going somewhere new.

As her excitement starts to fade, so does the sunshine. Droplets begin falling alongside her, and the light rain animates the lake with pixelated static.

She falls into the digital ripples, sinking down until it grows black. Light appears in the darkness, but it isn't the warm yellow of the sun. A cold, blue light frames her periphery, and moving images dance all around her—beautiful and captivating visions of life—some of them her very own dreams and hopes for the world. But as she continues to sink, they float away.

At last, her feet touch a sandy bottom. Some people come into view, a few that she knows, and others she doesn't. They're all looking at glowing orbs, captivated.

She sees something else too: Men in suits, hundreds of them, walking around with notebooks, peering over the shoulders of those she loves—writing notes, taking pictures, folding them up, then tossing them into a stream of others identical pieces of paper that formed a current of information moving through the water. It seems to go somewhere far away.

She walks around now, looking over everyone's shoulders, watching people tap and scroll endlessly. She sees one person writing a heartfelt message to a lover. One of the suited men makes some notes and sends them up. "Someone is watching you!" Eleanor shouts. But they don't look up.

A woman in a wheelchair researches chronic illness and disease. A man in a suit makes some notes and sends them up.

A teenager searches for answers to why he's so different from everyone else. A man in a suit makes some notes and sends them up.

On some screens, the first images of the Boston Marathon bombing appear. She watches people's faces turn to shock and horror as they're met with blood, gore, death, human suffering. The darkest side of humanity.

"Look away!" she yells. They don't hear her.

Now rows of desks with computers and people hunched over them come into *view. They're content moderators, all clicking one of two buttons as the gory images from the bombing roll across the screens: 'pass,' 'pass,' 'pass.'*

She thinks of the beautiful forest she left behind, "If I can just pull everyone up there, they will look away. I can save them." She screams, but no one hears her.

They melt away.

She turns around. One person has actually looked away from the image. His hands are shaking, and she tries to run to him, but her legs are leaden. A man in a suit reaches him first, holding something with electrical pulses arcing out that he floats to the screen. The trembling man looks down and becomes calm again. The observer makes some notes and sends it up into the stream of the world's consciousness.

Eleanor's only thought is that she must leave this place. She turns to run but comes face-to-face with another suited watcher.

He's been watching her the whole time.

She abandoned the safety of her private inner world the moment she jumped off that cliff.

"Where is your uniform?" he asks, "Your break is over."

A chill runs up her spine. "I am not one of you!" she yells.

The man snaps his fingers and an alarm begins to sound. "You have violated the terms of service."

A fleet of suited men are coming after her, but she can no longer breathe under water. She's kicking her legs, struggling, drowning...

Eleanor's body jolted awake, and suddenly she was in her apartment, tumbling out of her bed, drenched in sweat and gasping for breath. She whipped her head around to make sure she was alone, then gentle sobs shook her chest.

Everything she'd been grappling with these past few months became clear. It's like watching a street performer and not realizing you're being pickpocketed. But instead of stealing your wallet, they're stealing your private inner world and using it to keep you captivated in the street forever.

As the rumble of thunder from early spring showers filled the room, she knew today would be the last day she worked for Agora.

30

———

After staring out the window until the tears stopped flowing, Eleanor reached for the old touch-tone phone and dialed Avi's number, which she now had memorized. Her body felt weak and shaky as she listened to the phone ring long enough for her to check the time and realize it was 5:00 a.m. He answered groggily.

"I just can't do it anymore," she breathed into the phone.

She couldn't be Eleanor Crawford today. She couldn't give a two-week notice and find another job first. All the responsible things she would normally do didn't matter to her anymore. She was trapped in a nightmare and had to get out. Maybe she was crazy, but she didn't care anymore.

"I understand." He said without judgment in his voice. Avi understood her—or at least pretended to. He said he would help her exit as quickly and drama-free as possible and that he would miss working with her.

She set herself on autopilot as she went through the day—cleaning out her desk, turning in her laptop, meeting with HR, and then with Daryl. Avi convinced her to make a family emergency case for leaving immediately so she wouldn't burn any bridges, and she followed his advice.

She made the same rehearsed statements to everyone about how she needed to go home and help out her family as a result of Anne's accident. By the end of the day, she really believed that's what she needed to do. Had Avi read her mind? She knew Anne and her parents were struggling, that was certainly true.

She said heartfelt goodbyes to all her teammates, and Avi walked out with her. It was her last walk through the familiar twisting cubicles and elevator down to the lobby. She handed in her security badge at the front desk and suddenly started to cry. This place had been everything to her. She thought she would work here forever.

Avi said he would come over and check on her later, and with a quick hug they parted ways. Back at home, she sat alone in her room, thinking about what to do next.

An hour ago, I was a Senior Software Engineer at Agora. Now I'm nothing.

When the list of goals and achievements had been checked off, what was left? Eleanor didn't know anymore, but as she paced her room, one image was clear to her: Aska Valley. The only thing that she knew was that she was going home.

She began emptying her clothes from the cheap, pre-furnished dresser into a duffel bag. She set to work finding someone to take over the lease on her apartment; there were always plenty of college students looking. She told a completely crushed Emily she was sorry, but she had to move back home for a while.

Eleanor walked across the street to a grocery store and picked up a few boxes to pack the rest of her stuff in. She didn't have much: books, clothes, her computer. The furniture all belonged to the apartment. She was working in this way, boxes scattered, when Avi knocked on the door. It was a relief to not be alone anymore.

A look of surprise came across his face when he came in and saw the boxes. "Are you moving?"

"Yes, I'm going home." She said it like he should already know this. It *was* his idea.

"You don't actually have to do that," he said patiently. "I just thought it was a good way for you not to have to say anything bad about the company on your way out."

"Yeah, well, it made perfect sense once I said it a few times.

What else could I do? I have no job lined up. My sister is *blind*, and my parents need help. I may as well go home until I get things sorted out."

He hesitated, then said, "I don't want to see your talent go to waste."

"Well, it already has," she said sharply.

"Try not to think that way, Eleanor." He let out a deep sigh as he sat in her desk chair.

The room was silent for a while as she moved around, putting her things into the boxes. "Avi, don't you ever think about quitting, too?"

"It's not as simple for me. I'm on a work visa."

"But you could look for another job first?" She stacked the third and final box that held all her stuff by the door.

"Yeah, I could."

"But you didn't answer my question. Have you *wanted* to quit Agora?" She sat down on the bed facing him.

He closed his eyes for a moment, as if suppressing a level of frustration he had never let escape. "Of *course* I have, Eleanor, but I couldn't until—"

Their eyes met, and Eleanor's face flushed red with understanding.

He watched her silently for some time, his face increasingly reflecting his inner conflict. "I don't want to be selfish…"

Please do, for once. Eleanor thought and he seemed to hear her.

"But you're going back home… Well, what about us?" He looked as if he felt guilty even asking that question, but Eleanor found herself smiling at him. Thoughts of a new kind began to shine on her. She had freed herself from Agora and was going home. They wouldn't have to hide their relationship.

She said nothing but simply leaned in to kiss him, and he kissed her back with none of the restraint he had used every time before. As the passion between them ran free, Avi and Eleanor entered a world where only they existed and nothing else mattered. When they woke up the next morning in each other's arms, they were back in the real world. Wherever Eleanor was going next, she had Avi.

NEW EMAIL

SUBJECT: TALENT LOSS

Daryl,

I'm reaching out to learn more about why we lost one of our top performing developers under your umbrella today?

Matthew

31

Avi and Emily helped load Eleanor's boxes into her car, and after a blur of tears and heartfelt goodbyes, she was on the road north. She had not yet told her family that she was coming home or why, and she needed to before she appeared there. As overpasses and interstates twisted around her, she tried to figure out what she should say exactly.

It wasn't until her car climbed the hill revealing the first glimpse of blue mountains that she dialed her dad. He answered on the second ring, and Eleanor made it quick. She told him she'd quit her job and wanted to move home for a while. "I'm not ready to talk about all the specifics now, but I'll be able to help Anne… and at the Inn if you need it."

"Well, of course, we could use your help here for sure." She could hear him holding back on asking more questions, and she was glad for it.

"Thanks, Dad."

She hung up the phone feeling relieved and wondering why she had been nervous in the first place. She had the privilege of a loving family to return to. Her dad was probably already thinking of ways to convince her to take over running Grayson House—and for once, Eleanor didn't mind entertaining that thought. *Maybe I'm done with the world I'm leaving behind.*

When she pulled into the rocky driveway of her home, there didn't seem to be anyone there. She took the key from under the doormat and unlocked the door.

She lugged her boxes into her childhood bedroom and deposited her computer and monitor in the closet, shutting the door. Sitting on the bed, she was struck by the realization that she was unemployed. She had nowhere to go and no obligations to fill.

A wave of doubt made her feel as if she'd made a huge mistake. To just walk away from a Senior Software Engineering role at a top tech company? She had to be insane. Tears bubbled up again, but she stopped them. *This isn't the time to doubt myself.*

Instead, she went down to the basement and pulled out the camping equipment. A little time in the woods might do her some good. She filled her pack with the necessities and decided not to even bring the old flip phone. She left a note for her parents saying she'd be back in a day or two and that she wouldn't have a phone. She was determined to be truly alone for a bit. Just like that, she was back out the door and driving toward an entry point to the Appalachian Trail, Neels Gap, about thirty minutes away.

By mid-April, most of the thru-hikers would have already started, so she didn't expect to see many people. There were no cars in the parking lot when she got out and hoisted the large pack on her back. It felt heavier than she remembered, or maybe she was weaker. The weather was still cool, maybe low sixties.

As she approached the trailhead, she began to feel a bit lighter. Atlanta, Agora… they seemed so far away now. She took a deep breath and took her first step onto the trail. This particular part of the route had the highest peak to climb in the entire Georgia portion.

She started off slow at first, walking along a creek valley, focusing only on her feet, watching every step. The ground was brown with the old leaves of winter. After about a half a mile, she stopped to drink some water and take her jacket off. Her body felt warm, and the cool April breeze moved across it, standing her hair on end. She needed to conserve her energy for the steep climb to the summit. The dribbling sound of water leaking down the rocky mountainside filled her ears.

She kept on. As she felt more comfortable on her feet, she began to look up more, letting her mind wander. She began to see, for the first time, that the forest was just beginning to come alive with spring. Little white buds on the dogwoods prepared to show themselves to the world. The soft pink rhododendrons were beginning to bloom. How could she have not seen it before?

She approached an intersection with a white-blazed trail marker. She was connecting with the Appalachian Trail now. It grew steeper, and Eleanor found herself breathing heavily. She looked to the ground again, careful not to trip over rocks or exposed roots. She thought about how vulnerable she was, alone in the woods with no way to contact the outside world. Rocks jutted out here and there from the mountain side.

A canopy of pink and white mountain laurels hovered over her. Her legs felt warm and tired. She stopped to catch her breath then pressed on, thinking she was surely close to the top.

It was late afternoon when she reached the summit. She'd been focused on her feet when suddenly she felt bright, warm sunlight on the top of her head. When she looked up, the trees had dissolved from view, and she was met with the wide blue sky and a sweeping expanse of azure tinted mountains. They went on so far that their periwinkle hue began to blend with the sky like a watercolor painting. The hills were a blend of trees not yet bloomed and the fresh green of new life.

Sweat dripped from her forehead, and she breathed deep. She walked around the mostly flat stone top and felt her feet approach the ledge.

How large the world is, she thought, *and how small I am. Sometimes, things just have to happen. There are things we can't change... can't control. Life happens before, in spite of, and after us.*

She slid her pack off and sat down, her feet hanging over the precipice.

I can't help thinking like this…What's the point of it all?

All the most wonderful things mankind has done don't exist without other humans working together—when they help and teach each other. The writer doesn't exist without pen and paper. The artist doesn't exist without paint and pencils. Even when creativity is solitary, it's not.

Eleanor wanted to live in a world where each and every consciousness is valued for how special and rare it is. Because it is the rarest thing in the universe, despite it seeming abundant.

All this time, Eleanor thought she was helping unite people in the world, enhancing their ability to collaborate and come together. Undoubtedly, there were moments when that was true. But the cost was the violation of a most fundamental moral code. The cost was harvesting the private lives of those individuals to be analyzed and used against them to predict and nudge their behavior. She'd helped build a large-scale platform to violate and profit from individuals, using them as a means to an end.

What she had thought was the greatest achievement of her life now felt like her biggest regret. She watched the sky turn yellow, then orange and red, only somewhat aware that time was slipping away from her. She got up to gather some sticks and twigs to build a fire. As the last remnants of the sun disappeared, she had a warm blaze going. Despite the effort of hauling her tent this far, she didn't bother setting it up. The evening was mildly cool, and the sky was clear. She rolled out her mat and sleeping bag to sleep under the stars.

She took off her worn old hiking boots and slid into her sleeping bag, warm next to the fire. She stared into the night sky and counted each star as it came into view until she lost track of the number. A sparkling, swirling *beyond* dizzied her sight until she drifted off to sleep.

She slept through the night without stirring and woke with the sun the next morning. As she climbed down the mountain and walked again through the river valley, she felt like she had grieved the loss of her job and had to look forward now to the future. She had no idea what path she would follow, what her next mountain to climb would be. She only knew that she didn't want to make the same mistakes again.

THIS MESSAGE HAS BEEN DELETED

32

———

When Eleanor returned home from the mountain the next day, Anne was sitting on the porch waiting for her. Eleanor hopped up the porch steps and noticed an envelope sitting in her sister's lap that was promptly thrust in her direction.

"I got in. Or rather I've been told I got in. I can't actually read it for myself." Anne spoke with little excitement in her voice.

Eleanor took the envelope and read. Sure enough, Anne had been accepted to the Savannah College of Art and Design for the fall semester. She wanted to congratulate her and be excited, but that clearly wasn't what Anne needed right now.

"You *did* get in. That's what it says." Eleanor tossed the heavy pack down and collapsed onto the wooden porch. "This is a good thing."

"Maybe. Before we went to the CVI, I would have felt awful, but Mika made it seem possible still. I don't know if it is, but I at least feel there's a chance. But if I tell them I'm blind, could they withdraw my acceptance?"

"I'm certain they can't do that."

"But what if I'm just wasting a space that could be better used by someone else?"

"I don't think you should think of it that way. I looked up some of those artists Mika mentioned. Who was that one? Bramblitt, I think. His stuff is amazing. You're the one who told me there was more to art than what is seen."

"Art helps people see the chaos in the world as beauty," Anne whispered.

"So find a way to make your chaos beautiful."

"Yes, well, I'm not sure that drawing board is going to be the way."

"Oh, you've tried it?"

A hint of eagerness spread across her sister's face. "Yeah, you want to see?"

"I do! I also need a shower. I kinda stink."

Anne cracked a smile. "Just a little."

"Okay, I'll meet you in your room shortly." Eleanor went inside and checked her phone. A few messages from Avi. In a brief flicker, that world came back to her, and she imagined Avi working extra hours to make up for the team's sudden loss. But in that inner space where she would typically have felt guilt, she didn't feel anything.

She took a quick shower and put clean clothes on before heading into her sister's bedroom. Some sheets of paper were taped to the wall, and on closer inspection, she could see they had many tiny holes poked into the pages. They all formed relatively simple images: Mickey Mouse ears, a bunny, various fruits, and one attempt at a face.

There were sheets on her sister's desk where she'd drawn the Braille dots in abstract shapes like circles and squares and attempted to sketch more detailed drawings around them. Anne spread them out on the desk and waited for Eleanor's response.

Eleanor studied them. They were a good start but nothing like the drawings still on the wall from before the accident. Staring at one that Anne seemed to have put a lot of effort into, she noticed that at some point, the dots just got in the way or there were too many to make sense of.

"Well, I don't expect it will happen overnight," Eleanor said, trying to be encouraging.

Her sister let out an angry sigh. "I figured they were crap."

"I didn't say that." Eleanor looked again at the drawings on the desk and on the wall. "You know, Anne... I think you've always drawn what you saw more than what you felt. Most of your old drawings are of nature or people you know. I think you might have to find a way to express what you *feel* now. And you know what? I think you'll be able to learn that when you go to school."

"Thanks Ellie... I hope you're right." Anne swept the pages up and dumped them in a stack of other papers.

For the first time, Eleanor realized that Anne's goals were far nobler than her own had been at the same age. Eleanor had no idea what was next in her own career—or life for that matter—but she knew one thing for sure. The coming summer would be dedicated to making sure Anne could start college in August. She didn't yet know what that entailed, but she knew this was what she had to do.

Back in her own childhood bedroom, Eleanor began to unpack. She filled the dresser with her clothes, dusted off the furniture, and moved some of her mother's odds and ends to another room. Then she got her computer out of the closet and set it up on the desk.

She booted it up and connected to the home internet. She'd forgotten how slow the network connection was in rural areas until she sat staring at the loading wheel.

First things first. She navigated to the Agora homepage and through several vague menu options to get to the place where users could delete their accounts. It wasn't easy to find. It involved several warnings about "permanent deletion" and suggested deactivating the account instead. Once she had sufficiently reassured the system that she really wanted to delete her profile, she then had to go through a series of tasks to download all her pictures and posts from over the years. Then she was notified of a twenty-four-hour waiting period before her account would actually be deleted, and that logging in during that period would stop the process.

By this time tomorrow, I will be completely done with Agora.

She followed suit with several other platforms she deemed non-essential to her life. Then set up a new email address through an encrypted provider and set an automated message on her old account, giving her new address to anyone who contacted her. She deleted Chrome, downloaded Firefox, and switched the browser to Duck-Duck-Go. She put a sticker over her monitor's webcam.

She was beginning to feel like a conspiracy theorist, but it felt good. She was well aware she couldn't evade all the invasions of her privacy, but she could avoid some of them. And that gave her peace of mind that she could think for herself. The door to her behavior, her thoughts, and her inner world was now locked.

NEW DIALOGUE

Eleanor "Ellie" Crawford

As of today, you will no longer find me on Agora. My phone number is still the same.

Eleanor Crawford, signing off.

33

———

Over the next couple weeks, Eleanor fell into a rhythm—helping out at the inn in the morning, studying with Anne in the afternoon, and visiting Avi on the weekends. She spent her free time researching everything she could think of that would be of help to Anne. She read success stories about blind artists, about people who were able to go to college despite visual impairments, and most of all, what resources they found most helpful.

The month of May crept in, and the Crawfords got to watch Anne walk in her high school graduation ceremony. Afterward, everyone—all Anne's friends as well as the family's long-time neighbors, community members, and customers—gathered at Grayson House to celebrate. Eleanor and Emmett had decorated the place with school-colored balloons and confetti. The chef had prepared Anne's favorite foods (mac-and-cheese and country fried steak), and their mother had even made her a SCAD t-shirt by sewing thick, tactile letters onto it.

Eleanor went out front to meet Avi and was glad to see he'd taken her advice to dress down. Even in jeans and a polo, he looked like what Emmett would call a city-slicker, but she didn't care. He looked good. Avi picked her up in a hug and kissed her on the nose. "I love this place."

"I'm glad you could come. Wanna take a walk?"

"Sure."

She took off in the direction of the gardens, eager to show Avi how different things looked this time of year. The last time he was here, everything was brown and decaying. Now the place was bursting with new beginnings. The herb and vegetable garden had been planted and was already full of sprouts.

"How's work?" she asked.

"Fine, fine. All the usual." He wrapped his hand in hers.

"I'm sorry if I made more work for you."

"Nah, we brought in a new contractor last week, so it should calm down."

Eleanor felt as if she'd been poked in the belly with a paring knife when she heard this. She'd gladly focused on her family these past few weeks, but now she realized she also missed programming and solving problems. She couldn't stay here forever.

As they continued walking along a trail, Eleanor looked up at him. "I'm just trying to help Anne start college. Then, I'll have to figure out what's next for me."

"Do you have any ideas?" Avi asked.

"Honestly, I've been spending a lot of time looking at accessibility tools, and I feel like the resources available are underwhelming. I mean, I'm glad there are some, but I feel like there should be more... or better..." Eleanor tripped over her words. "Have you ever used a screen reader? It's appalling."

Avi stopped and pulled her close with a kind smile. "Can't say I have, but I'll have to look now."

"It's like the bare minimum is being done in this area, and when I think about all the resources funneled into ways of advertising and manipulating behavior..." Her voice trailed off. Her face was flushed, and despite the cool temperature, she started breaking a sweat.

"Then *do* more. You have the skills." His face was serious now.

"You mean build something myself?" She considered her skillset

—building mobile apps, writing algorithms, and dabbling with machine learning. *How could I use those here?* She felt her mind slip into that familiar place where problems were deconstructed and reconstructed with solutions.

"You've lost sight of the promise of technology, Eleanor. It's how we design and build these systems that matter." His words lingered in the air. They were familiar to her, yet she'd refused to believe them for some time now.

"You're right, Avi."

He gave her a peck on the cheek then said, "I believe in you."

The trail wrapped around the estate and deposited them back in front of the inn again, so they went inside. The party was in full swing, and they went over to a table full of gifts where her sister was sitting, surrounded by some friends and her mom. Eleanor smiled at them. "Mom, Anne, you remember Avi."

"Nice to see you again, Mrs. Crawford." He shook her hand gently. He reached into his back pocket and pulled out a white envelope that he handed to Anne. "Congratulations on graduating, Anne!"

"It's nice to see you again, too." She gave Eleanor a knowing smile as Avi placed the card in Anne's hands. She opened it and found a thick card with textured lettering on the front and a graduate popping out. There was also a gift card for an art supply store. Eleanor watched Anne run her hands across the card, and her heart felt too full for words.

"Thank you, Avi." Anne reached out to squeeze his hand, and he returned the gesture.

The party continued on with great success until light stopped coming in through the windows.

Later that evening, Eleanor was already in bed when she heard some rustling and banging in the bathroom. She tiptoed out of her room and could hear Anne clearly looking for something. She was about to tap on the door and ask if she needed help but then hesitated. Should she give her space to try and figure things out?

Then the door flung open revealing her flustered sister. "I heard you coming."

"Can I help with anything?" Eleanor said.

"Is this Tylenol or Aspirin?" Anne held up a bottle of allergy medication.

"Neither, which are you looking for?" Eleanor rustled around in the cabinet.

"Honestly, either at this point." She shook her head in frustration.

Eleanor found the bottle of Tylenol and gave one to Anne with a hug then went back to her room.

What if something could help Anne identify things with a camera? On a smartphone?

She started scribbling down some ideas in her notebook, her problem-solving gears turning. For the first time since she left Agora, she let herself think about how to solve a problem with technology, with algorithms.

First she thought about developing an app that would allow users to upload images that sighted moderators/volunteers could then identify. She quickly dismissed the idea. It could be unreliable both in accuracy and in how much time it took.

Perhaps if Anne could hold her phone camera up to things, the app could use computer vision to identify them? She made a list of examples: soup cans, letters, medicine bottles. It might even help with her art if it could recognize colors.

She jotted down some thoughts on how to approach these problems. For many products, she could have the app scan barcodes and search known databases for the item. She could use optical character recognition to read text. These two functions would probably be the most powerful and useful to start with.

She considered more of the technologies she'd learned about or used at Agora. She could try to train neural networks to recognize objects and ultimately describe scenes the camera was capturing. It would take some time and some more learning on Eleanor's part.

An hour slipped away in what felt like a minute while Eleanor tossed ideas around and researched and read information on the internet. She soon felt confident this was something she could make and that it would help Anne and others in her situation.

In the dead of night, she went right to work getting the basic features of the mobile app built. She started with a basic interface, camera access, as well as methods for scanning barcodes.

Around four in the morning, she used the emulator on her computer to test the app and check for any crashes or major bugs. It quickly became clear to her that the emulator was not going to be sufficiently effective for an app that required pointing a camera at things.

She was going to have to get a smartphone again.

NEW EMAIL
SUBJECT: EXPOSE AGORA

Miss Eleanor Crawford,

I am a journalist at The Atlantic working on an article to expose negative business practices at Agora that I fear have become rampant. From my network of colleagues, I heard of your recent (and sudden) departure from the company. I would love to interview you to hear more about your experience there. Rest assured, you will be kept anonymous. I have no desire to subject you to libel or slander charges or to leave you open to legal penalties if you signed a non-disclosure agreement. I always protect my sources. Please let me know if you're interested.

All the best,

Alisha Buchanan
Senior Writer at The Atlantic
Real Journalism for Real People

34

The next day, Eleanor retired the chunky flip phone that had been her trusted companion since Anne's accident and purchased a smartphone once again. The same smug employee helped her at the store. He rolled his eyes when she insisted she didn't want to restore her data from backup, that she would set it up as a new phone—and she could do it herself, thank you.

She followed the same routine she'd done with her computer, keeping the things installed to a minimum. She hurried back home to continue working on the project she'd started the night before. Eleanor thought she might get the barcode scanning feature working today. She was using a UPC lookup database and the built-in voice-over.

This current setup will require an internet connection to work, though… But this is just a prototype. I can solve efficiency issues later.

She installed her prototype on the new smartphone and went to the bathroom to try it with the medicine bottles. Eleanor held the bottle up to the camera, and a loading wheel spun around a few times before the robotic voice announced the words: "Aspirin Pain Relief. Coated Tablets. Three hundred milligrams. Five hundred count."

Eleanor yelped with joy. It worked. She then began thinking of what to do next. *It took too long for the camera to focus on the barcode. What if Anne is turning the item around, trying to focus it?*

She ran to her room and scribbled down some notes then back to the kitchen to test it with a few more items. This became her pattern for the next couple weeks, iteratively adding something, testing it, then refining it. She spent a week learning how to use a framework for optical character recognition. Her app was beginning to read words off papers.

Once these basic features were working smoothly, she set to work on the artificial intelligence she envisioned as the powerhouse of this tool. Her goal was for the app to be able to describe a scene in detail. She would start simple. If there were a dog or a cat, it would say so. Eventually she hoped it would be able to identify the breeds and even tell the user if the dog was sitting or standing.

After she configured the architecture of the neural network, she needed to train the model. The framework could mostly run on its own, feeding images to the system.

She told no one what she was working on, although since she was awake and active at all hours of the night, her family knew she was up to something. She hadn't driven herself so hard on so little sleep since her college days. She wanted to get a stable, minimum viable product before she showed anyone or got Anne's hopes up.

June was a busy tourist season for Grayson House though with families taking trips on summer break. So Eleanor continued to work and help out during the days and saved the midnight oil for the project she had begun calling A.Eye in her mind.

One morning, she found herself hosting a river-rafting outing that had been arranged as a team-building activity for a large corporate party. Eleanor laughed to herself thinking that before she'd left Agora, she could just as easily have been on the other side of the equation.

Helping out with rafting parties had always been one of her favorite summer activities at the inn. The party on this particular morning was large enough to need two rafts, so while she led one team, Emmett handled the other. It would be the first time they'd been working together all season. She wasn't eager to tell him about what had happened at Agora and, for that reason, had been skillfully avoiding him.

They all piled into the small bus prepared to take them a few miles up the river where there were some low-level rapids. Emmett slid into the seat next to her. "You ready?"

"Yeah, they're all here." She said, looking down at the list of names.

Emmett nodded to the bus driver, and they were on their way. "So, uh, how's your summer been?"

"I quit my job." She awaited the, "I told you so."

"Yeah, your dad told me."

"Well?"

"Do you *want* me to say I told you so?" He raised his bushy brown eyebrows at her.

She couldn't help laughing. "No, I don't. We can be Luddites together now, at least."

"Well, pitchforks and torches won't be enough to take that down." He snorted, and they found themselves laughing together. When he finally stopped, he turned serious. "But what'll you do? You're not going to stay here forever, are you?"

"Well, I don't know just yet. My main priority is helping Anne, and I've been working on something."

"Oh?" Emmett looked genuinely curious, but she didn't say any more about it.

The bus arrived at their destination, and everyone piled out, clipping on puffy orange life jackets and helmets while Emmett went over the safety rules.

" ...Unhappy is the land that needs a hero." Emmett looked at the corporate crowd, and when he received spurts of low chuckles, Eleanor wondered how many of them actually understood what he meant. He raised a finger. "I'm serious," he warned them. "Do not try to be heroes here today. If we turn over, keep your hands and ankles above the water as much as possible so they don't get stuck under rocks. We'll fish you out."

Once all the safety precautions were in place, everyone gathered into the two rafts at the edge of the river. Emmett shoved off with his party first. Eleanor felt a rush through her chest as her raft pushed into the water and was swept away. With the warm sun on her skin and the roar of the water in her ears, she stood proudly at the front of the boat, moving her paddle from side to side and shouting instructions or warnings. The regular sprays of cool mountain water kept her from breaking a sweat. She felt like an explorer leading an expedition to a new world.

Eleanor took in everything—the large granite bedrocks jutting out of the water, the glimmers of mica in the riverbeds. Shouts of excitement came from behind her, and every so often, Emmett would look back to make sure Eleanor and her passengers were doing okay. Each time, she waved back with excitement. Like most joyful experiences, the rafting expedition seemed simultaneously to last a lifetime and end in the blink of an eye.

They reached the end of their course in a calm area of the river where the rocks formed a wading pool. Eleanor slid off the raft into the deep, cold water feeling it all over her body before the tension of her life jacket pulled her back up. She reveled in the way that mountain river water could be so icy even in the heat of summer. This water purified her in an existential sort of way.

She looked around at all the people she'd just led down the river, watching their faces radiate exhaustion and euphoria. This place had brought them closer together even if they hadn't wanted it to. It gave them a bond that merely sitting in a nearby cubicle could not. She waded out of the river, dripping for a few minutes and letting the sun warm her before helping load up the equipment.

It was late afternoon by the time they were bouncing on the bus back to the inn. Eleanor was dreaming of snagging some food from the kitchen. There was nothing more satisfying than a heavy meal after an outdoor adventure.

Emmett sat next to her again. "You know, you're different out here."

"Am I?" She raised an eyebrow.

"You don't care so much about expectations or… perceptions."

"I guess I'm more focused on just experiencing living." Eleanor wasn't entirely sure where these words came from, but she believed them.

"We spend too much time in our own heads sometimes."

"Yeah." She smiled. "It's weird. Anne talks about how her other senses are growing in intensity. But I think we've all lost that in a way. The digital world is this flat, desensitizing force… numbing and intangible. It's so visual that it blinds us to anything else. It's impossible not to see. But the world holds so much more to be experienced. Haptics can't even begin to communicate all there could be to touch…" Eleanor knew she was mumbling her thoughts out loud, using a word like 'haptics.' She was making a point, but did Emmett even know that every time his cell phone vibrated, he was experiencing a haptic?

"I agree." Emmett smiled.

She hoped he was beginning to understand her better. Before he had seen her as nothing more than a mindless soldier of society. Was it possible he now recognized her as the leader of a rebellion? Is that how she saw herself? Someone strong enough to climb the first mountain only to get swept off it into a dark valley at the first obstacle? No, she wasn't going to waver. Eleanor smiled back at Emmett, but her eyes looked beyond him, up towards the second mountain, the one she was about to start climbing.

SMS CONVERSATION

Eleanor
Can I come visit tomorrow? I have something to show you!

Avi
Of course! You want to stay the night?

Eleanor
Sure, if you don't mind driving me back up to AV?

Avi
No problem see you tomorrow :)

35

———

By the start of July, Eleanor felt like A.Eye was sufficiently developed to justify her showing it to someone. Anne hadn't used a phone since her accident, but maybe if she saw how this could help her, she'd change her mind.

After dinner one evening, when everyone was in a particularly good mood, Eleanor decided it was time. "Mom, Dad, Anne—I've been working on something, and I need your feedback." She pulled out her phone.

"So we finally get to see what you've been working on in there," her dad chuckled.

"Yeah, I wanted to get it working reliably first."

She explained how the app could use the camera to recognize and read things out loud and did a few examples. She held up a book, and they heard a robotic voice say, *"The Fault in Our Stars."* Her dad opened the book and tried to have it read a page, but it tripped up on all the words.

"Might have to stick to audiobooks for that," Eleanor laughed.

"It's still impressive, Ellie." Her dad beamed at her.

Her mom held up various food items to the phone, and the voice identified them all pretty well. When she panned the phone around the room, it described things aloud: "chair," "sofa," "cup with liquid."

Anne's face lit up with excitement. "That's amazing, Ellie!"

An idea occurred to Eleanor. "Be right back."

She ran to Anne's room and found her college acceptance letter on her desk, then dashed back to the living room. "Let's try with this."

Anne held up the paper, seeming to know what it was, and for the first time since the accident, Eleanor placed a phone in her sister's hand. Anne positioned it in front of the page, and the choppy mechanical voice filled the room: "Dear Anne Crawford, I am pleased to announce that you have been admitted to the Savannah College of Art and Design. Congratulations."

For a moment, the corners of Anne's smile reached her cheekbones, and her eyes crinkled with joy, but then the grin vanished, replaced with open-mouthed shock. "Ellie—" she breathed.

"What?" She noticed Anne's eyes blinking rapidly.

"I see… something?"

"What!" Eleanor's heart began to race, and their parents exchanged excited glances.

"What do you… see Anne?" her father asked hesitantly.

Anne's voice quieted. "It's not like before, don't get your hopes up, but I see, like, little dots of light."

Eleanor looked at Anne and then the smartphone in her hand. "Coming from the phone?"

"Maybe." Anne was breathless as she moved the phone around the room, the voice-over still reading out the things it saw, but no one was paying attention to that anymore.

"They're moving! It *is* the phone!"

Eleanor was both interested and confused. "It's dots of light? No more detail than that?"

Anne nodded, pulling the phone closer to her eyes.

How odd. I wonder what it is about the phone. Eleanor ran to grab a flashlight and came back. "Can I try a flashlight, Anne?"

Her sister nodded and put the phone down. "Okay, it's back to nothing."

"I'll shine the flashlight now." She pointed it straight into Anne's eyes. "Anything?"

"No."

Eleanor moved the light around, back and forth, up and down, and into the periphery. "Still nothing?"

"Nope." Anne said.

Eleanor could see the disappointment in her mother's face.

Their father, however, seemed more cautiously optimistic. "Hmm, very interesting."

Anne took the phone back out and held it up, her face brightening once more. "I see it again!"

Feeling slightly dizzy, Eleanor took a seat next to her parents.

"I think we should definitely see a doctor about this," their mother said.

Anne's eyes began to water as she set the phone down and pulled Eleanor into a hug. "Ellie, your app—is amazing. I didn't mean to detract from that."

"What? No! This is exciting! We have to figure out what's going on—it could be a breakthrough, the next phase of what I can do with this app." She hugged her sister tight.

"Thank you," Anne whispered. "You know, you should bring this to the CVI and show people. I bet they would be excited too."

"Yeah." Eleanor realized that what she had done was not just for her own sister. There were probably lots of people who could benefit from what she had built. "Maybe someone there will know why you can see bits of light as well."

"I think that's a great idea," their dad said. "Everyone was so helpful there. I think we should pay another visit."

"Okay, let's do it." Reenergized by the possibilities her family had presented, Eleanor couldn't wait to get back to work. She turned to her sister. "In the meantime, let me get you set up with my app so you can play with it more and get me some feedback.

"Yeah, okay!" Anne said brightly.

• • •

The next morning, their mom called the Center for the Visually Impaired to make an appointment at the clinic. They had an opening that afternoon, so the Crawfords loaded up and drove toward Atlanta.

The four of them were crowded in an examination room when a youngish-looking doctor came in and introduced himself as Dr. Z.

He listened intently as the Crawfords explained what happened the previous evening. "That's very interesting. I will say, most people think blindness means pure darkness, but it's not at all uncommon for individuals to experience some kind of visual irregularity. I've had patients who report seeing blobs of color, specks of light, and even cartoon-like images."

Eleanor felt a sudden cold chill imagining strange or disturbing shapes constantly bouncing around in her field of vision.

Dr. Z. rubbed his chin. "But you seem to have identified something here in terms of a specific source of the visual impression, rather than a disruption." He smiled kindly. "Let's take a look."

He pulled a large contraption in front of Anne and began to narrate what he was doing. "So first I'm going to use an ophthalmoscope to take a look at the interior of the eye. Then I'll use a retinal camera to get a few pictures."

The Crawfords all held their breath, and the room was quiet except for the sound of the machine clicking.

"So what I'm seeing is that the retina is indeed damaged severely, which you already knew, but it seems the optic nerve might still be processing some light signals."

"What does that mean exactly?" their mother asked.

He pushed the device away from Anne now. "If we think of the eye like a camera that takes in images, the retina is the part that turns the light into electrical signals or pixels, and the optic nerve sends those signals to the brain." He pulled up the photos he had just taken on a computer screen and pointed out Anne's damaged retina compared to a normal one.

"So how does this affect her vision capabilities?" Eleanor asked.

"Well—" He hesitated, probably trying not to crush anyone's

hopes. "Usually not at all. Just that it would be part of Anne's new way of being. This is relatively unknown territory."

"But does this mean we could still find a way to send signals to her brain?" Eleanor pressed.

He nodded. "Maybe… Let's do a little test. You all said a smartphone was the trigger for these visual stimuli, correct?"

They all nodded, and he rustled around in a drawer and pulled out something that looked like a pen. "This is a spectroscope—it separates light by wavelength, which means I can shine a specific color of light into Anne's eyes and see if her optic nerve responds to it."

Anne's eyes grew wide and eager.

"Anne, are you okay with trying that?" Dr. Z. asked.

She nodded quickly. "Yes, please."

"Okay, I'll start with red and move up the spectrum." He shined the light in front of her eyes and moved it back and forth. "Anything?"

"No."

"Okay." He twisted the knob at the top, then shined it again. "Yellow?"

"No." Anne bit her lip.

"Green?"

"No."

The whole room sighed.

"Okay, let's try blue," he said reassuringly before holding the device up to her eyes once again.

The whole room took a deep breath.

"I see something!" She squeaked.

Eleanor restrained herself from jumping out of the chair.

"Okay, this is great!" Dr. Z moved the light around in different directions. "Do you see it in your entire field of view, over here to the right?"

"Yes!"

"And can you describe what you see exactly?" He continued to move the small light around.

"I see little dots of light in a circle. Just like with the phone, but those were in a rectangle."

"Fascinating." Dr. Z made some notes in the computer.

I wonder if there's a way to make simple images that Anne could see. "Do you think blue light could be projected into her eyes to… make images maybe?" Eleanor asked.

Dr. Z ran his fingers along his jaw. "Well, I don't think it would be images exactly, since it's only taking in one color…"

"But maybe abstract shapes or outlines?" Eleanor's problem-solving gears were turning.

"Well, that sounds possible, but again this is very experimental. Even if you could, I'm not sure what it would help really. The complex neural network that processes visual data is what's damaged."

But what if I could replace that with my own algorithm? Eleanor looked at her parents, who still seemed to be processing this information. "But I *could* project blue light into her eyes then?"

Dr. Z. frowned slightly. "Typically, blue light can be damaging to the retina, but since that's already damaged, you could…" He looked at Anne. "With Anne's consent, of course."

Anne beamed. "Ellie's brilliant. I bet she'll find a way to make use of this."

Dr. Z. made a few more notes then clicked his pen. "I'd love to know if this goes anywhere. If it could help other patients too, it would be invaluable."

Her father spoke. "My daughter's already one step ahead on that too. Ellie, show Dr. Z. your app."

Eleanor flushed. "Well, it's just a prototype."

"It's amazing already." Her mother encouraged her with a smile.

"I'd love to see." Dr. Z. said.

Eleanor took out her phone and gave a quick demo of what A.Eye could do.

Dr. Z.'s eyebrows went up. "I think you really might have something here. This could help so many people… You know, you should really talk to our president, Cecilia."

Eleanor's heart was racing, and her thoughts tumbled over themselves. "Do you think so? I mean, at the very least, I'd love to get some more feedback on how to improve it."

"Yeah, actually, let's go see if she's in her office real quick." He looked at Anne and their parents. "If you'll wait here just a moment, we can talk a little more when I get back."

Eleanor followed him down the hallway to a door labeled Cecilia Murphy. He tapped on it gently, and the sound of, "Come in!" came through.

"Hey, Cecilia! I've got something really cool to show you, or rather *someone* really cool." He waved Eleanor in.

She stepped into a cozy office whose walls were decorated with children's artwork, cards of appreciation, and several framed college degrees. Eleanor introduced herself. "My sister, Anne, has already been helped so much by the services here."

Cecilia stood to shake her hand. "I'm so glad. It's nice to meet you! Have a seat if you like."

"Eleanor is building something really cool that might help everyone here, so I'll let her show you, and with that, I'll get back to Anne." Dr. Z gave Eleanor a wink of encouragement then slipped out the door.

Cecilia seemed eager to listen to whatever had excited Dr. Z.

Eleanor took a breath. "Well, I've been working on an app that can do object and text recognition through the camera of your phone. Right now, it can read short bits of text, recognize simple objects, scan barcodes, and describe scenes at a rudimentary level— that's what I'm working on improving at the moment." Eleanor took out her phone, gave a demonstration, then handed it to Cecilia to try.

"This is definitely more advanced than anything we have available currently," she said while waving it around the room. "Just imagine… reading ingredient labels, medicine bottles, reading restaurant menus… The possibilities are endless."

Eleanor smiled. "My sister was trying to read a medicine bottle when I got the idea!"

Cecilia held it up to some papers on her desk to test it out, and the robotic voice filled the room.

Eleanor started talking almost as quickly as the voice-over. "I'd love to find a way to make the language voice-over sound more natural, and I have tons more training data to run through it still, but I'd love to get any feedback I can from real people."

Cecilia smiled wide. "My first advice is *please* keep working on this! There are so few people willing to work on accessibility tools... not a lot of money in it."

"Yes, I've noticed that." Eleanor nodded.

"Second, I'd be glad to put out an announcement about it and see if anyone is interested in testing it. I'm sure plenty of our clients would be."

"That would be amazing." A year ago, Eleanor never would have imagined herself here, and yet, she felt a warm glow inside her chest. *Is this what it feels like to actually be helping people?*

"Also, let's exchange contact info so we can stay in touch on this." Cecilia handed Eleanor a business card and a notepad to write her information on.

Eleanor tucked the card in her pocket. "I'm so glad to have met you."

When she returned to the lobby, her parents and sister were waiting with huge grins of excitement on their faces.

"Anything interesting happen after I left?" Eleanor asked.

"Nah," Anne said, "but, Ellie, do you really think there's anything you can do with what we've learned?"

She didn't want to give false hope, but she was determined to do whatever she could. "I don't know, but I'm going to try." She gave her sister a hug, and her parents joined in for a Crawford family embrace.

The family made their way back outside to the bustling Atlanta streets where the dense heat of summer fell onto them.

"I'm going to visit Avi. He's driving me back up tomorrow."

When her family waved good-bye, Eleanor started walking in the direction of Avi's apartment, thinking about what she was going to tell him first.

FORUM
CONTENT MODERATORS ANONYMOUS

Bluesterid
Have you seen the latest bullshit rule they
gave us

Dailyphoter
Which one I can't keep track...

Bluesterid
The literal flow chart of questions to
determine if something is hate speech
or not

Dailyphoter
oh lord I didn't even read that

Averstor
I can tell when something's hateful

BurntWomanLittle
If it seems hateful to me I'm deleting it
anyway

<h1 style="text-align:center">36</h1>

When Eleanor reached Avi's apartment, he greeted her at the door with a kiss.

"I've been working on something. I want to show it to you." She entered the room with a bounce in her step.

"I know you have." He chuckled.

"How?"

"It's that look in your eyes. I know that look."

"Am I such an open book?" She laughed, and the two sat down on the couch.

Eleanor took out her phone and showed him A.Eye, explaining what it could do so far. When showing her family, she'd felt a childlike pride, but now she felt more like she was presenting her work at Agora.

"Eleanor, this is incredible." He shook his head.

"You think so?"

"For sure, this has a lot of potential. I mean, your object recognition is fast, and with even more training data, it could be very powerful." He stopped and closed his eyes in thought. "Too powerful even… You need to file a patent for this."

"Patent?" She leaned back on the couch. "Really?"

"Well, your object recognition could be useful to more than just the visually impaired. People will want this… another company might want to buy it… or you might get funding to start a company or grants to keep working on this." He was speaking so quickly Eleanor half wondered if he might start speaking in his native language.

"I hadn't thought about any of that." She suddenly felt overwhelmed by how fast everything seemed to be moving today.

"You need to protect what you've made." He took a deep breath and smiled at her.

"But I don't really want to sell this. I want anyone who needs it to be able to use it."

"Yes, but do you want *anyone* to be able to use your object recognition algorithm?"

She thought about what he was saying, or implying really. *As usual, Avi sees the bigger picture.* "No, but I mean what I have here can't be that special. Plenty of people are working on algorithms like this, right?"

Eleanor had always been driven by curiosity. She had lived in an idealized world of innovation with the naïve belief that everyone had wholly good intentions. But now that she had learned to see good and evil on a spectrum, things were different.

"I think you're underestimating what you have here," he said gently.

She considered this and realized her mind didn't have to go very far to think about how Agora might want to use something like this, or probably were already trying to. She no longer had any right just to build something with good intentions and expect everyone else to use it the same way. She would be forced to wade through the world of patents, copyrights, lawyers, and finance if she wanted to secure this thing she had made. She knew there was no turning back to the way things were before either—only forward.

"Okay, what should I do?" she said decidedly.

Avi smiled. "Well, first things first, you should type up a simple non-disclosure agreement and only discuss the project with people that have signed it. We can do that now, and I'll sign it before you go." He stood up to get his laptop.

"But Avi," she hesitated. "What could really come of this?"

His voice came from the other room. "Well, that's up to you." He sat back down on the couch with his laptop. "There are several possibilities."

He opened the computer and typed in his password while Eleanor waited for him to clarify what these possibilities were.

"Well," he continued, "the simplest scenario is that an existing company might want to buy your product, but we've already agreed that's not on the table."

She nodded.

He leaned in closer. "You could start your own company, a non-profit maybe. Then you would have access to government grants. I bet there are plenty available for accessible technology." He paused to think. "I have no doubt you could build other things like this too."

That was something Eleanor hadn't thought of. While Avi tapped on the keyboard, she thought about it some more. *I could assemble an actual team of people, make this better, and maybe even design other tools in the future. But it won't be easy, and I won't make a lot of money.* She cleared her throat. "Speaking of building other things, I have something else to tell you."

He looked up from his computer. "There's more?"

Eleanor filled him in on the eye exam and the blue light test, and he listened attentively, nodding. "How interesting...."

"And so I was thinking—"

He looked up and smiled at her.

"What if I created a neural net that handled the job of the retina?"

He nodded slowly, waiting for her to say more.

"It wouldn't be able to process fully detailed images, of course, but, well, I'm still trying to work it out in my head—some kind of abstract representation of the space that Anne can know where she's at and maneuver around?" Eleanor pulled her legs up onto the couch and took a deep breath. "And I was thinking about—have you seen how autonomous cars work at all?"

Avi nodded furiously in a way that told Eleanor he was following her train of thought.

"Well, most of them use lidar or computer vision to map 3D models of space, but I wouldn't need that much detail even. I could make simple point clouds since she seems to be processing light— almost like pixels maybe?"

"I love this line of thinking, Eleanor—abstract point clouds of the space around her—but I don't fully understand how we'd then get that information to her?"

"That's where I'm stuck too." Eleanor laughed. "I was hoping you might have a suggestion."

"You overestimate me." He shook his head. "But let me think."

He typed on his computer, looking up information about how the eye works. When he landed on a diagram, he snapped his fingers. "Oh! What about projection mapping?"

"Like what they do on the side of buildings?"

"Well, kinda, but instead of making a small image larger, we'd make a bigger image smaller."

She thought hard about this. *Might just be crazy enough to work.* "So, we'd need some kind of glasses with a camera to take in information, a small microprocessor to convert it to light signals, and a small blue light projector."

"Worth a shot, I think. I can work on the projection mapping part if you want." He was getting swept up in her excitement.

"That would be great! Then I can work on the point cloud models."

Eleanor felt like she could just work and work until the image in her head was built, and the fact that Avi was now in on the project made her even more hopeful. "I want to help as many people with this as I can," she resolved.

"I know you do." He set his laptop aside and gave Eleanor his full attention. "I'll print some of these NDAs out and email them to you. Then let's order some stuff to start our experiments." He kissed her on the top of her head and went to get the papers from his printer.

She stood up and looked out at the city through Avi's windows —at the concrete jungle where grassy areas are considered a luxury and tiny ants shuffle through crosswalks. The sound of an emergency siren wailed somewhere in the distance.

But today, she caught the smallest glimpse of the remaining hints of natural life: trees, flowers, bushes. The things that ran wild in Aska Valley were meticulously placed here. People didn't invent grass, trees, and flowers. Those were here long before these buildings took their places. But they did change them, or master them, perhaps.

As Eleanor looked out on this smoggy, hot summer afternoon, she saw more than just the regular old skyline. The ugly tower cranes still hung over the city, but they had new meaning for her now. Opportunity and growth.

She thought about the person who went up into that box at the top every day and moved mountains, clearing the way and helping to build the giants that will house the future. Eleanor hoped in some way she had just climbed into one of those boxes herself.

RECEIPT FROM SPARKNOW
ELECTRONICS

1x LidarLight V3
1x Arduino Pro Mini
1x Pixy Cam
1x RGB LED Controller Box
1x Laser Mapping Sensor
10x Blue laser diode

37

Eleanor was looking at a simple photo of a tree in a field. She took a deep breath and then clicked "run code." In the square black window on her monitor, blue dots began to appear, creating a 3D representation of the image. The dots spread out to indicate the grassy field, and then little clusters of light floated abstractly above it, but the image was still clearly recognizable as tufts of leaves. She could see the little repetitive patterns of nature.

For several weeks now, she'd been working almost non-stop to create an algorithm that would take in images and create point cloud representations of them. But now that she could see it working, she felt the way she imagined Anne did when she created a new piece of art.

She pulled up another photo, this time of a small waterfall and river, and ran the code again.

It's beautiful. Blue dots outlined where the water ran, and a few specks of light indicated where the water crashed and fell over into the river.

She ran it with another image—this time it was of the kitchen inside their house—a line of dots ran along where the countertop was and up across the cabinets. She could see where the fridge, oven, and sink were.

She had done it. She'd made simple point cloud models of the world based on image input. If Avi's prototype worked to project this simple light map into Anne's optic nerve, then her sister might be able to see again, albeit in a new way.

It's not perfect, but she won't be completely in the dark anymore. Combined with the object recognition, she can have a pretty good sense of what's around her in real time.

Anne had already been making use of A.Eye these past few weeks, gaining back more and more independence, and the family was turning toward Anne's future with renewed hope. Her sister also had several meetings with Mika at the Center for the Visually Impaired where the two talked about how to make Anne's transition to college a successful one.

Eleanor had been in regular correspondence with Cecilia, who now had a long list of people from CVI interested in testing out A.Eye. She'd been so focused on this new project, which in her mind she'd started calling Second Sight, that she hadn't done anything other than feed training data to A.Eye. Now she'd have some time to work on that again.

The next day, Eleanor got up early and drove into the city to test her algorithm with Avi's prototype. Then she'd go to CVI to run some tests with A.Eye. When she got to Avi's apartment, the counter and table were scattered with electronic parts, and Eleanor felt a surge of excitement in her heart.

"Welcome to my laboratory." Avi smiled and pulled her close.

"It's amazing! I'm so excited, I could barely sleep last night."

"I've missed you." He playfully blocked her vision from the project area with his body.

Eleanor bounced on her toes. "You know I've missed you too, but c'mon, let me see it!"

Avi laughed. "Oh alright, remember, it's just a prototype … Not very fashionable."

She followed him over to the table and watched him pick up a pair of oversized sunglasses with a small camera clipped to the front and a wire running to a microprocessor attached to the frame. He turned them around so she could see that where the glasses would cover the eyes, two round lenses protruded that looked kind of like binoculars.

"Hideous, isn't it?" He laughed nervously.

"I think it's wonderful," she said—and meant it. "How's it work?"

"Okay, well, the camera on the front of the glasses takes in the images, of course. We'll put your code on the microprocessor, which will convert the image to the point cloud, then…" He paused for a moment to increase suspense. "Well, this part is pretty brilliant. I'm really excited about it."

She clapped her hands then pulled them to her mouth.

"I'm using a LIDAR laser for optical projection, but instead of projecting an array of points, I'll project the ones your algorithm tells me to." He looked proud of himself.

Eleanor took the device from him and turned it over in her hands. "Avi, it's brilliant! Genius!" She had to catch her breath.

"Only way to know if it works is to let Anne try it, though, right?"

"I guess so." She sat down and plugged the microprocessor into her computer to upload her code on it.

"You want some coffee? Breakfast?" He asked her. It was only 8:00 a.m.

"That sounds great," she said without looking up.

He clanked around in the kitchen while she clacked on her keyboard. Finally, she said, "Done!"

The two sipped coffee and ate blueberry muffins that Avi had clearly baked fresh.

"Are you going into work today?" she asked.

"Yes, I said I'd be in a little late."

She didn't know what to say next.

"Everyone misses you. I think Daryl got in trouble for letting you leave."

Eleanor cracked a smile. "Poor Daryl. You know I actually got this weird email from someone wanting to interview me about why I left."

"You didn't respond, did you?" Avi sat straight up.

"Lord, no."

He breathed. "Okay, good. Have you started looking into any grant funding yet?"

Eleanor nodded as she sipped coffee. "That's next on my list. I just wanted to try and get this working first." She gestured to the glasses.

"And the patent for A.Eye?"

"Yes, I filed that. I'll probably do one for this too if it works."

Avi nodded and drained his mug.

"Have you been looking for jobs at all?" she asked hesitantly.

"A little, but I haven't really found the right thing yet." He didn't seem able to meet her eye.

"Well, let me know if I can help at all." She started to pack up her stuff.

"Alright, I'd better get ready for work. You can stay as long as you want."

"Thanks! I'm actually going to CVI to test A.Eye a little bit before I head back to Aska Valley. Do you want to come up on Saturday so we can all test Second Sight together with Anne?"

"That sounds great!" he said.

She kissed Avi goodbye then packed the device gently into a box and put it in her car. As she walked up Peachtree Street, she saw the familiar sharp-edged Agora building in the distance, and a twang of loss went through her.

I left that behind? She shook the feeling off. What she was doing now… could be incredible.

When she got to CVI, she went straight to Cecilia's office and tapped on the door.

"Come *iiin!*" She heard her sing from the other side.

"Hey, it's Eleanor." She slid around the door and set her bag with all the testing materials on a chair.

"I'm so happy to see you. And I've got some other people

excited to see you as well." Cecilia's smile was wide enough to form lines around her mouth.

"I'm really glad to test it out and get some feedback." Eleanor only managed a slight nod in return as the butterflies in her stomach threatened to break free.

"Follow me. We'll set up in the demo room. I think you saw it when you came for the tour."

Eleanor nodded and followed her up the hall.

"So how do you want to run this?" Cecilia asked.

"Well, I think it would be easiest to have one person come in at a time, and I have a set of three tasks for each person to try and complete using the app."

"That sounds doable." She nodded. "I'd love to stay and observe if that's okay."

Eleanor felt relieved. "Oh, yes, that would be great." She hesitated before admitting, "I'm a little nervous actually."

Cecilia looked surprised. "After working at a place like Agora? This will be a breeze."

Eleanor smiled reluctantly but didn't vocalize that she thought this was different. That these were people with a much different set of problems than Agora users, and that Eleanor's app wasn't perfect, it might not work in all situations, or that she might be giving people false hope.

"Okay, I'll go get the first person then." Cecilia gave a thumbs up before leaving the room.

Eleanor took out her phone with the app, her laptop, and a clipboard. She'd prepared three tasks:

1. Navigate to the room's exit
2. Find the correct medication from a series of bottles
3. Identify a snack from a set of boxes

She set out medicine bottles, a few boxes of cereal and granola bars, then took a deep breath.

Cecilia re-entered the room with a middle-aged Black man, a baseball cap on his head and a cane in his right hand.

"Eleanor, this is Isaiah. He's been coming here for about ten years."

"Hi, it's so nice to meet you," Eleanor started, "and thank you so much for taking time out to test my prototype."

"Well, thank you, Missy, for taking an interest in folks like us."

Eleanor felt a twinge of sadness at his compliment and decided not to mention that she only wound up here because her own sister needed help. She explained what the app did and what they were going to do to test it, then gave him the phone to play around for a few moments to figure out how it worked.

The voice-over began to fill the room:

"You are in a room. North facing wall, one window. Objects: table, chairs, books."

Isaiah's face lit up as he turned the phone in different directions. *"West facing wall."*

He pointed it down. *"Brown loafers."*

"My goodness!" he grinned wide. "This is something else."

The excitement she felt from seeing Isaiah use the thing she built began to settle her nerves. "For the first task, I'd like you to navigate to the room's exit using the phone." She jotted down some notes.

"South facing wall. Objects: poster, door, shelf…"

He stopped with the camera pointed towards the exit and said, "Navigate to door."

"Door is five feet northeast."

He turned slightly to the right.

"Door is five feet straight ahead."

Isaiah began to walk towards the door—without using his cane. Although Eleanor knew he probably had a mental map of this room anyway, he still seemed excited to have done it.

"You have reached a door. You are exiting a room."

"Well, I'll be." Isaiah looked ecstatic. "Could I use this to get through city streets, places like that?"

I could integrate with Google Maps… and I could see about connecting to traffic lights and street crossing signals… Eleanor scribbled furiously. "Not yet, but those are great suggestions!"

He nodded eagerly as he made his way back over to the table.

"Okay, for the next task, I'd like you to identify which of these medications is a bottle of Acetaminophen."

"Alright." He pointed the phone in the direction of the table.

"Table top with assorted bottles."

He reached out to pick one up and held it to the camera, but nothing happened. Eleanor watched as he moved the bottle around and twisted the orientation, trying to get some kind of reaction.

Her heart began to skip again. *Maybe it crashed… or it can't find it…* She made some notes.

His mouth turned into a slight frown, and he set the bottle down before picking up another one.

"Acetaminophen, 500 milligrams."

Isaiah shook the bottle with a little wink. "Ah-ha! What happened with the other one, though?"

"I'm not sure, I'll have to check the error logs." She pushed the medication bottles out of the way, glaring at the offender. But since she didn't see anything abnormal about it, she moved on. "Okay, last thing. I'm laying out some different snack items here. Go ahead and find the one you'd like to eat."

He went in a similar way, holding each item up to the camera and listening intently to what the voice-over said it was, before setting it down and checking the next one.

"NutriGrain Blueberry. Strawberry. Chocolate Chip. Peanut Butter."

"Ah!" His face lit up. "I have a peanut allergy, relatively mild compared to some folks, but I can't tell you how many times I've spent the day all puffed up from a granola bar I didn't know had peanuts in it. Could this read ingredients?"

"Oh, that must be awful. It can read things, but sometimes the ingredients are kind of small and can be difficult."

That's another feature to work on! Allergen data might be part of the barcode data. I could read out the allergens when it identifies food.

"That would be something great to have," Isaiah said.

"Absolutely. I should be able to do that." Eleanor set down her notes and made eye contact with him. "Thank you so much for your time, Isaiah. This has been so helpful in figuring out what you need."

He nodded as he picked up his cane. "No, thank you. I can't wait to see what you do with this." He tipped his hat and left the room.

"That went well." Cecilia said from behind her laptop.

Eleanor nodded, feeling exhilarated but anxious.

The rest of the afternoon went just as well. Each person seemed just as excited and eager to provide feedback as Isaiah was. When they finished up, she had pages of notes and tons of new ideas.

Cecilia closed the door behind the final volunteer. "Well, I think this has been really productive, don't you?"

Eleanor pointed to her notes then began to pack up her equipment. "For sure. I can't wait to get started on some of this."

"Do keep me updated on how it's going, and let me know if there is anything else I can do to help."

"I will. Thank you so much." She smiled and shook Cecilia's hand before they parted ways.

Walking back to her car, Eleanor didn't even look in the direction of Agora this time. Instead, she spent the whole drive home thinking about all the work she had ahead of her.

NEW EMAIL

SUBJECT: INTERESTING OBSERVATION FROM DR. Z

Eleanor Crawford,

I have some news to share with you that I'm sure you'll be very interested in hearing, and I'm too eager to wait until your next visit to CVI.

After what we saw in your sister, I've been screening my other patients who express interest with the spectrometer, and it seems that many of them are still able to process a specific wavelength of light, much like Anne. Oddly, the color they can process does vary. I'm not sure what progress you've made on this yet, but perhaps the idea that others may benefit from it too may inspire you!

Would love to hear an update from you.

Best,
Dr. Z

38

Saturday morning came, and the Crawford house began, full with the smells of Southern brunch food, hosting eager observers to the testing of Second Sight. Avi and Emmett showed up for the occasion, and Eleanor was at the counter with her computer, getting what she had begun to call her Franken-prototype ready.

Her father was in the kitchen making cheesy grits and eggs in a basket while her mother assembled a tray of fruit and pastries. Anne was showing A.Eye to Emmett, and Avi had taken up washing dishes. Eleanor couldn't help but think what a strange sight it was to see him there, but it also gave her a warm happy feeling.

She took a deep breath. It was good to go, and she was too eager to wait any longer to see if it worked. "Okay, Anne, are you ready to try it?"

Anne nodded and felt her way over to the counter where Eleanor had everything set up. She carefully placed the prototype on Anne's head, making sure to line up the projectors in front of her eyes. There wasn't a sound to be heard as everyone gathered to watch.

"This window on my computer will show what the projection

should look like to Anne." Eleanor pointed to the screen then took another steadying breath. "You ready Anne?"

"Let's try it already!" Her sister said impatiently.

Eleanor clicked "run code" and watched the point cloud of her living room appear on the screen. She watched Anne's face intently, waiting for something—or worse, nothing—to happen. She held her hands in mid-air in anticipation of having to rip the device off her sister's face in a panic.

Anne's mouth began to part, and she held onto the frames at the side of her temples as she began to take some steps around the room. She reached out and ran her hand along the edge of the kitchen table and then the chairs. She let her hand guide her to the front door.

Everyone was holding their breath… waiting.

Avi smiled in Eleanor's direction as if to say, *You've done it.*

Eleanor fidgeted her fingers. "Well?"

Anne turned to face her sister, tracing Eleanor's features in the air with her hands. Although Eleanor couldn't see Anne's eyes, she knew that the device worked.

"It's like walking through a galaxy, but when I reach towards the stars, there's something there. I feel it. It's the real world. And suddenly, I'm in it more. I feel like I'm grounded in a place instead of drifting along in a black hole." Anne's voice shook slightly.

Eleanor exhaled and felt champagne bubbles dance across her skin.

Anne put her hands on her sister's face. "It's you, Ellie. I can see your outline." Eleanor pulled her sister into a hug. She could see Anne's tears forming behind the glasses, and Eleanor knew the same was happening in her own eyes as well.

Her parents began to clap with excitement along with Avi and Emmett.

"This is so exciting." their father said.

"I'm so proud of you both." Their mother dabbed at the corner of her eye with her apron.

Eleanor even got a nod of approval from Emmett.

As the excitement settled, the family sat down to brunch. Anne was still wearing the Second Sight glasses and couldn't be convinced to take them off.

"So what will you do now?" Emmett asked before shoveling a big spoonful of grits into his mouth.

"Well, patents, testing, testing, and more testing." She laughed. "And probably work on building a better prototype. Look for grants."

Avi nodded in agreement, his mouth full of peach puff pastry.

"Do you think Anne will be able to use this when she starts school?" her mother asked.

"I hope so. I've got a lot more work to do, though." Eleanor popped a mini-muffin in her mouth.

After they finished eating, the party moved outside to test what the device could do in a larger setting. Eleanor sat on the swinging bench with Avi, talking and making notes about the project.

She watched her sister with the device covering her eyes as she walked around the magnolia trees, the large white blooms scenting the air. In this moment, there was so much hope for the future, and she overflowed with happiness.

WIKIPEDIA ENTRY
OCULAR PROJECTION TECHNOLOGY

The means by which images are projected directly onto the retina. This is an experimental technology for patients with vision loss, currently being developed by Second Sight Technologies.

Last edited by E. Crawford

39

———————

Throughout the month of July, Eleanor spent more time on Second Sight and A.Eye and less helping out at Grayson House. She watched every day as her sister gained more independence.

Eleanor hired a lawyer who specialized in technology patent law and began the long process of filing a patent for Second Sight. She spent time researching and learning more about starting a company as well as what grants were available. She filed articles of incorporation and began crafting a mission statement.

She decided that starting a non-profit was the best path for something like Second Sight. Going forward, her goal was to continue producing accessible technology, and she wanted to make sure that helping those in need with the new technology always remained the top priority.

She began filling out applications for grants, and once her attorney told her that her patent had been approved, she sent them out. After some research, she decided to seek out an accountant and develop a budget.

In between all these activities, she continued to improve the A.Eye app. She trained it to recognize and count currency, starting with U.S. Dollars then advancing to some of the other more common mediums of exchange. When she had time, she worked on methods to optimize and make the recognition run more efficiently.

She wanted the app to be able to function pretty well without the internet, but this was not something she could do on her own. When she dreamed about the future, she found herself listing the professionals she'd need to hire for the positions that would have to be filled. But not right away. At least for the first year, she'd have to keep the business lean.

Most importantly, she would need someone to help market and inform the public about A.Eye. She was already working with the Center for the Visually Impaired in Atlanta and was certain there were centers like this all over that would be eager to set up and train people to use the app.

Eleanor was beginning to make so many trips back and forth to Atlanta that it occurred to her that it might be time to move back. With Anne going to school there too, it also made sense. She brought the subject up at the dinner table that night.

"So Anne, I've been thinking… What do you think about getting an apartment together in Atlanta? We can get one close to the school."

"Really?" Anne looked up with a smile.

"Yeah, I mean, I know it might not be cool to live with your sister, but—"

"No, Eleanor, I *need* that… I'm so nervous," Anne admitted. "Going off to college was already going to be a bit scary, but… this situation… I have no idea what to expect."

The relief in their mother's eyes was unmistakable. "Oh, Ellie, that would make me feel so much better too." She grabbed her husband's hand, and he nodded in agreement.

"It's decided then." Eleanor liked the idea of being able to look out for Anne as they both embarked on new journeys, separately but together. "I'll start looking for an apartment, and if any of my grants get approved, I'll be hunting for office space too."

"Wow." Anne marveled. "So you're really going to take this somewhere?"

Eleanor finished a bite of food. "I think so."

"We're so proud of you, Ellie," her dad started, "and we're so grateful for all your help this summer."

Eleanor beamed. "Thanks for letting me stay here while I figured things out."

"Of course." Her mother's eyes were glossy. "This will always be your home, Ellie."

A week later, Eleanor Crawford received news that she had been awarded one of the grants she'd applied for. She now had enough money to officially start the Second Sight Foundation. She read the email several times before it really sank in, then she ran to Anne's room where the two jumped for joy like they were ten years old again. She told her parents then called Avi and told him.

That afternoon, Eleanor drove up to Atlanta and signed a lease on a two-bedroom apartment close to SCAD and looked at a small office space available nearby. As she drove back to Aska Valley that evening, she thought about how much had changed for her in the past year. Realizations seemed to come tumbling over her in waves, again and again. She was used to working hard, but until that moment, she didn't realize how exhausting the past couple of months had been. Knowing that very soon she might be able to hire some employees to help carry the load was a relief.

The Executive Director of Second Sight. She let that title roll around in her mind trying to digest what it really meant. She knew it was going to be a small team at first. She was planning to hire a chief technology officer and a few developers. She also had to establish a board of directors. She tried to picture herself in an office, interviewing people and telling them what to do.

She laughed to herself thinking how impossible that image would have been just a year ago.

The next week was a whirlwind. The office space was rented and furnished, job postings went up, and boxes were packed. There was an anxious and excited energy in the Crawford house, her parents experiencing all the sentimentality of their final child leaving the nest.

Eleanor's phone seemed to ring every five minutes with business-related calls. Between those, she worked on packing and watching her mom and Anne argue about what clothes to take to college. She'd chosen another student-style apartment, primarily with the hope that Anne's classmates might live in the building too, but also so that they didn't have to move or buy furniture.

When moving day came, Eleanor loaded up her car with boxes, and her parents loaded theirs. Everything was ready to go. She took one last look at her house and waved goodbye to the valley that would always be there between every mountain she climbed.

The car was quiet except for the white noise of interstate driving. Eleanor broke the silence first. "Are you nervous?" she asked her sister.

"A little. I could ask you the same." Anne was fidgeting her fingers.

Eleanor's posture was stiff, her lips parting slightly. "I am. This is unknown territory for me. I always thought I'd be hiding in a cubicle, writing code for the rest of my life."

"But this is better, isn't it?"

"In some ways, yeah. It feels heavier though. More responsibility. I'm not sure if I'm worthy or qualified to have that much responsibility, I guess." Eleanor tapped the steering wheel.

"Well, I think you are," Anne announced with conviction.

Eleanor turned her head. "You think?"

"Ellie, you were smart enough to see past all the glossy prestige of Agora and find out the truth, and then you were brave enough to leave a company many people only dream of working at."

"Some might call that irresponsible." She laughed lightly.

"Maybe… but I don't see it that way. You've learned to see the greater promise of technology *and* found a way to share it with the world… to help me see again…."

Eleanor raised her eyebrows at this description of her actions.

"And I'm grateful," Anne continued, "and other people will be too. Plus you don't have to do it alone now. I have no doubt you'll hire people that share your vision." She nodded confidently, seemingly relieved to have said words she'd wanted to say for some time now.

Eleanor felt her eyes water, both from the kind words and the joy she felt. "Thank you," she whispered.

They arrived at the apartment building, which was already bustling with other new college students moving in accompanied by their sniffling parents. Eleanor had managed to secure them a room on the main floor when she explained Anne's situation to the leasing office. The Crawfords made several trips back and forth from the parking garage with boxes and such, moving a bit faster than others who had to wait in line for the elevator.

When the boxes were all inside, they set to work unpacking. Eleanor set up her computer first, making sure the internet was working. She was planning a soft launch of A.Eye tonight that some people at the CVI were going to test tomorrow. She figured she could get some more feedback this weekend, then come Monday, she would officially start work.

She dumped all her clothes in the dresser and closet and made up the bed. The place was similar to her old apartment, and she found herself setting it up exactly the same. Emily was coming by with a box of kitchen equipment that she'd left at her old place.

When Emily called, Eleanor went down to let her in. Her friend's familiar face and cheery smile were waiting out front. "Ellie! I'm so glad you're moving back. I've missed you." She dropped the box and pulled Eleanor into a hug.

"I've missed you too!"

The two friends walked down the hall, chatting about all that had happened, Eleanor filling her in on details she hadn't conveyed over text message. When they came into the apartment, her mom was in the kitchen sticking Braille dots on the appliances.

"Mom, you remember Emily?"

"Oh, yes! Nice to see you again sweetheart." Her mother smiled kindly.

They started unpacking dishes, pots, pans, and Tupperware and putting it into cabinets. A little while later, Avi arrived with pizzas and drinks, and everyone was relieved to take a break. They all gathered around the living room table, the late summer sunset warming the room.

Eleanor felt like she was watching the scene from above. After all that had happened, to see Anne laughing and living her life was a dream come true. She couldn't help but think that Anne was climbing her first mountain with way more courage and grit than Eleanor had—and she was proud of her. From his seat at the table, Avi sent her a mischievous smile.

Before she knew it, the Crawfords were hugging their girls goodbye and wishing them luck. The sun set. The apartment grew quiet, and come Monday, Eleanor and Anne would both start new adventures.

NEW EMAIL

SUBJECT: RFA-EB-21-001 GRANT SUBMISSION UPDATE

Eleanor Crawford,

We are pleased to inform you that the National Institute of Health has granted the requested funding to Second Sight Technologies for the continued development of supportive software for the blind. Please find terms and next steps in attached documents. Congratulations!

Thanks,

This is an automated message from Grants.gov. Please do not reply.

40

Eleanor spent the weekend fixing some bugs that came in for the app and exploring the college campus with Anne. They walked around, finding out where her classes were and trying to determine the easiest routes to get to them.

Eleanor watched with delight as Anne used A.Eye to read signs on the buildings, find room numbers, and generally take in the sights of the campus. She was also wearing a new model of the Second Sight eyewear, one with fewer protruding wires that also had headphones built into the frames to connect to the app. Eleanor thought about how one of the first projects would be to make the voice-over sound more natural and less robotic. Like most things, she figured people got used to it, but that didn't mean they had to.

They stopped at a sandwich shop for lunch, and she watched Anne use the app to read the menu and decide what to order all on her own. She knew her sister would never have the same level of freedom she'd possessed before the accident, but Eleanor thought back to Thanksgiving, less than a year ago. They had rocked back and forth on the porch at Grayson House, and Anne believed that she wouldn't have a life left to live. But here she was now, chasing her dreams.

Eleanor believed now, more than ever before, that her work mattered. That conviction filled her with the energy to keep going.

Monday morning arrived, and Eleanor woke early, spending extra time fixing her hair, applying her makeup, and getting dressed. She'd bought a brand new outfit—black pants and jacket with a blue blouse. She slung a grown-up, black leather bag over her shoulder and took one last look in the mirror.

Eleanor Crawford, Founder and Executive Director of Second Sight. She turned her glossy lips up in a smile then slipped on her black pumps.

She went into her sister's room, finding her performing her own first day ritual. "You ready for today?"

"Yes!" Anne beamed at her, flushed with her own excitement. "You look good."

"How can you tell?"

Anne placed a hand on her chest. "I can feel it… Your presence is intimidating." She laughed.

Eleanor dropped Anne off at the campus, giving her a tight hug and wishing her luck. She stayed a moment and watched as Anne took her first steps, backpack in tow, swinging her white cane along the sidewalk. But she no longer looked embarrassed or awkward with it. In fact, she used it only casually. She stood tall and walked confidently, relying on Second Sight to show her the world in specks of blue light.

Good luck, Anne, Eleanor whispered to herself.

She got into her car and drove up the road to a tall office building that housed several smaller companies and start-ups. She waved to the receptionist then stopped to look at the building's directory.

Suite 1024. Second Sight Foundation.

She took a deep breath and stood up straight. Her heels clicked down the hallway as she approached the suite. She pulled out a key and unlocked the door, taking in the office space, plain and typical as office spaces go, but it was hers, and, therefore, it felt different. It was where she would gather with others who shared her vision to build something that would make the world a better place.

She walked past four cubicles, a few small windows, and the

single conference room toward the set of two executive offices. Her fingers ran across her own name on the door. With a smile, she pushed the heavy door open and went into the windowed corner office, looking out at the city skyline. She was now in her own tower crane box, helping build the future.

She sat down in the sturdy leather chair with a little spin. A grin broke into a joyful laugh, and then she got to work.

Eleanor spent the morning organizing her office and setting up her computer. The assistant she'd hired showed up around lunchtime, bringing her something to eat. They talked some and went over the schedule of interviews for the afternoon. Eleanor wanted to get people hired as soon as possible, and her assistant had already arranged several interviews for her that day.

She went over the list of prepared questions, adding a few others, and after lunch, the first interviewee arrived. Eleanor had never interviewed anyone before and was convinced she was just as nervous as the person across from her. As the interviews went on, she found that she was even interviewing people older than her and more experienced. She got better as the day went on, but by 5:00., she was feeling tired.

She had interviewed some good candidates for sure. A young programmer she particularly liked had already worked for another non-profit and had a specialization in machine learning from her university. A few candidates hadn't seemed to understand they had applied to a non-profit and weren't thrilled about the salary. Eleanor herself was taking only living expenses until the company got off the ground.

She had interviewed two candidates for the CTO position that she was unsure about. They were knowledgeable for sure but had much more traditional corporate experience, and she wasn't entirely convinced of their reasons for applying to Second Sight.

This person would take the office next to hers and be her main partner in leading the company. Whoever she picked had to not only believe in her vision but share it with her. This was important, but they also had to be a good leader as well as have a strong technical background. Eleanor knew she was expecting a lot for not a lot of money. If some of her other grants came in, that might change, but there were no guarantees.

Her assistant popped her head in the door. "The last interviewee for the day is here. Should I send him in?"

Eleanor let out a deep sigh and then straightened her posture. "Yes, send him in."

"Good afternoon." A familiar staccato speech reached Eleanor's ears, and her lips parted in a wide smile. "I'm here to interview for the CTO position."

The eyes of Avi Kumar met Eleanor's, and she shook his hand, familiar warmth and comfort surging through her. "Welcome, please, have a seat."

He closed the door and sat across from her with a playful look. Eleanor wondered if he was just having fun with her until he produced his resume and handed it to her. His face turned serious.

She wasn't quite sure what to say, but she did feel happy he was here. Her team lead, a person she had trusted in, confided in, learned from, and then fell in love with, was sitting across from her asking to be led by *her*.

He loves complicating our relationship, doesn't he? Her cheeks warm, Eleanor looked down at the first question on her sheet and tried to keep a straight face while asking, "Can you tell me a little about what brought you here?"

He seemed relaxed, like this was the exact question he had come prepared to answer. He looked into her eyes. "There is a person I've promised to help. She has a big heart and dreams about making the world a better place, much like myself. But she's far better at following her purpose. She will jump off any cliff to make her dreams real. So I've chosen to follow her."

Eleanor hesitated. "And you're prepared to jump off that cliff after her?"

He leaned back. "I already have."

A smile spread across Eleanor's face as she stood up and shook his hand formally. "Avi, Welcome to Second Sight."

DIGITAL ART EXPERIENCE
CREATED BY ANNE CRAWFORD

Welcome to the future of sight for the visually impaired. Artist in residence, Anne Crawford, is the first person to pioneer a new technology to restore partial sight after losing her vision in an accident.

Through virtual optic display technology, Anne's vision was restored in an abstract way that helps her to navigate spaces and experience the world. She created this installation so everyone could experience the world the way she does.

The same points of light that sketch the world for those who use Second Sight will guide you through a sensory experience unlike any other. Feel free to reach out and use all your senses as you move through the exhibit.

Special Thanks to:
Second Sight Technologies

ACKNOWLEDGMENTS

First thanks goes to **you**, the reader! A story can exist inside my head or on my computer drive, but it doesn't really come to life until it's out in the world being read, thought about, and talked about. I hope you enjoyed the book. If you could take a moment to leave a review on Goodreads or Amazon, that would be so helpful to an indie author like me.

Of course I also have to take a moment to thank those that helped bring the book to readers. There are always so many that deserve thanks, and know that if you've loved and supported me at any time in my life, you deserve thanks.

A few people bear specific mention for this project. The time and motivation to write would have never been found without the love and encouragement of my best friend and partner in life Clifton Malecki. Thank you to Susan Rosenbluth and Maddy Owen who devoted an incredible amount of time and thought into beta reading and editing.

A few of my professors from Georgia Tech must also be mentioned. Kathleen Goonan, an incredible author and teacher, helped this lost STEM undergrad feel like she had permission to write again. Lisa Yaszek and Amanda Weiss gave their precious time to read my early manuscript and help me workshop and improve the story. Thank you so much to everyone who helped me tell the story I wanted to share.